A Heart for Freedom

by

Janet Grunst

SMITTEN
HISTORICAL ROMANCE
LIGHTHOUSE PUBLISHING of the CAROLINAS

A HEART FOR FREEDOM BY JANET GRUNST
Published by Smitten Historical Romance
an imprint of Lighthouse Publishing of the Carolinas
2333 Barton Oaks Dr., Raleigh, NC 27614

ISBN: 978-1-946016-58-4
Copyright © 2018 by Janet Grunst
Cover design by Elaina Lee
Interior design by Karthick Srinivasan

Available in print from your local bookstore, online, or from the publisher at:
ShopLPC.com

For more information on this book and the author visit: https://janetgrunst.com/

Scriptures are taken from the KING JAMES VERSION (KJV):
KING JAMES VERSION, public domain.

Brought to you by the creative team at Lighthouse Publishing of the Carolinas
(LPCBooks.com): Eddie Jones, Shonda Savage, Robin Patchen, Pegg Thomas,
Brian Cross, Judah Raine, Jennifer Leo

Library of Congress Cataloging-in-Publication Data
Grunst, Janet.
A Heart for Freedom / Janet Grunst 1st ed.

Printed in the United States of America

Other Books by Janet Grunst

A Heart Set Free

PRAISE FOR *A HEART FOR FREEDOM*

A stirring tale of America's tumultuous beginnings, *A Heart for Freedom* is both historically and spiritually rich, a poignant reminder of the high cost of freedom that we continue to enjoy today. Janet Grunst inspires, educates, and entertains in this second in the series.

~ **Laura Frantz**
Author of *The Lacemaker* and *A Bound Heart*

Janet Grunst has written another fine inspirational historical romance in *A Heart for Freedom*. As the American colonies struggle for freedom from British oppression, Ms. Grunst shows how much sacrifice takes place on not just on the front lines but also on the home front. This well-crafted story engaged me with its plot, the realism and depth of its characters, and the historical detail which kept me in the world of the 18th century. Ms. Grunst has developed the family relationships nicely in her continuing saga, showcasing the beautiful power of love between a husband and a wife, especially when they trust in the Lord and His promises, despite the chaos in the world around them—a message relevant even today. Highly recommend!

~ **Kathleen Rouser**
Award-winning author of *Rumors and Promises*

A Heart for Freedom continues the love story of Matthew and Heather from *A Heart Set Free*. Janet Grunst weaves romance, friendship, and intrigue into a delightful and well-written yarn that will keep you yearning for a happy ending until the last page.

~ **Denise Weimer**
Multi-published author and
Lighthouse Publishing of the Carolinas editor

A Heart for Freedom is a historically-accurate novel that depicts the quandary of the colonists in 1776. While many Americans desired freedom from England, an equal number desired to remain loyal to the King. What is often missing from historicals of this time period is the other third of the colonists—those who desired freedom yet desired peace as well. Their simple lives as farmers and merchants were about to be turned upside down by war and they knew the consequences would be life-changing. They could no longer ride the fence of indecision.

This novel is a riveting look at the rippling effects of events that force the main characters to choose one side or the other. They long for peace that can no longer be, as the discontent of the Patriots and the military response of the King's Army force the issue.

In *A Heart for Freedom*, a sequel to *A Heart Set Free*, Ms. Grunst shares the lives of Heather and Matthew Stewart, who struggle to remain neutral as farmers and owners of an ordinary (a Colonial-era hotel). They, along with their children and their circle of friends, become impacted by the Revolution in ways that disrupt their peace of mind and challenge their faith. A compelling read that makes me look forward to Book Three in this series!

~ **Elaine Marie Cooper**
Author of *Saratoga Letters*

A Heart for Freedom is an inspiring story of love and courage in perilous times. Four years have passed since the end of *A Heart Set Free,* book one of the series, and the colonies are teetering on the verge of rebellion against heavy-handed British rule. With a young son in addition to Matthew's son and daughter from his first marriage, he and Heather are joyfully looking forward to the birth of another baby. But Heather's fears that the turmoil pitting their neighbors against one another as the colonies edge toward war will upend their peaceful lives soon comes agonizingly true.

Grunst affectingly portrays the trials families were forced to deal with during the American Revolution and keeps readers turning pages, hoping for happy endings for this appealing cast of characters. The story doesn't disappoint, and I'll be looking forward to another book in the series to carry Heather and Matthew, their children, and their friends into the future.

~ **J. M. Hochstetler**
Author of the *American Patriot Series*

Author Janet Grunst puts flesh and blood on the dead bones of textbook history in *A Heart of Freedom*, her second book in her historical trilogy about life in late 18th century Virginia. The author easily draws readers back in time. She also does a wonderful job juxtaposing the simplicities of life against the complexities of a pre-war political era. Her characters' relationships, conflicts, joys, and hardships become ours.

~ **Clarice G. James**
Author of *Manhattan Grace*, *Party of One*, and *Double Header*

A well-researched book, *A Heart for Freedom* puts the reader into the everyday life of the Stewarts as rural farmer Matthew Stewart is forced to choose between the Tories or the Patriots who want to break away and be free of England's control. Through the lives of Matthew and Heather Stewart, the reader is immersed into the growing tensions of the pre-Revolutionary War and how it impacted their family and their community. Underlying this historical tale is the love story of a couple impacted by the struggle, and how their faith carried them through.

~ **Carol Grace Stratton**
Author of *Lake Surrender*

Acknowledgments

A big thanks to Eddie Jones at Lighthouse Publishing of the Carolinas for his enthusiastic commitment to publish books that shine a light in a dark world. Thanks also to Pegg Thomas, Managing Editor of LPC's Smitten imprint who saw the potential for this story and to General Editor Robin Patchen for her tireless work to make it better. And thank you to the whole team at LPC— hard at work behind the scenes.

The encouragement, patience, and tenacity of Linda Glaz, my agent with Hartline Literary Agency, has been a blessing. She's a generous lady who encourages and works hard for her clients.

Many thanks to all who took time to read the story and offer helpful suggestions, and for friends who lifted me up in prayer throughout the process.

I'm so appreciative for my husband, Ken, who, armed with a red pen, is my first reader. His wisdom and ongoing encouragement to never give up on my dream to write stories has meant so much.

I've loved the feedback from those who read my first book, whether it's by a comment or by taking the time to write a review. My heart is to write stories that communicate the truths of the Christian faith that will entertain, as well as bring inspiration, healing, and hope to the reader.

I am most grateful for my Lord and Savior, Jesus Christ, for His provision, mercy, and grace in my life. He put this story in my mind and guided me throughout the process.

"Trust in the Lord with all your heart, and
do not lean on your own understanding.
In all your ways acknowledge him, and
he will make straight your paths."
Proverbs 3:5-6

Dedication

To my sons, Jeff and Jim
Your willingness to serve our nation in the armed forces to
preserve the freedoms we enjoy is an inspiration.
I'm proud to be your Mom.

"Have not I commanded thee? Be strong and of a good courage; be not afraid, neither be thou dismayed: for the Lord thy God is with thee whithersoever thou goest." Joshua 1:9 KJV

CHAPTER 1

April 1775

Matthew removed the three-cornered hat and wiped the sweat from his brow as he headed down the narrow alley just off King Street. Every step felt like a drumbeat accompanying Lucas Stephens' remarks from the day before.

"Sometimes we have to put aside our personal interests and be faithful to a greater principle," Stephens had said. "If our cause is just, then God Almighty will equip us to answer His call. Some will take up arms. Yours is a different charge. What will you do?"

What will you do?

For the past twenty-four hours, the man's question had tormented him. When Stephens had taken him aside yesterday outside of Brady's mercantile and asked for the meeting today, He should have said no. But he'd hesitated, and then, for some reason—likely a sense of obligation—he had agreed. And regretted it ever since.

He would meet with Stephens and hear him out, just to get that task behind him. It wasn't as if he owed this man anything. They had only just met. He and another man, Jones, had been introduced to him at the Cameron Street Tavern the last time the family was in Alexandria. The men had expressed a keen interest in the cause for separating from England. Matthew wasn't against it, but he certainly did not intend to be put in the middle of it.

Yet here he was, meeting a practical stranger in a dark alley. He put his hat back on and continued down the alley.

Stephens stepped away from the brick wall. "Glad you came."

Matthew froze a good ten yards away. "I don't have long. A friend is waiting for me at Brady's Shop. Was this so important that we had to meet before I left Alexandria?"

"We have a proposition for you."

"We?"

Stephens walked to within three feet of Matthew and whispered, "Me, Martin Jones, and some other Patriots."

Matthew closed his eyes. "I have no time for, or interest in, politics."

"We need you, Matthew."

Matthew opened his eyes at the emphatic words.

The man's passion burned in his gaze. "You have strong ties to influential people in Philadelphia."

"It has been five years since I was last there, and that was only to sell my parents' property."

"Your family was close to the Fergusons."

Matthew took a step back. Why bring up that family? Fond memories of hours of hunting and merriment with John and Henry Ferguson flooded his mind. "What of it?"

"The Fergusons are Tories. Their daughter is married to a major in the British Army, and the family socializes with other Tories and a significant number of British Regulars."

Matthew looked over his shoulder at the relative peace of the street beyond. No one was in sight. Still, he kept his voice low. "What has that to do with me?"

"You could have access to the Fergusons and their friends. The younger son, Henry, is a different sort, sympathetic to the Patriot cause. He would be your contact. You could gather information needed in Virginia as well as the other colonies without drawing suspicion."

"It's been years since I last saw Henry or his family," Matthew said. Stephens' machinations made no sense. "My suddenly appearing after all these years would seem odd."

"It wasn't odd five years ago when you went to Philadelphia after being gone so long. A strategy could be devised to make it plausible."

Matthew slapped his hat against his thigh. "I don't know what kind of a scheme you and your Patriot friends are up to, but I'm not your man. I have a family, a tenant family, a farm, and an ordinary to oversee."

Stephens stepped back, shook his head, and pursed his lips. "Is there anything you believe in enough to inconvenience yourself? Civil unrest is growing. The Crown's men killed dozens of our countrymen that day at Lexington, Concord, and Menotomy. Everything has changed."

"It's not my fight."

"'Twill be all of our fight soon." The man raised his voice. He glanced around, then stepped within inches of Matthew's face. His next words were quieter but somehow laced with even more passion. "The question is, will you serve the cause of liberty or the Crown's oppression?"

The Crown? How could he fight for the Crown against his fellow colonists? This was his home, and the Crown had done nothing but take their money and impose unnecessary and repressive restrictions. To remain neutral—that was his goal. He had no desire to choose a side. But could neutrality be an option? And what would happen if they did fight? The carnage that would be suffered by his neighbors and friends could be devastating. "Against the world's strongest army and navy? We would be crushed and robbed of even more liberty. And countless lives."

The man pushed his shoulders back. "If our cause is just, and many believe it is, then God Almighty will equip us to answer His call. Many will take up arms. What will you do, Matthew?"

Heather Stewart relished the peaceful atmosphere in Parker's Millinery Shop. It was the perfect antidote for Adam Duncan's rant that morning about the recent fighting near Boston. Growing up in Scotland, she had witnessed the ravages of war, and the prospect of a war with England terrified her. This excursion to the shop to find fabric for her fourteen-year-old stepdaughter Mary had provided the escape she needed. The fabrics, trimmings, and hats reminded her of all the years she had worked in her family's dry goods shop a lifetime ago. The gentle hum of women's voices soothed her nerves. Margaret Lamont, the wife of a prominent local solicitor, was speaking with the mistress of Blakemore Hall.

The ringing of the bell on the shop's door drew Heather's attention away from the bolt of fine green muslin she had been examining. Mary and her friend Jean Duncan came in.

"I'm glad you made it." Heather lifted the fabric, and Mary joined her. "What do you think of this for a new dress?" She lifted a corner so it rested near Mary's face. "The green sets off your amber eyes and brown hair."

Mary's smile was encouraging. "'Tis beautiful." She held the bolt up to show Jean. "Do you like it?"

"It flatters you." Jean Duncan, Mary's longtime ally, was thirteen, a year younger than Mary.

Heather rested the bolt of muslin on a chair and pointed to a stack she'd collected earlier. "I set those aside for you to look at. Choose two or three, but if you see something else that—"

"Heed my words, Margaret." Mrs. Blakemore's shrill voice pierced the serenity of the shop. "The colonies will be at war before the year ends! And they will reap the consequences of their treason!"

Heather stared at the two other customers in the shop. Why was Mrs. Blakemore so irritated with Mrs. Lamont? She looked across the counter at the proprietress, Mrs. Parker, whose mouth was agape.

Mrs. Blakemore banged her cane on the floor. "The recent skirmishes in Massachusetts are only the beginning. Edwin and I leave for England in a fortnight, before the fighting comes to Virginia. Your husband still has family near London. Why would you and George remain here amongst people who are determined to defy the king?"

Fighting in Virginia? Heather put her hand to her chest. Hopefully, the woman was wrong.

"This is our home." Margaret Lamont's plaintive voice was heart-rending. "We have always lived in Virginia. My children and I have never even been to England."

Heather tried to ignore Mrs. Blakemore's response as Mary and Jean stepped nearer to her. Mary handed her a bolt of calico and one in amber linen. She leaned in close, a stunned expression on her face. "Mama, what—?"

"Not now, dear," Heather whispered. "Are these the only other fabrics you want?"

Mary nodded. "May we wait outside?"

"Aye. I will join you after I settle with Mrs. Parker."

The girls wasted no time in departing the shop.

Still attempting to ignore the argument at the far end of the shop, Heather dipped the quill in ink and wrote on a piece of parchment how much fabric she wanted. A glance at Mrs. Parker confirmed the poor proprietress was clearly embarrassed.

Mrs. Blakemore's gown shimmered in the sunlight streaming through the window. "Your excuses for staying in the colonies will seem foolish when war lands on your doorstep. Your husband can practice law in England. You and George will be received by all in good society. Surely he will decide in favor of his family's well-being."

Margaret's face grew flushed and nearly matched the pale coral of her bodice. "You needn't concern yourself about us. George will know if and when we should leave. He believes our grievances with the King may still be settled."

"After the battles up north, any Loyalists remaining in Virginia or any of these colonies will not be safe for long." Mrs. Blakemore walked to the counter and nodded at Mrs. Parker. She retrieved her purchases and shuffled out the door as swiftly as her cane would take her, leaving Margaret Lamont visibly upset.

Heather spotted a chair nearby and sat. Feeling lightheaded, she closed her eyes. Mrs. Blakemore's commentary had been unnerving. She was still haunted by her father's tales of wars with England and the family members who had been lost. Scotland had been crushed. That the Colonies would wage a conflict with England was unthinkable.

Mrs. Parker finished cutting the fabric and put down her shears. "I'm sorry for the disturbance, ma'am." Her voice was low and her cheeks crimson.

"'Tis fine." Heather returned to the counter. "Would you be able to have these packages delivered to the Duncan home within the next couple of hours? We will be leaving the city later today."

"I will have my son make the delivery," Mrs. Parker said.

"I appreciate that."

With her purchases paid for, she approached Mrs. Lamont, who was seated in a chair near the window, her cheeks still reddened from the confrontation.

"'Tis good to see you again, Heather." Mrs. Lamont stood and curtsied. "I hope you and the girls were not distressed by the fracas."

"Please, don't give it another thought. These days there is constant talk of the hostilities wherever one goes. It seems to have everyone in short temper. I'm headed back to the Duncans', but please give our regards to your husband and children."

"Your kind words are appreciated."

Heather curtsied and joined Mary and Jean outside. They walked toward Fairfax Street.

Mary picked a blossom from a tree planted along the road. "I cannot believe how rude Mrs. Blakemore was to Mrs. Lamont."

Jean shook her head. "And loud. Why would she say those things in such a public place?"

Heather took a deep breath. "Perhaps Mrs. Blakemore was having a bad day. We need to get back to the house and see if Jean's mother needs any help with dinner preparations."

The warm breeze energized her. Children's voices playing in the distance and the rhythmic clacking of horses' hooves on the cobblestone streets reminded her why she enjoyed their family's visits to Alexandria. They had just crossed to Princess Street when angry shouts and a loud noise, like wood shattering, echoed from the nearby alley.

Mary reached for Heather's arm. "I think the sound came from over there." She led them to some bushes, where they could observe without being seen.

Five boys pounded and kicked each other ruthlessly amid angry accusations and strangled yelps.

Heather put her hand to her throat. "Jean, 'tis your brother." Why was Donald fighting? At seventeen, he was well past the age of schoolboys' rows.

The warring factions broke apart at the sound of an approaching chaise.

Donald's voice boomed. "Go running home to your mother, you Tory."

Three boys stormed off, their derisive retorts becoming less audible with each step.

Donald and Braden stooped, picked up their hats, and brushed the dirt from their clothes. They dabbed at their cut and bruised faces.

Donald's chest heaved as he beat the dust from his breeches. "Do you think we convinced Everett and his friends?"

Braden brushed the dust from his stockings. "This settles nothing, but I doubt we shall be bothered by those cowards again. Hey, your face is bleeding. Want to stop by my house and wash up before going home? No one will see us. My uncle will not be there, and Aunt Lucy has gone to visit her sister."

"Sure. I'm in no hurry for my parents to see me this way."

Heather and the girls watched the boys leave in the other direction. Mary's eyes followed their departure as she adjusted her cap. "Donald and Braden were brave to take on those bigger boys."

"Come, girls," Heather said. "We need to get back."

Within minutes, they arrived at the modest two-story house on Oronoko Street. They were halfway up the walk when Mary turned to her. "Mama, are you going to tell Donald and Jean's parents about what happened just now?"

"Nay, I think it best Donald tells them."

Jean had a sly expression. "I cannot wait to see how Donald explains this."

When the front door opened, Maggie Duncan's smiling face greeted them. "Were you able to find everything?"

Heather glanced at the girls. "We found fabrics for some new dresses for Mary. Mrs. Parker will have them delivered soon."

They followed Maggie past the parlor into the large kitchen. Tables had been pushed together to accommodate the two families.

Jean tugged on her mother's sleeve. "I want to show Mary something upstairs."

"After you set the table."

The smell of roasting chicken made Heather's mouth water. "What can I do to help, or would you prefer I gather the children?"

"Adam and Matthew should be back soon." Maggie wiped her hands on her apron and tucked a few loose brown curls back into her cap. "I'm about finished here. Care to check on the boys out back? Mark is supposed to be supervising the younger boys."

Heather smiled. Her nine-year-old stepson was most likely avoiding or bossing the younger children. "Aye." She headed to the service yard, where she spotted Mark perched in a crook of the apple tree, reading a book.

The two youngest Duncan boys and her four-year-old Douglas

played with marbles underneath the sprawling branches.

Mark closed his book when she sat on the bench behind the house. "Miss Maggie asked me to 'watch over the boys.'"

"You have taken that quite literally."

"Have Pa and Mr. Duncan returned yet? I'm hungry."

"You are always hungry, son. They are due back soon. Come down from there and sit beside me."

"Ma, I climbed the tree to get away from the boys, and they are still there." Mark climbed down from the tree, managing to bring twigs and leaves with him, which disrupted the younger boys' game.

The boys scowled as Mark walked past them and sat beside her on the bench.

She brushed some pollen from Mark's dark wavy hair. With each passing year, he looked more like his father.

"Where is Donald?"

She bit her lip. "I'm sure he will be home in a bit."

"Are we still going home this afternoon?"

"Aye, we must get back. Managing the ordinary and making sure the guests are cared for is a big responsibility, so we need to return to the Green and relieve the Gordons."

"I wish we could stay longer."

"I know, but Polly has not been well lately, and their boys only help with the horses and carriages. We are blessed to have them as tenants. Were they not there, we could not get away."

"Philip and Todd asked if I wanted to go fishing with them when we got back."

She shook her head. "'Twill be too late when we get home today, but tomorrow, perhaps when the chores are finished. I think some fresh fish would be more than welcome."

"There are no guarantees we will catch any, Ma."

She smiled and patted his leg. "I need to get back to the kitchen. Please see that you and the boys wash before coming inside."

Maggie opened the door and stood in the doorway. "Matt and

Adam are back." She handed Heather a bowl and a slotted spoon. They stepped inside, and Maggie pointed to the steaming pot of water hanging from the trammel over the hearth. "You can put the vegetables in there. The men are in the front room mulling over the latest rumors from Boston."

Heather sighed. "Will this political fuss never end? Did the girls tell you about the confrontation we witnessed at Parker's Millinery?"

"Aye. It seems everyone is at odds these days."

Heather placed the bowl of vegetables on the table. "Mary and Mark will be in a pout this afternoon when we leave for home. The children still speak of the year they spent with your family. There are many interesting diversions and friends in town, but farm life with all the chores is a mite less appealing to young people."

Maggie handed her a wooden trencher of bread. "They would miss their life and friends in the country. They enjoy coming here for visits, but they favor the freedom of farm life."

Heather laughed. "But not all the work."

Maggie spooned butter into a bowl and placed it on the table. She counted the settings—four adults and seven children. "But the Gordons have proved to be reliable help."

"Polly and Thomas have been a treasure helping to manage the farm as well as Stewart's Green these past four years. They are hard workers, and their sons have been good friends with the children. Todd is very responsible, and Philip is as strong as many a man." Heather gazed out the window. "We have all benefited from the arrangement. I'm a bit worried about Polly. She has had a rough time carrying this babe." She took a deep breath, and her hand grazed her stomach. New life. She lifted her head as a familiar heaviness formed in her chest. *This time will be different.*

Maggie gave her a gentle hug. Her soft brown eyes were full of love and compassion.

Maggie had probably attributed her melancholy to the death of her six-month-old. Painful memories of wee John as well as an earlier miscarriage continued to surface.

God had been faithful in the past by blessing them with Douglas, so she would trust that this babe would live. She had so much to be thankful for, particularly now with the new bairn growing in her belly. Should she tell Maggie about this expected child? Nay, she would wait another month or so, just in case.

Jean and Mary entered the kitchen just as Maggie peered out the window again. "Girls, please ask the boys to wash for dinner. Jean, do you know where Donald is?"

"Perhaps he has gone to visit Sally Lamont." Jean gave Mary a knowing grin before they went outside in pursuit of their brothers.

Heather tilted her head. "Is Donald sweet on Sally?"

Maggie chuckled as she cut up the roasted chickens and placed the meat on a platter. "The lad takes notice of any budding lass, even your Mary. She certainly is growing to be a lovely young lady."

"Mary is not yet fifteen, a wee bit young for courting. Aye, she is bonnie and a delight most of the time." Heather took the bowls to the table. "But she can also be as prickly as a porcupine."

Maggie's lips quirked up. "Raising boys is so much easier."

Matthew sat in the Duncans' parlor, gazing out the window. Stephens' pleas continued to haunt him. He would weigh the consequences of accepting or rejecting the assignment and seek the Lord's direction.

Adam took a puff from his pipe. "I wonder if Virginia will be next. The recent attacks near Boston will require the colonies to respond." He got up from the chair and closed the parlor door. "No need to upset the ladies."

Matthew shook his head. "An assault on Virginia, the most British of all the colonies? Perish the thought. And what do you think the response would be? Most of us have family in England or Scotland. I suspect we will have a reaction before Virginia is targeted."

Adam slammed down his pipe. "'Twill be David fighting Goliath, and the outcome will be the same. Fortunately, our militia has General Gage and his lobsterbacks on the defense now."

"An interesting analogy," Matthew answered. "But Britain has the largest navy in the world and a strong army presence, particularly in the north. Our untrained colonial militias operate independently and have no unifying command. If war comes, it will tear our communities in two and cause a civil war that knows no boundaries."

"There can be no retreating after what happened in Massachusetts. Lord North and the King must understand they have pushed us too far this time. They shall realize the folly of fighting three thousand miles across the sea."

Folly. Indeed, both sides might soon realize their folly in this fight. Matthew stood and waited for Adam to do the same. They headed toward the kitchen. "My friend, you and I cannot solve these problems. The Continental Congress meets again next month. I venture much will be determined there in the way of organizing our forces. Whatever the outcome, all the colonies will have a representative say in our destiny."

But what would his role be? Could he remain neutral as he had hoped, or would he—and his family—be pulled into this fight?

A few minutes later, the Stewart and Duncan children gathered for the meal. Just thinking about her affection for this family brought tears to Heather's eyes. It had been Maggie, as well as the Reverend Mr. Northrup, who had convinced her she should marry the widowed father, Matthew Stewart, that warm April day five years before when he purchased her indenture.

Maggie drew back the curtain at the window and looked outside. "Now, if only Donald would come home." She turned to the children. "Do any of you know where Donald might be or why he is late?"

Silence.

Mary approached Heather and whispered, "Will you say anything if he does not return?"

"Aye."

"Must we go back to the farm this afternoon?"

"We leave shortly after dinner, as planned," Heather said. "Your father will be eager to get home if those clouds in the northwest mean a storm is gathering."

Heather watched the men enter the room. Adam Duncan wore a solemn look, and Matthew had a clenched jaw. *Please, no more talk of conflict with England.*

Matthew's fleeting glance at her and the subtle shake of his head forbade any inquiry.

Heather watched Adam, the stouter of the two men, take his place at the head of the table. His usual jolly disposition had changed considerably. The flush on his face showed from the top of his steenkirk to the sparse growth of brown hair that began well back on his forehead.

They all lowered their heads as Adam, still standing, offered a prayer. "Heavenly Father, we ask Your blessing for this meal. All we have comes from You. May this food strengthen our bodies to Your service." Most eyes around the table looked up, expecting the prayer to end there as it usually did. But he continued, and they looked down again. "We ask for wisdom to know Your will, guidance as we pursue it, and courage to accomplish the task ahead. In our Lord's name, we pray. Amen."

Matthew's brown eyes locked on hers when Heather raised her head.

Adam glanced down the table to the empty seat. "Where is Donald?"

Maggie patted Adam's hand. "I'm sure he will have a good explanation, dear. It is not like him to be late for dinner."

Adam's lips did not even twitch toward a smile. "Donald will answer for his absence later."

Jean looked at her father. "Why are you angry, Papa? Surely not because Donald is late."

"My ill temper has more to do with a discussion Matt and I had with some men at Brady's, lass. Some people's inability to reason beyond their own self-interests infuriates me."

Mark passed the bread to Matthew. "Are you also angry, Papa?"

"Our conversation was irritating." He looked at Maggie. "I'm thankful to the Duncans for hosting our family these past two days. I hope we can reciprocate soon."

Maggie smiled. "We shall visit in June when we go to see my sister in Leesburg."

With the mention of a visit in just a couple of months, the heavy mood lifted, and the two families enjoyed the dinner. When the meal ended, Matthew and Adam retreated to the parlor. Maggie and Heather were at work in the kitchen when the delivery boy from Parker's Millinery Shop brought the parcels. Heather set them on the table and returned to her work.

Maggie handed her a towel. "What are you going to do about the letter from Boston?"

The letter. Another thing that weighed heavily on her mind. "We still have not come to a decision."

"Do the children know about it?"

"Nay," Heather said. "We will address that when we have settled on what to do."

The kitchen door that led to the service yard opened and closed.

"Donald!" Maggie's shout pierced whatever peace remained. "Your face!" She rushed to her eldest son. "What happened? Who did this to you?"

CHAPTER 2

Matthew watched Adam flinch at Maggie's shriek. The Duncans' oldest had obviously returned. He followed Adam to the kitchen. Inside, Heather touched his sleeve and pointed to the clock on the mantel. He nodded.

Adam approached his son still standing by the door, a grimace on his bruised face. "Son, where have you been?"

"I'm sorry I'm late." Donald took a deep breath. "Braden Campbell and I ran into some trouble a few blocks back, and I wanted to wash before coming home." Two deep cuts and several swollen and reddened bruises were a vivid contrast to his pallor. "We went to Braden's house."

Heather moved a chair closer to Donald, and he entered the kitchen. "Here, sit down."

Donald sank into the chair and turned his face toward his mother. "It really hurts, Ma."

When Mark and the younger boys rushed into the room, Matthew reached out and caught Mark as he passed him. Jean and Mary stood in the doorway.

Maggie shifted her son's face gently to better inspect the damage. "How is Braden?" She used a damp cloth to clean the wounds.

Donald winced and groaned. "He got some cuts and scrapes, too."

Adam's brows furrowed. "What provoked this?"

"May we talk about it later, Pa?"

Mark's brown eyes were wide with excitement. "Does Braden look as awful as you do?"

Matthew shook his head at Mark, then rested his hand on Adam's shoulder. "I think 'tis time for the Stewarts to ready for our return home." It was evident that the Duncan family needed some privacy.

They gathered their things and took them outside while the children made their farewells. Adam and Matthew loaded the wagon for their departure. Nearby, Donald stood deep in conversation with Mary.

Heather and the boys positioned themselves on the seats and shared final parting words. Maggie squeezed Heather's hand. "I withdraw my earlier comment on the relative ease of raising sons. They are *all* a worry."

"I know, Maggie. Each child has a fierce grip on our hearts."

Mark's voice rose above the rest. "Well, I think it is fine that Donnie and Braden gave those stinkin' Tories a beating."

All eyes turned to Mark before shifting to Donald.

Adam approached his oldest son, who pulled his attention from Mary reluctantly. "So, is that what this is all about?"

"We argued over whether Virginia should send the militia up to take on the redcoats. We were fighting with Everett Hastings and some of his friends."

Matthew's heart sank. The fight was getting closer than he wanted to admit when young men in Alexandria were getting into fisticuffs. Stephens' scheme had to be given serious thought ... and soon.

⊚⅋⚜⅌⊚

As they reached the outskirts of Alexandria, his conversation with Lucas Stephens continued to weigh heavily on Matthew's mind. Stephens said that he would be in contact with him for his answer. His answer. *And what should that be, Lord? Are You calling me to serve by being part of this scheme?*

His goal had been to remain neutral, but how could he if

England continued to impose their repressive restrictions and kill his countrymen? He certainly could not fight for the Crown against his fellow colonists.

Heather leaned her head on his shoulder and pointed to the sky. "I love to watch the way the sunlight shines through the clouds onto the hilly landscape. The visit with the Duncans was precisely the tonic I needed." She slipped her arm through his as he held the reins steady. "I'm grateful. You probably had your mind on the farm the whole time."

Her comment lightened his heart. She delighted him in so many ways, and her buoyed spirits encouraged him. "Not the entire time." He reached over with his free hand and patted hers. "'Twas a pleasant visit, just what we needed."

They headed west on the well-traveled road that stretched on for miles, away from the friendships and diversions of Alexandria. The ever-changing landscape, with its homes and outbuildings scattered amongst the rolling hills, was beautiful in the late afternoon. As they traveled farther from the city, they passed through wooded areas not yet cleared. The leaves on the trees were in full leaf with the new green that came early every spring. Dark clouds moved in from the west. In a few short hours, they would reach home. *Will we escape this other approaching storm or be drawn into it? Surely our safe haven will withstand any coming tempest.*

In the back of the wagon, Mary, deep into a book she had borrowed from Jean, was oblivious to everything around her, and Mark and Douglas had both fallen asleep.

Heather was unusually quiet. Was she upset by Donald's conflict or concerned about the child she was carrying?

"Are you ill, Heather?"

"Nay. I am well."

"You had such a distant look about you."

"Did I now?" She grinned. "You caught me daydreaming, remembering ... remembering that first day five years ago with you on this very route."

"That is a day I shall never forget." He chuckled. "I wonder which one of us was the most terrified."

"Terrified? You?" She poked him in his side. "What a confession. I had no idea. You were so sure of yourself, so serious and determined."

"Determined to be sure. I needed someone at home caring for the children. Any anxiety I may have harbored about our marriage was worth the risk I believed had to be taken." He brought her hand to his lips. "The most pleasing bargain I ever made."

"I was a bit suspicious of a man who would marry a complete stranger when there had to be plenty of eligible ladies looking for a husband, particularly in Alexandria."

"How might I have courted a lady in Alexandria while stealing time from the children and trying to work the farm twenty miles west? I had no desire to go courting anyway." He put his arm around her shoulder and drew her to him. "And you, my sweet … Your charm and beauty as you stood there shaking on the quay, broke any resistance I might have had to taking a wife."

Their laughter woke Mark and roused Mary from her reading. Douglas slept on.

Mary turned in her seat to face them. "What is so amusing?"

Matthew grinned. "We have been reminiscing about the day we met and married."

Mary put down her book and leaned forward. "A day I shan't forget, Papa. I was angry when you brought that 'strange woman' to the Duncans' house and said you planned to marry her."

He turned to Mary and winked. "I remember your response very distinctly."

Mary touched the back of Heather's arm. "Forgive me, but I never understood why Papa favored you, for you looked … well … so poorly."

Heather laughed. "Very diplomatically stated."

"Yet you forgave me for being so dreadful to you for months."

"You were a challenge, lass," Heather said, "but I understood your fears."

After a moment, Mary returned to her book.

Matthew reached for Heather's hand and brought it back to his lips. "I am glad the trip to town and time with Maggie and the clan brought the smile to your lips. You called it a tonic. I hope it continues when we return home."

"Please forgive me, Matthew." She kept her voice low. "I know my moods and nerves have ... well, I keep thinking about our John and the unborn bairn we lost."

"There is nothing to forgive. Give yourself time to heal. All will be well again."

He smiled at her and caressed her cheek. She had a gift from God growing and resting close to her heart. This child would never take the baby's or John's place, but this new life was a reminder that God truly did restore the years the locusts hath eaten.

"Pa," Mark said, "what do you think the people will do in response to the battles near Boston?"

"We do not know all the details yet, son. We shall have to wait and assess what transpires in the next days and weeks. The recent uprisings in Massachusetts may very well change all our lives."

Mark said, "Donald believes we shall go to war with England. If we do, he and Braden Campbell plan to join the militia."

"That is troubling. I'm sure the idea of joining the fight sounds very heroic to you boys." Matthew turned to look into his son's eyes. "However, you must consider how many losses would result were we to go to war."

"You said Virginia and the other colonies cannot continue to obey England's demands."

Matthew focused on the road again. "'Tis true, we may soon be at the point of war. But anyone who thinks it will be easy or clean without families and friends being torn apart by death, injury, or politics had better think again. England has a trained, experienced, and well-equipped army and navy. We do not. War is not a boy's game, Mark. The casualties would be enormous. In any event, I doubt we will need to send young men of Donald's and Braden's age off to battle."

Mary's voice trembled. "As British subjects, how could Virginia go to war with them?"

"A good many Virginians, as well as people from the other colonies, believe we should not remain under British rule. They are tired of being subjected to the heavy taxes and the harsher laws and restrictions Parliament imposes on us without any real representation in Parliament. Boycotting British goods has been about the only way we have made our point of view known." He removed his hat and handed it to Heather in an effort to cool his forehead.

"The King views us as rebellious children, and I fear the point may have been reached where neither camp will back down."

Heather clutched his damp hat. "Surely war can be avoided. Too many people would suffer great loss if war broke out. My father never let us forget the Jacobite Rising of '45 and the last stand at Culloden Moor in the spring of '46. Both had lasting consequences for all Scots. I lost a grandfather and four uncles."

The look of terror on Heather's face was a punch in the gut. "No need to be anxious, my dear. Judging from the way you have crushed the side of my hat, our discussion has alarmed you."

"I'm sorry." She smoothed the stiff fabric out. "All this talk of war is troubling. I'm used to Adam being stirred up by political discussions, but 'tis unusual to find you so concerned."

"Events are unfolding quickly. Our entire world may soon be turned upside down. The time is approaching when each one of us will have to determine where our loyalties lie." *And I will have to determine what role I will play. I am trusting You, Lord, to make that very clear and to equip me to answer Your call.*

Heather slipped her free hand into the crook of his arm again. "Perhaps we should speak of this later so as not to distress the children."

"We cannot insulate the young ones from the events going on

around them. They are going to hear it discussed, and they need to understand. Today's incident with Donald and the Campbell boy proves that."

"But all this talk of war makes it seem so much more inevitable. I dread how all our lives would change. The consequences would be heartbreaking."

He patted her hand. "Whatever transpires between Britain and the Colonies is beyond our control. We shall pray that God would give the delegates wisdom and direction."

Heather gazed up at Matthew. His dark hair was beginning to grey at the temples. Was he more concerned than he was admitting? She must calm her own fears. 'Twas not doing her or the babe any good to fret over what she could not control.

"Be careful for nothing; but in every thing by prayer and supplication with thanksgiving let your requests be made known unto God. And the peace of God, which passeth all understanding, shall keep your hearts and minds through Christ Jesus."

Thanksgiving. Aye, she had so much to be thankful for—a husband, two children, and another on the way. She had survived that miserable Atlantic crossing and had her indenture purchased by a godly man whom she loved dearly. She survived the birth of two children and the death of John and another babe. They had a farm, a home, and the ordinary. Whenever she felt anxious about what was happening around her, she must remember that in thankfulness she would find peace. She would do all she could to care for her family, keep the ordinary running smoothly, and help Matthew oversee the farm. These were all blessings from God, and she would do her part to protect them. The Lord and Matthew had seen her through dark days. Together they could face all that would come.

She glanced behind her and saw that the children were listening.

She leaned close to Matthew and whispered, "We need to discuss the letter."

"I know. We will ... later."

CHAPTER 3

It was dusk by the time they approached Stewart's Green. The filtered light through the leaves on the trees cast muted shadows, and the harmony of crickets and bullfrogs reminded Heather how different the sounds of country evenings were from those in the villages. The light shining through the window in the Gordons' smaller cottage situated to the left of the ordinary drew her attention.

"It's been a long day," Matthew said. "I will check in with Thomas once we have unloaded the wagon and taken care of the horse."

Years earlier, when they were the sole residents of their farm, a day spent away from the property meant they would find it in the same state when they returned as when they had left it. Now, with the Gordon family living there as tenant farmers and the ordinary with the possibility of guests, returning home often came with surprises.

Heather reached for his arm. "There is a light burning. I want to see how Polly is feeling before we settle in for the night." She turned to the children "Mary, please take Douglas inside and ready him for bed while I go to the Gordons'. We will unload the wagon later."

"Yes, ma'am."

"You two are angels."

"Hungry angels," Mark said.

"Aye. Get yourselves a bite to eat."

When the wagon came to a halt, Matthew helped Heather and Mary down, then lifted Douglas into Mary's waiting arms. Mark carried a bag and headed inside the Green with their father. From the back of the wagon, Heather retrieved a basket and made her way toward the cottage.

The door opened before she reached the porch.

Polly's right hand rested on the back of her hip. "I heard the wagon." Her ample belly and the telltale dark shadows under her eyes suggested exhaustion. She stepped aside. "How are the Duncans?"

"They are fine. We had a bonny time. They send their regards and"—she lifted the basket—"some treats for you."

"How kind of them."

"Do sit down. I hope 'tis not too late to stop in for a quick visit."

"Nay, please come in."

Heather set the basket on the table and sat across from her friend. "I believe there is something in here for the baby. How are you feeling?"

"Tired, and ... so different from when I carried Todd and Philip. Being older, I s'pose."

She took Polly's hand in hers. "I'm praying for you and the babe. You need to take things a bit easier. I'm here, so please rest tomorrow. I can see to the meals and cleaning. Many thanks for helping with the Green while we were gone. Tell me, have we any guests?"

"Yesterday, two gentlemen on horseback and a family from west of Leesburg stayed the night, and midday today, your friend from Fredericksburg, Mr. Macmillan, arrived."

"Oh, 'twill be so good to see Andrew again. Anything else I need to know?"

"It has been quiet here. Alexandria must have been exciting. I s'pose a lot of goings on about politics. 'Tis all most folks want to talk about these days."

"Aye, and the talk is growing increasingly heated. Where are Philip and Todd?"

"I think they are in the barn, caring for the animals."

"There are sweets in the basket for them. I shall stop by in the morning. Good night."

She left and walked toward the Green, only stopping at the sound of voices nearby.

Even with his lantern, Philip's amber hair appeared darker at night. "We saw you coming from our place. Do you think Ma is in a bad way, Mrs. Stewart?" The fifteen-year-old's expression suggested he feared for his mother.

Both boys were lanky, but Philip stood a head taller than his thirteen-year-old brother Todd.

"She is tired. Come and get me if she needs help ... for any reason."

"Do you think the baby will come soon?" Philip asked. "Ma is mighty big and groans a lot like Bessie did before she delivered her calf."

Todd winced. Though he was the younger brother, he had already matured beyond Philip and would probably far surpass him soon enough. "Ma won't like you comparing her to a cow."

"She may be closer to having the babe than we thought," Heather said, "so do what you can to help her. And plan on eating at the Green tomorrow. No need for her to prepare meals."

"Yes, ma'am," Philip said.

When she opened the door to the main house, the soft lights in the large center hall welcomed her. Men's voices came from the parlor, and muffled sounds of the children's conversation drifted down from upstairs.

She glanced up the stairs and then headed to the parlor.

Matthew poured two tankards of cider and handed one to Andrew, who was leaning against the mantel over the hearth. Andrew's gaunt face and the dark circles under his eyes were reminders of his loss.

"Heather will be pleased you came for a visit," Matthew said. "She has been concerned about you and James since Rebecca's death."

Andrew rubbed the rim of the pewter tankard. A frown formed before he looked up. "We are doing as well as can be expected."

Heather entered the parlor, made her way across the room, and clasped Andrew's hands in hers. "What a joy to have you here again. It has been too long. Will you be with us for a while?"

"Tomorrow I will catch the ferry to western Frederick County, Maryland. I have a meeting with some chaps at Hungerford's Tavern."

"Hungerford's?" Matthew motioned for Andrew to sit. "That place has a reputation for being a hotbed of Patriot activity." Wherever he turned, it seemed that people were taking sides. His hopes of remaining neutral were beginning to seem farcical. "Are you involved with the independence movement?"

"You might say so, ever since the Hungerford Resolves and Fairfax Resolves last year." Andrew dropped a copy of the *Gazette* on the table. "Look, another Continental Congress will meet in Philadelphia next month, and Lord Dunmore is challenging the proceedings."

Matthew put down his tankard. "That is no surprise. He is in a precarious position. Patrick Henry's speech last month at the House of Burgesses only added to the discontentment. Each day it seems we move closer to a conflict."

Heather removed her shawl, folded it, and placed it on her lap. "Andrew, we were so saddened to get your letter telling us of Rebecca's death. We had so hoped she would recover. You and James have been in our prayers. How is he?"

"James is well and back in Williamsburg."

"Studying the law at the College of William & Mary?" Matthew asked.

"Yes, though his interests seem to skew." He focused on Heather again. "Your letter and generous sentiments meant a great deal to both of us."

"We were very fond of Rebecca, and she will be missed by all who knew her. You have had a rough time. 'Tis good to be around friends and keep busy. We're so glad you came to visit."

"I would not come west without a stop at Stewart's Green. My increased involvement in this squabble between Britain and America has given me a new purpose," Andrew said, "something to pour my energy into now that Rebecca is gone."

Voices came from the top of the stairs.

Heather arose. "I must go to the children. I will look forward to a longer visit in the morning, Andrew."

Upstairs in the boys' room, Heather sat in the chair and scooped Douglas into her arms and nuzzled her four-year-old's sandy blond curls. "I see Mary helped you change into your night clothes. Ready for bed, young man, or do you want a bite to eat first?"

Mary pulled back the coverlets on the boys' beds. "I brought up some biscuits and milk. Is that Mr. Macmillan I hear in the parlor with Papa?"

"Aye."

"Did he mention James? Is he well? I mean, the loss of a mother can be so painful."

She spotted the blush on the girl's cheeks. "He said James is well and at school. 'Tis thoughtful of you to be concerned about him."

"Concerned?" Mark laughed. "She is smitten."

"What you are talking about?" Mary's narrowed eyes looked as though they would bore a hole through her brother's head.

"While we were at the Duncans', you told Jean you hoped James Macmillan would visit and that you welcomed his attention."

Mary picked up a pillow, threw it at Mark, and stormed out of the room.

Heather had assessed Mary correctly. This budding young woman and her youthful annoyance with boys had changed into something entirely different.

CHAPTER 4

The next morning, Matthew and Andrew took seats at the window table in the public room. There was plenty to be done, and he would get to it later, but Andrew's visits were rare, and it was good to have some time with him. Losing a wife was a lonely business. Mary must've finished her chores early because she slipped in and sat in the window seat with a book.

Heather joined them carrying a tray of food.

Andrew looked around the room. "This is the most pleasant ordinary I have visited. Others are dark, dreary places, but this is a warm and inviting room, filled with light."

"'Tis all Heather's doing." Matthew placed his hand on hers. "She wanted Stewart's Green to look like a residence, not a business establishment."

"'Tis our home." Heather set a plate of eggs and another of biscuits and bacon on the table. "We lived beside and above the family's dry goods shop in Scotland, separate from our business. Here, the family and business areas are merged. Since Stewart's Green caters more to travelers than those seeking entertainment, we chose to make the common areas a parlor and dining room." She backed toward the door. "I will be back with the coffee."

Andrew slid the *Gazette* he had been reading the evening before across the table. "The freeholders and citizens of Williamsburg unanimously elected Peyton Randolph to represent them at the Convention next month."

Matthew glanced at the printed page. "He is a good man and doesn't hesitate in supporting the colonies, not at all like his brother John. The Convention will be a lively place with everything that has taken place this past month. You probably have associates who will be in attendance." Matthew considered all of Andrew's business colleagues. Andrew might have influential contacts of his own.

"Yes," Andrew said. "George Washington grew up on the other side of the Rappahannock River, just a few miles from my home. He crossed the river to where we both were educated by the rector of St. George's Parish."

"Washington, hmm. He has quite the reputation for leadership. I have no doubt he will have a significant role if an army is formed. Do you still have contact with him?"

"Occasionally. He sold Ferry Farm last year but comes to Fredericksburg to see his mother and sister. My guess is that he will be put in charge of organizing a unified military force."

Heather returned with coffee and another plate of bacon, which she passed to Andrew. "Will James be spending the summer in Williamsburg or Fredericksburg?"

"He will be coming home in May when his classes end and plans on returning to Williamsburg in July."

"Why so soon?" Heather sat and passed a dish of spoonbread.

"A number of his friends believe they can be of some use in the Capitol while Randolph and the others prepare for the convention in Pennsylvania."

Matthew put down the news journal. "Not a bad idea. Students are in a better position to keep their eyes and ears open to the machinations of Governor Lord Dunmore without as much scrutiny as others would receive. It appears the Governor had the Royal Marines take a dozen or so barrels of gunpowder from the magazine there last week."

"He fears an insurrection," Andrew said. "James and I plan to visit friends in Leesburg, Fairfax, and Alexandria while he is home, so perhaps we can stop here for a visit."

Matthew studied Andrew. He was tempted to take him aside and seek his wisdom regarding his choosing to get involved in Stephens' scheme. But what he was considering had risks, and he could best protect his family and friends by remaining silent. He glanced to where Mary sat in the window seat. The sun shone brightly through the window onto the open book on her lap. Matthew smiled at his daughter, who seemed quite attentive, but not to reading.

While Thomas and the boys transplanted tobacco, Matthew worked the rest of the day in the cornfield. He needed solitude and physical activity and time to weigh the wisdom, benefits, and risks of agreeing to Stephens' proposition.

The scheme Jones and Stephens had cooked up had eaten away at him. And Stephens' words prodded him like a battering ram. "If our cause is just, and many believe it is, then God Almighty will equip us to answer His call."

"Many will take up arms," Stephens had said. "Will you serve on the side of liberty or will you serve the Crown's oppression?"

Liberty was a just cause, and he genuinely believed that God would equip those He called. But was Stephens' scheme God's call? The men's request had come right on the heels of the letter from his late wife's parents suggesting a visit with their grandchildren in Philadelphia. The timing could be a sign. Was that a fleece the Lord had provided? If so, then there would need to be conditions.

On the one hand, it wasn't as if he were joining the militia. This assignment would be limited. And it seemed, with his established relationships in Philadelphia, he was uniquely positioned for this service.

Is this what You would have me do, Lord?

Because of the smallpox epidemic, his late wife's parents were leaving Boston to spend the summer in Philadelphia with family. They had written to him requesting that the children join them there. That would have pleased Elizabeth.

The relationship with Henry and his family could be an open

door.

And the children's visit would provide him the cover he needed. Coincidental? Or the hand of Providence?

He did not believe in coincidences.

On the other hand, he had responsibilities, and he did not want to be away from his family. And there were risks. Were he captured or killed, what would become of his family? Might his actions put them all at risk?

But what were the chances he would be found out?

Maybe slim, but if he were caught, his actions could put his family in jeopardy.

The anticipation of such a venture had cost him sleep, but it had drawn him closer to God, because he knew if he were to aid the Patriot cause, he would have to put his complete trust and dependence on the Lord. His appreciation for all the blessings he'd been given had grown immeasurably.

Matthew reached for the jug of water and took a drink. He looked around at his farm, its beautiful rolling hills, lush meadows, and a stream teeming with fish. God had been very good to him. The years with Elizabeth had been a treasure, and though the Lord had taken her home, He had brought Heather into his life, an unexpected gift. Soon he would have four children. Yes, he had been blessed indeed.

With all his heart, he wanted to stay here and enjoy those blessings. To work his land, raise his children, and hold his beautiful wife every night. He wanted the world to stay away and his life to remain just like this, forever.

But the world wouldn't stay away, and the dreams he had for the future were shifting. His countrymen, his friends, were preparing to fight the King. A battle he feared was inevitable. Yes, he believed the Colonists were in the right. The trouble was, he didn't believe they could win. Not on their own. To take on the greatest army and navy in the world would be complete madness. Or unconditional and sustained faith that God would bless their endeavors.

Were he to accept Stephens' challenge, he'd have to keep it to himself. As much as he hated the deception, he would not allow his family or friends to know anything about what he was doing. It was the only way he could protect them. Stephens would have to ensure that and answer Matthew's other questions satisfactorily. Those boundaries must be assured.

Did he truly want to remain safe at Stewart's Green while others fought to protect all that was dear to him? Or was he willing to do his part to help? Could he live with himself if he ignored this call?

Those questions still plagued him as he picked up the hoe and returned to work.

Not my will, Lord, Your will. If you lead me to accept the assignment, I trust You will provide what I need.

Heather had no time alone with Matthew until they retired that evening. She studied him as he readied for bed. He had that look again. She'd seen it a lot lately, that faraway look as if he were lost in thought. She pulled back the coverlet. "Andrew has been through so much with Rebecca's illness and death. 'Tis good he is keeping busy, particularly with James' absence. What is your impression of his visit?"

"Andrew's visits are always good. Time is a great healer, and activity and purpose help."

"Matthew, what should we do about the letter from Boston? We need to answer the Moores."

He set the oil lantern on the candle stand beside the bed and reclined beside her. "Their request is reasonable. The children have spent so little time with their grandparents since Elizabeth's death."

"You don't worry about the children being so far away for months?"

"They lived in Alexandria for almost a year following Elizabeth's death, so I'm familiar with the pain of separation. But Mary and

Mark thrived with that arrangement, and I genuinely think they would benefit from a visit with their grandparents also."

"I know, but Philadelphia? Is it safe from the smallpox epidemic?"

"Safer than Boston was, or the Moores wouldn't have chosen to go there." Matthew patted her on the hand, his voice gentle. "John and Louisa would not ask the children to spend the summer there if they feared for their safety. While I'm reluctant to have them go, I prefer the children go to Philadelphia rather than Boston, three hundred miles further north, especially considering the recent troubles there."

"What do you think the children will say?"

"I suspect Mary will be thrilled to have the chance to experience Philadelphia. Mark may not even remember his grandparents. I will write to the Moores and tell them I will bring the children in June."

"But what about all this talk of rebellion?"

"That is another reason I prefer they visit them now. We do not know what the future might bring." He put his hand out to her. "Don't worry."

She pulled up the coverlet, still studying him as he put out the light and motioned her to cradle in his arm.

"You seem distracted lately. Is it the letter, the farm, the Green, or something else weighing heavily on your mind?"

"Do not fret, my dear." He pulled her close and held her in the shelter of his arms. "Nothing is weighing heavily on my mind."

She drifted off to sleep remembering the Scripture, *"Take therefore no thought for the morrow: for the morrow shall take thought for the things of itself. Sufficient unto the day is the evil thereof."*

CHAPTER 5

The warm May sun soothed Heather as she stood and relieved her stiff back. She removed her gloves and fanned herself with her straw hat. Weeding and tilling the kitchen garden had energized her initially, but now she needed a rest. The three weeks since their trip to Alexandria had gone by quickly. She must look in on Polly to see if she needed any help.

Tears filled Heather's eyes, and sorrow, her heart. No surprise Polly had delivered early since she had carried two babes. Seeing Polly's distress, Thomas had gone for Dr. Edwards. Laura, born first, appeared healthy, but wee Frank lived only an hour. Heather grieved for Polly. Nothing compared to the pain of losing a child.

Leaning the potato hook against the side of the whitewashed picket fence, she glanced at Douglas, who was playing with blocks on the back porch.

Mary came out the back door. "Two riders are approaching. We may have boarders. I will find the boys to take care of the horses."

Heather wiped her hands on her apron and tucked the loose strands of hair into her cap before placing the straw hat back on her head. She headed to the front of the Green. The travelers slowed their horses as they approached.

Philip attended to the gentlemen's horses while she escorted them inside.

Heather stood in the upstairs hallway and directed Mr. Jones, who appeared to be about fifty, and Mr. Stephens, possibly a few years younger, to available rooms. These were well-dressed guests and new to the Green. "There is a *Gazette* in the common room," she said. "Supper is served at seven. In the meantime, may I offer you cider, water, or coffee?"

"Appreciate it, ma'am." Mr. Stephens, the taller of the two, walked to the end of the hallway and peered out a window that looked down on the barn. "Is Matthew Stewart around?"

"He should be back from the fields later. Do you need him before then?"

"It can wait." Mr. Jones, the older and shorter man, looked around. "We will take that coffee you offered in the common room. Do you have any other guests?"

"Nay, none others yet."

Polly was working at the table when Heather got to the kitchen. "We have two gentlemen for supper. For now, all they want is coffee." Heather bent over the basket resting by the table and smiled at the sleeping newborn. "How is wee Laura this afternoon?"

"She is an easy one so far, very different from the boys. Laura has charmed us all. 'Twill be the same, no doubt, with your family when we welcome your little one this fall."

Heather sighed as she prepared a tray for their guests. "When you finish, please get off your feet. It has not been long since the birth."

Laden with the tray of coffee and cakes, Heather returned to the common room. The men halted their conversation and smiled as she served them. Odd. Male guests typically ignored her and talked when being served. These gentlemen were not only well dressed but had fine manners.

Back in the kitchen, she started working on supper.

A few minutes later, Thomas came in, wiping his face with a rag. "Is Polly here?"

"She went to the cottage with Laura to rest. I'm getting this tray ready for you to take a meal to her. Shall I prepare a plate for you, or do you want to take supper here with the boys?"

"I will eat with her. No wonder she is tired. She is up all hours of the night with the girl."

"'Twill get easier as the babe grows." She sent up a prayer of protection for Laura and rubbed her own belly. Fear of losing her babe was always just below the surface. With two gone, she couldn't bear losing another. *Protect this one, Father, and the three children we have.* As long as she and Matthew and the children were safe, she could handle anything.

Matthew carried the hoe and pitchfork back to the barn. The sound of Philip mucking out the stalls caught his attention. "'Tis nearly time for supper."

"I'm almost finished."

Two figures cast a large shadow into the barn near where Matthew stowed his tools. He turned and felt his neck tense. It was Stephens and Jones, the men he had met in Alexandria. "I'm surprised to see you gents here."

"We wanted to—"

"Wait." Matthew held up his hand. "Philip, go on in now." Any conversation with these men had to be private.

Philip walked out from one of the stalls. "Something wrong, Mr. Stewart?"

"We can finish this later." He patted the adolescent on the back as he walked by.

When Philip was halfway to the house, Matthew turned to the men. "Gentlemen."

Lucas Stephens glanced at Martin Jones before focusing on Matthew. "Have you given any more thought to our earlier conversation?"

"Some." He had prayed and searched his heart and mind on the matter ever since.

"You have any questions? We can begin making some initial plans ... a reason for you to be in Philadelphia around June."

Matthew rubbed his chin. June. Exactly when he had planned to go, though they had no knowledge of that.

Jones took his hat off. "No one is asking you to take up arms or join the militia. Your role will be more discreet and take far less of your time. You can still run your farm and the ordinary."

Stephens added, "You are the perfect man for this, Stewart. You know that."

Matthew glanced to the grassy area leading to the Green. Heather would be expecting him soon, possibly even sending one of the children to get him. He turned back to the men. "If I agree, 'twill be on the condition that nobody knows anything about this."

"Agreed." Stephens appeared to be the lead man on this assignment. "When will you decide?"

"Tomorrow, if you answer my questions satisfactorily. I will make my decision then."

Jones put his hat on. "Fine."

"'Tis supper time. *None* of this will be discussed. Understood?"

"Of course," Stephens said.

Matthew watched the two men walk back toward the Green, heaviness pressing on his chest. *Lord, if this is part of Your plan, I need You to show me a sign. And if this is Your call for me, please equip me to execute it.*

◎❧❀☙◉

Later that night, Matthew entered their bedroom and began removing his shirt. He glanced at Heather as she sat on the edge of the bed braiding her hair. She was captivating.

She cocked her head. "Our guests seemed eager to speak with you when they arrived."

He put his clothes away without comment.

"Where do you know Mr. Stephens and Mr. Jones from?"

"I met them in Alexandria."

"Do the Duncans know them?"

"Not sure." He hung up his shirt and turned to her. "I think they are from Philadelphia."

She tied a rag at the end of her braid and watched him ease himself into bed. "Are you going to tell me about your conversation with them or am I supposed to guess?"

He leaned back onto his pillow, regarding her. Would her questions ever cease?

She lifted her eyebrows.

He opened his arms. "Come here, my sweet."

Reclining on the bed beside him, she searched his eyes.

He wrapped his arms around her. "All the talk of turmoil between the colonies and the Crown upsets you. They were passing on news about the friction between the Royal Governor and the locals. The Randolph brothers are opposed to each other. John is remaining loyal to the Crown, and Peyton is leading the Virginia delegation to the Second Continental Congress."

"Matthew, what does that have to do with us here, so many miles away?"

"The conflict is not just between the Crown and the colonies to the north. Virginians are taking sides." He held her close, caressing her back. "I say we sleep now."

Her warmth and the scent of her hair were intoxicating. He knew she would have enjoyed living closer to civilization these past five years, but he was more grateful for their distance from town than ever. If nothing else, the miles would make her feel safer.

The next day, Heather was in the kitchen to begin dinner preparations. Glancing out the window, she spotted Matthew speaking with the two guests outside the barn. They seemed intent on whatever they were discussing.

Mary came through the door and set the tub with the chickens she had just plucked on the counter. "I thought Father planned on going to the Whitcombs' place today."

Heather picked up the fowl. "I believe he is taking the ox over there after dinner."

"May I go with him? I told Martha I would help her finish sewing her gown. You don't need me for anything this afternoon, do you?"

"By all means, go. When does Martha leave to visit her aunt and uncle in Williamsburg?"

"The end of next week. Martha said she will be attending teas, assemblies, and concerts."

"That sounds enjoyable."

"Much more interesting than doing chores on the farm. I suppose I should be thankful to have a friend who lives nearby who will have interesting stories to tell when she returns."

Heather fought the impulse to roll her eyes. "True."

Mary's brow furrowed. "I would settle for going to Alexandria or even Fredericksburg."

Heather placed the chicken pieces in two large iron skillets. Matthew planned to let the children know at dinner about his intention to take them to Philadelphia in June. Soon enough, Mary would have her own exciting news to share with their nearest neighbors.

Thoughts of Hannah Whitcomb made Heather shudder. She was grateful the Whitcombs lived but a ten-minute walk from Stewart's Green, giving Mary and Mark neighbors close to their ages. Tobias and Martha were sixteen and fifteen, and Teddy was only a year older than Mark. But their mother, Hannah, could only be described as difficult. While at times the woman demonstrated a tender and generous heart, more often she was a busybody and gossip. Hannah's lack of tact set many folks in the community on edge.

When they finished dinner, Mary cleared away the plates. "May I go with you to the Whitcombs' today, Papa? Martha and I have some sewing to finish."

Heather caught the wink in Matthew's eye when he set his napkin down and held up his hand. "Yes, but first I have a matter to discuss with you. You too, Mark."

Mark had been pushing back in his chair but stopped at Matthew's words. Both the children regarded their father.

"We received a letter from your mother's parents."

"The ones who live in Boston?" Mark asked.

"Correct. They are planning to spend the next few months in Philadelphia at a cousin's home and have asked if the two of you might like to visit them. I responded that I believed you would."

Mary leaned forward, eyes wide. "Do you mean it?"

Mark looked back and forth between the adults.

Matthew reached over and tousled the boy's hair. "We mean it. We agreed you both should spend some time with the Moores. We are just waiting to hear back from them with more details. If 'tis still convenient, I will take you to Philadelphia next month."

Douglas crawled onto Heather's lap. "Do I go too?"

Heather ran her fingers through his sandy blond curls. "No, son, you are to stay here with us. I am grateful I do not need to part with you."

He looked relieved but remained in her arms.

"Mary, I will get out those fabrics we purchased in Alexandria. We need to begin sewing those new dresses for you right away. You can share your news with Martha this afternoon."

"Philadelphia." Mary stood and smoothed her dress. Her amber eyes sparkled. "Martha will be so jealous. I will get my needlework and be ready to go."

Heather got up and placed the dinner dishes on a tray. The sound of Mary running upstairs made her laugh and brought Matthew to his feet. "The drama of adolescence."

Still seated at the table, Mark had a pensive expression on his face.

Heather untied her apron and hung it on a nearby hook. "Is something wrong?"

"No ... well, perhaps, a bit."

"Are you anxious about going to Philadelphia?"

"I don't remember much about my grandparents."

"I'm sure once you are there a couple of days, you will be reacquainted with them, and everything will be fine. There will be so many fascinating things to do and discover. And Mary will be with you, so you will always have her company. Go on out and finish your chores." She watched him through the window as he walked to the barn. They would be gone a long time, up to two months. Would they be in danger from the escalating conflict? Would this visit satisfy Mary's curiosity for city life or only make her more dissatisfied living in the country when she returned?

Why do I allow all these doubts to plague me? Is my faith in You, Lord, so fragile? She leaned against the sideboard, closing her eyes and wrapping her arms around herself. *Perfect love casteth out fear.* She remembered her mother saying that. It must have been from the Scriptures. Aye, she would hold onto that. God had always been faithful. He would provide her with whatever she needed to face any situation that would confront their family.

CHAPTER 6

Matthew headed home, enjoying the clear skies. He had been glad to loan the ox to George and Tobias. Two plows would cut the men's plowing time in half. It had been a good day. The children seemed pleased about their trip to Philadelphia, Mary more so than Mark. The look on her face before she ran ahead of him to the Whitcomb farm warmed his heart. She was becoming a young lady with all the transitions of a normal fourteen-year-old.

Had he given Stephens and Jones the right answer? He hoped so. He had certainly prayed enough about it. He would not question his decision now.

As he turned the corner and entered his yard, he spotted the Gordon boys leading two horses to the barn, one that looked like Andrew Macmillan's bay.

At the kitchen door, he heard voices coming from the common room.

Andrew and James stood when he entered the large room.

Heather joined Matthew. "Look who arrived about thirty minutes ago. I told them of the children's upcoming adventure."

James grinned. "Good to see you again, sir." The young man had grown in the past ten months. Now eighteen and about six feet tall, his refined manners would serve him well.

Andrew shook his hand. "I hope our arrival is not an inconvenience."

"Not at all. We are delighted to see you both."

Matthew turned toward Heather. "Mary will be home by six to help you with supper."

"Good. Now, gentlemen, if you will excuse me, I will see to the meal."

Matthew turned toward James. "So, you are back at William & Mary. We understand Williamsburg is becoming a hotbed of controversy between the Whigs and the Tories."

James nodded. "Yes, sir. We all are wondering what Lord Dunmore will do now that he is feeling more threatened with each passing day."

Andrew looked at his son with pride. "Hopefully, the governor will realize how serious we colonials are and act prudently."

Matthew pointed to the Gazette. "Have you seen Dunmore's proclamation?" He picked up the paper and began reading.

"'Whereas I have been informed, from undoubted Authority, that a certain Patrick Henry, of the County of Hanover, and a number of deluded Followers, have taken up Arms, chosen their Officers, and styling themselves an Independent Company, have marched out of the County, encamped and put themselves in a Posture of War, and have written and dispatched Letters to diverse Parts of the Country, exciting the People to join in their outrageous and rebellious Practices, the great Terror of all his Majesty's faithful Subjects, and in open Defiance of Law and Government; and have committed other Acts of Violence, particularly in extorting from his Majesty's Receiver General the Sum of 330l under Pretense replacing the Powder I thought proper to order from the Magazine …'" Matthew set the newspaper on the table. "And the proclamation continues from there. If Dunmore feels imperiled, he may abandon the capitol. That would present an interesting opportunity."

A sly grin appeared on Andrew's face. "An interesting opportunity indeed. That would change everything in Virginia."

Matthew glanced toward the kitchen doorway. He must end this topic. Heather did not need to be rankled now, particularly with the baby she carried. The danger was mounting. This latest news just solidified his choice. He wished he could share what he was doing with Andrew, but that would only put his friend in danger.

He was on his own.

In the kitchen, Heather tied her apron on and began preparing the cock-a-leekie soup.

Mary walked through the door and set her sewing basket on the table.

"I'm glad you are home. I want to hear all about your visit with Martha, but 'twill have to wait." She handed Mary a knife. "Please go fetch me a few more leeks."

Mary's shoulders sagged. "I wanted to tell you about Martha's—"

"The Macmillans arrived this afternoon, so we'll have two—"

"James is here?" Mary's face lit up. "If I had known, I would have come home sooner."

Heather looked up from the kettle, eyebrows lifted. "The leeks, please."

"Right." Mary picked up a basket from the larder before going outside.

Heather shook her head. After she sliced bread, she glanced at the boiling pot hanging from the trammel. How long could it take Mary to fetch a few leeks?

While she waited, she'd find the porcelain tureen. Now, where had she put that? Aye, the front parlor.

When Heather went to the parlor, she was startled by movement outside the window. Were there birds nesting in the holly again? Nay, not birds at all. She edged to the side of the room to better observe the activity in the overgrown holly hedge. James and Mary were breaking off sprigs of the dark shiny green leaves. Had the girl gone daft?

Heather marched back to the kitchen. She would get the leeks herself. She opened the door, and there were James and Mary with a basket of holly.

James grinned in that charming way of his. "Mary and I were

bringing in the holly."

Mary winced. "For the table arrangements, Mother."

"Aye … holly to decorate the tables in May. Why did I not think of that? Let me take those." Heather tilted her head and peered at Mary's squinting eyes. "Mary, would you mind picking two or three leeks to add to our supper?"

"Leeks? Certainly. Do you want to come along, James?"

"Sure."

Heather watched as James and Mary walked around the side of the Green to the kitchen garden in back. *Oh, my!* Mary's trip to Philadelphia could prove challenging for the Moores.

❦

Matthew ushered the Gordons, Andrew, and James to the common room for supper before offering the blessing.

On the heels of the "amen," Mark assaulted James with questions. "Is the college near the capitol? How do you get about? Do you have a horse with you or do you use a carriage or trap?"

James looked flattered by the attention. "We need no conveyance. The college is right in town. We walk everywhere, even to the capitol at the other end of the street."

Matthew spotted Mary glaring at her brother before she focused on James. "I thought when you spent time at sea last summer you were destined to become a mariner."

James and his father exchanged smiles. "Since Father is a merchant and reliant on the shipping industry, I needed to become familiar with that part of the business. The ship remained in the bay, landing at various ports. It was hard work, but I enjoyed it."

While James was getting a diversified education, Matthew's bet was that he would go into trade like his father.

Andrew glanced at Mary. "Are you looking forward to your visit to Philadelphia? I'm sure you will find the social life there exciting."

"I am very excited about the visit. There will be so many interesting things to do."

He chuckled. "I expect there is a great deal a young lady would find appealing. And you too, Mark. Hundreds of Patriots turn out each day for military exercises."

Mark's eyes lit up. "That will be something to behold."

Heather exchanged an anxious glance with Matthew.

Mary's eyes grew wide. "Whatever maneuvers take place in Philadelphia will not affect us, Mr. Macmillan. Our time will be spent in educational and social pursuits."

Philip, who had silently followed the conversation, spoke up. "Can you swim, James?"

James nodded at Philip. "Why, yes, I can." He winked at Mary.

Philip nodded. "Good. If you are going to be on a ship, you should know how to swim."

⊙⅋⅋⅋⅋⊙

The next morning, the Stewarts, Macmillans, and Gordons breakfasted and prepared for Sunday services, loading the wagons for the fellowship meal that would follow.

Matthew came alongside Andrew. "I'm glad you and James will meet Spence Grayson and hear him preach."

Andrew mounted his bay, Stirling. "I'm looking forward to it, as well as meeting your other neighbors."

"Other than a barn raising, our services and fellowship meal is our only social time with friends. It gets the day and coming week off to a positive start." Matthew climbed up into the Stewart wagon and joined the others on the three-mile journey to church.

When the service was over, people made their way to the grassy yard by the schoolhouse for fellowship and a meal. While the men talked with Reverend Grayson, the boys brought out tables and benches from the schoolhouse and the women set out food.

Reverend Grayson offered the blessing, and the congregation

gathered near the tables laden with food.

Matthew pointed to a shady spot under a tree where his family and James were spreading blankets on the ground. "It looks like James has already met the Turners. Aaron Turner, the chap you just met speaking with Reverend Grayson, was the first friend Elizabeth and I made when we settled here nearly sixteen years ago. Our families have been close ever since."

Heather approached them and took Andrew's arm. "Come meet some friends." She introduced him to Amelia and Aaron Turner. "And these are their sons, Cole and Logan." The two lanky youths, one a full head taller than the other, smiled and nodded. "And these are their eight-year-old twins, Emily and Ellen."

Matthew looked around at neighbors gathered in groups, laughing and savoring friendships. On a day like today, it was easy to forget Philadelphia and the marching orders Stephens would give him. Well, he would do his part.

Everyone seemed to be enjoying the mild spring day when some neighbors got heated about the current political climate. Charles Whitney, owner of Whitney's Mill, bandied about terms like "treason" and "treachery," while George Whitcomb and Aaron Turner argued that the colonists not only should separate but had every right to do so.

The sharp remarks traded back and forth silenced everyone seated nearby.

Charles Whitney's face reddened. "We are British subjects, and going to war with fellow subjects is untenable."

Aaron Turner yelled. "We are already at war, Charles. Colonists have been murdered by British soldiers at Lexington and Concord. This will only end by separation."

The men stood nose to nose and looked like they were about to come to fisticuffs. Matthew arose and got between them to separate them. "Calm down, Charles. Nothing is to be gained fighting amongst ourselves."

Aaron slapped his hat against his leg. "I am ready to go to

war with England, but I had not anticipated fighting with my neighbor."

Matthew shook his head. So much for the peaceful afternoon.

CHAPTER 7

The next morning after the Macmillans left, Matthew took a tankard of coffee and joined the ladies in the common room. He studied some receipts as Heather and Mary sewed and exchanged ideas on clothing design. Polly was seated at one of the round tables, rocking the cradle on the floor at her feet.

Heather held up her yellow gown. He smiled, remembering how it had once belonged to Elizabeth but was later given to Heather since she came from Scotland with few clothes.

"I thought we could also alter this gown," Heather said. "'Twill be quite elegant if we add some lace to the neckline and the edge of the sleeve. Would you like that?"

Mary dropped her work. "It looks so pretty on you. Surely you wouldn't part with it."

"I have enjoyed it, but now, you need new garments that will serve you for your social engagements in Philadelphia."

Matthew went over to Heather, placed his hands on her shoulders, leaned down, and kissed her head. "A very generous gesture, my dear. Two Stewart women looked stunning in the gown, and you will also, Mary."

Heather looked up at him, her eyes glistening. "I can only imagine how delighted Mary's mother would have been for her to wear the dress." Heather pulled a handkerchief from her pocket and handed it to Mary after a tear rolled down the girl's cheek. "I would love to refashion it for you."

"It would mean so much to wear a gown both of you favored."

The sound of a coach approaching the Green interrupted their conversation.

Matthew walked out to the center hall and called out. "It appears the Duncans have arrived."

Heather followed him outside and hugged Maggie. "What a treat. You said you might come by when you visited your sister."

"Aye, we were with her and the family for a couple of days. Look at you, Heather Stewart." Maggie stepped back and gaped. "When were you going to tell me that you had a wee one on the way?"

"I wanted to wait, to make sure. Sometime in October, we will welcome this wee bairn." Heather ushered Maggie inside to the common room. She'd best tell Maggie about the Gordons' loss.

"I am happy for you and Matthew." Maggie noticed Polly. "Oh, I must peek at Polly's new babe."

Heather pulled Maggie aside. "First come help me get the coffee."

In the kitchen, she told Maggie about the death of the Gordons' baby boy.

When the women returned to the common room with the coffee, Heather fought back tears as she watched Maggie go to Polly and share a few moments alone.

Maggie joined Heather in the kitchen a few minutes later. "I would be happy to assist you with any sewing for Mary."

"Bless you. There is much to do before she leaves."

"Time with the Moores will be good for the children, but you will miss those two."

"I already dread their absence, and I worry for their safety. Matthew said 'twas better for them to make the trip now rather than later when the situation might be worse."

"'Tis in God's hands, Heather, and He is faithful. Trust that He will protect them. The Moores will always have Mary and Mark's best interests at heart, and I suspect they will only have them in very sheltered circumstances."

Heather nodded. "My mind knows that. 'Tis my heart that is anxious."

After the supper, Maggie and Heather took tea and some hemming to the back porch to take advantage of the light.

Mary and Jean ran up to them. "We are going to play blind man's bluff."

Heather shook her head. "William and Douglas are too little to be running around the yard blindfolded with you older ones."

Mary grabbed a kitchen cloth. "Get them playing quoits, Mother. That will hold their interest and not make them feel left out."

"We will keep the boys out of your way, but once they are in bed, keep an ear open for them since we adults plan to take a walk."

The five young people laughed as they each were caught and forced to don the blindfold. And the tots were satisfied with playing quoits near the porch where they remained out of harm's way and supervised.

"I got you, Donald," Cameron yelled as he pulled off the blindfold, looking very pleased with himself.

Mary took the blindfold from Cameron and ran to Donald to tie it on him. "I saw the way you let Cameron find you."

The laughter in the yard continued as they tried to simultaneously tease and avoid Donald. Mary ran behind him laughing. She looked stunned when he suddenly turned and accidentally tripped her.

Mary cried out as she dropped to the ground. Donald, blindfold intact, toppled on top of her.

Donald took off his blindfold, smiling. "Look what I caught."

Jean ran over to them. "You are supposed to grab the person, not fall on them."

Mary gasped. "Get up. You are crushing me."

Donald got his footing, still grinning. He reached down and helped Mary up.

"What is going on here?" Adam called as he and Matthew joined them on the porch.

Heather laughed. "'Tis nothing. They are playing blind man's bluff, and Mary tripped." She reached up and took Matthew's hand. "If you gentlemen are ready to take a stroll, Maggie and I will put these lads to bed."

Later, enjoying the smell of maturing wheat in the air, she and Maggie strolled along the well-worn path a few feet behind their husbands.

Heather's eyes were on their husbands, deep in conversation and strolling ahead of them toward the Potomack. "What are you two chatting about?"

Adam glanced back, never breaking his stride. "Decisions to be made."

Maggie looked resigned. "The constant yammering about the conflict with the English. 'Tis more tranquil here than in town, but I fear 'twill not escape any of us soon."

Heather shook her head. "'Tis not as peaceful here as it used to be. Yesterday after church, grown men were fighting like schoolchildren. Even out here we cannot get away from the continual fracas."

Matthew stopped abruptly and faced her, his expression intense. "We may have an insurrection before long. Ultimately, all colonists must take a stand on where their loyalty lies—with the Crown, or with those who desire freedom."

Color rose to Adam's face. "Virginia and Massachusetts are not the only colonies impacted by this. And ladies, England will not let us separate without a fight."

Both women, now only five feet from their husbands, stood still and speechless.

Heather stared at Matthew. "But we are British subjects."

"That is the problem. We are subjects who no longer want to be subjected to English rule."

Heather suddenly felt light-headed. Darkness enveloped her, and voices grew distant.

Gradually, the light and sound returned. Heather opened her

eyes. Matthew was kneeling over her, his hands cupped behind her head. Maggie knelt at her side, wiping her brow.

Heather pressed her hand to her throat. "What happened?"

Matthew helped her rise to a sitting position, never letting go of her. "You fainted. We'd better get you home. I can send Adam for the wagon."

"Nay, I can walk. I stood still too long, and it made me faint. I had the same experience a few times when I carried Douglas and John. I will do better if I walk. I am well, dear, really."

Matthew helped her to stand and held her arm, and their conversations took on a gentler tone as the couples walked back to the Green. Adam and Maggie strode quietly behind them.

CHAPTER 8

Heather sat by a window in the common room studying the dress on her lap. "I think we are progressing well with the sewing.

Mary sat across from her. "'Tis only a week till we leave."

"'Tis enough time. You will spend a night with the Duncans on the way to Philadelphia."

"Hmm. Yes."

Something was amiss from the look on Mary's face. "Is something wrong?"

Mary sat silently a moment. "I should probably tell you since it may be known before long." A crease had formed on her brow. "Donald told me he plans to join the militia."

Heather leaned back in the chair, stunned. "His parents said nothing. Do they know?"

"He did not say, but I don't believe so."

"Yet he told you."

"Donald told me early the morning the Duncans returned home. He said that after the killings in Massachusetts, Patriots needed to take a stand, put their words into action, and be willing to fight, even die if it came to that." Tears flooded Mary's eyes.

Heather got up and drew Mary into her arms. "Did he say when he planned to join?"

"No"

Mary's expression suggested there was more to tell. "Donald must count you as a very special friend to share that with you before he has even told his family."

"I believe he does. And I care a great deal about Donald also.

I'm frightened for him."

On the night before their departure for Philadelphia, Matthew bid Mary and Mark good night and took their trunks downstairs so they would be ready to load first thing in the morning. He walked back to the common room and sat at the table where he had left his lamp and Bible. After running his fingers over the worn cover, he opened it, read for a while, then mentally checked off the tasks he had to accomplish prior to their departure. The children's time with the Moores would be good for everyone. Meanwhile, he could contribute to the efforts to secure liberty for his family and countrymen. No regrets. It wasn't easy leaving Heather under any circumstances, but now with the new baby on the way—well, he had prayed enough about this decision not to second-guess it now. He felt strongly that the Lord had encouraged this, and he trusted that God would work everything that happened for their good. When he'd finished his Bible reading for the night, he closed the book and carried it upstairs.

He opened the bedroom door just as Heather was struggling to open the jammed window. "Here, let me do that."

She smiled and moved away from the window. "I wanted to let in some of the fresh air."

Matthew opened it, put his arm around her shoulder, and took a deep breath. The sounds of tree frogs and an owl nearby invaded the room, accompanied by a breeze carrying the citrus scent from the boxwood.

She sat at her dressing table, removed the combs from her pale blond hair, and rubbed her fingers over the delicate silver thistles embossed on them. He had given the combs to her five years earlier when he declared his love for her. What precious memories.

He removed his shirt. "I checked on Mary and Mark before I came in. They finally fell asleep." He made eye contact with her in the mirror. "All should be in fit order for you. The Gordons, as well as George Whitcomb, will be around to assist you." He stood behind her and wrapped his arms around her, nuzzling her neck. "I promise not to stay away a moment longer than needed. Please rest and try not to do too much. I am concerned for you and the baby."

"I shall be fine. Polly and Thomas will be good company and do anything I cannot do."

He took her hand and led her to their bed, where they sat facing each other. "Your fainting during the Duncans' visit alarmed me. Shall I stop by the Edwards' tomorrow on our way out and ask Thomas or Betsy to look in on you?"

"Nay, do not trouble the doctor. The baby is moving. I only seem to get light-headed when I stand still." She placed her hands on each side of his face and drew him to her for a kiss.

Her kiss warmed him. Thoughts of days of travel and Philadelphia were drowned out by contemplating more desirable activities. He returned the kiss with an equal amount of passion. "You are already luring me back with your charms." He caressed her face. "I could never stay away from you for very long, beloved."

"Just reminding you." Her playful grin returned.

"I will be back within a fortnight."

"Oh, Matthew, I need to tell you about a conversation Mary had with Donald when the Duncans were here, though I suspect Mary told me in confidence. But you need to know if by chance 'tis addressed when you are in Alexandria." She glanced at the closed door.

"What is it?"

"Donald told Mary he planned to join the militia, and I am not sure he has told Maggie or Adam yet."

Matthew sighed and shook his head, which did nothing to ease her distress. "We all need to prepare ourselves for what is coming."

"Donald's decision does not surprise you?"

"I expect the fight ahead will require many men." He began getting ready for bed.

"Why must you assume there is no other answer than going to war with England?" The pleading tone of her voice tore at him. How could he make her understand?

"Beloved, you must reconcile that there is no other outcome."

She picked up his pillow and held it close to her. "The cost is too great. How can we possibly defeat England? We would be annihilated. Will you leave us to fight?"

He took the pillow, set it aside, and drew her to him. "I have no plans to join the militia." He shifted so they could look into each other's eyes. "However, we have been pushed far enough, and people throughout these colonies will put everything aside to fight for our freedom and the right to establish our own nation."

"England will view that as treason. They won't leave a land where they are so heavily invested."

"If we are too frightened to take on the giants in the territory, we will continue to be their slaves. God is faithful, and He will equip us to do whatever He calls us to do. 'Tis time to trust that God will fight for us and provide a way for committed people to form a free nation."

He turned down the lamp and held her close, unwilling to let her go just yet. How he wished he could tell her what he was doing, but that wasn't an option. Keeping her and the children safe was his priority. He kissed her forehead then her lips. She responded the way he hoped, with as much passion as he felt. For a while, all concerns of children, the farm and ordinary, travels and strife, fled. Tonight was only about the love they had for each other.

After a hurried breakfast early the next morning, Heather watched Matthew load the wagon. Mary and Mark were excited as they climbed to their seats. As sad as she was to see them leave, she was pleased for all the new experiences this visit would provide for them.

Matthew checked the horses and stepped to her side. "Please take care of yourself and give Douglas a hug when he wakes. I will give the Duncans your love and return as soon as I can." He wrapped his arms around her and held her close. "I love you, my precious."

"I love you, too. Be careful."

She allowed herself to rest in the comfort of his embrace for a moment. Finally, she stepped back and turned toward the children. "Have fun, you two, and remember your manners."

They smiled and waved as Matthew climbed aboard.

As Heather watched the wagon head down the lane, she recalled Matthew's assurance that he would not join the militia. Poor Maggie. How she would worry about Donald. Would Matthew and their neighbors not also be drawn into it? How would she muster enough faith to believe as Matthew did and confront all that might lie ahead? *"Thou wilt keep him in perfect peace, whose mind is stayed on thee: because he trusteth in thee." Thank You, Lord. I will trust in You.*

CHAPTER 9

Heather got up after cleaning the kitchen floor.

Polly shook her head as she entered the room. "I know what you are doing. You are keeping busy and pushing yourself to cope with Matthew and the children's absence."

"Am I that transparent?"

"Aye."

Matthew would be back in a fortnight, but the children … "I cannot imagine this place without Mary and Mark for the next couple of months."

Polly stood across from her at the large worktable. "The time they spend with their grandparents will be good for them." She washed the beans in the half-filled bucket. "And most likely Philadelphia will remain safe this summer."

She looked up from cutting the cabbage and glared at Polly.

"I am only saying the chance of a war starting in the next couple of months is remote. I am sure the Moores will take good care of them, so stop fretting."

Polly took a seat and began snapping the beans. "Philip and Todd moped around all of yesterday, missing Mark and Mary."

"Hmm, I had not considered that they are suffering the loss also."

The day after Matthew and the children left, Heather drove the cart to the schoolhouse to meet Amelia Turner and hang the new curtains they had sewn. They hoped curtains would preserve some of the heat during the cold winter months. When she arrived at the schoolhouse, there was no sign of Amelia. Heather gathered the linsey-woolsey curtains and carried them to the large door and went inside. Fresh air would go a long way to dispel the mustiness in the large room. She glanced around to assess where to start.

Mr. Martin, schoolmaster, was away for the summer visiting his family, so he would be of no help to her hanging curtains. She'd need something to stand on. A bench placed under the windows would make it easy to reach the poles. She dragged one to the first window. Holding the folded curtain in her right arm, she climbed on the center of the bench, being careful not to overturn it. She reached up and dislodged the pole from a bracket to slide the coarse woolen and linen fabric loops onto it, then returned the pole to its brackets. She pushed the loops along and edged her way along the bench to even out the fabric.

She stepped off the bench and looked up at the curtain. It was not only useful, but it looked nice.

Why had Amelia not arrived?

No matter. Heather could manage it herself. She pushed the bench to the next window and grabbed the next folded curtain and climbed back up on the bench. She slid each loop onto the pole and raised it far above her head to place it on the wooden bracket, attempting to smooth it out as she went. Her arms were tiring, but only a few loops were left.

Had a cloud hidden the sunlight? It had grown so dark so fast.

She sank into the darkness.

"Ma'am, are you ill?"

Heather's eyes opened slowly. A stranger's face hovered not even a foot above hers. His pale blue eyes were wide with concern. What appeared to be an old scar ran across his cheek.

She moaned, startled and acutely aware of a throbbing pain in the back of her head. The man leaned over her prone body and took one of her hands.

"Be still, ma'am. You have had a fall."

She pulled her hand from his and placed it on her belly. "I ... I beg your pardon, sir, but who are you?"

"Forgive me." He rocked back on his heels. "I rode by and

noticed the cart. Then I spotted you in the window as you fell. I came in to be of assistance." He reached for her hand and placed his other hand behind her back. "Do you think you can sit up?"

"Aye, I think so."

"Here, let me help you." He drew her to a sitting position. "Are you in any pain?"

She rubbed the sore spot on her head. "I will likely have a lump." But her child. Her child.

As if summoned, the babe moved in her belly. Thank God. "Other than that, and my pride, I believe I am fine."

He helped her to sit on the bench, then stepped back, watching her.

"I do not believe we have met. I am Heather Stewart. Are you from around here?"

"I am passing through. Are you dizzy or faint?"

"Nay, nay. Just a little pain. I'm grateful, Mr. ..."

"Cranford, John Cranford."

"Thank you for your help, Mr. Cranford. I am grateful you were here. I am expecting a friend to arrive at any moment to help. Perhaps I should not have been trying to hang the curtains by myself."

His eyes shifted to the door, then back to her. "Would you like me to assist you with the curtains?"

"Nay, but I appreciate the kind offer." She rubbed the bump on the back of her head again. It was pounding in rhythm with her pulse. "Perhaps I will head home. I do not live far from here."

"I will be on my way if you think you can make it home without my aid." He walked with an odd gait to the door and glanced to the left and right before turning and facing her again.

"I do appreciate your aid, Mr. Cranford." She got up from the bench and followed him as far as the doorway. Though her hip and shoulder would be bruised tomorrow, her fall could have been much worse.

Mr. Cranford's reddish blond hair glistened in the sunlight

before he placed his hat back on his head and headed toward a large chestnut horse. The man walked with a definite limp.

She lifted the crumpled curtain from the floor and folded it, then prepared to head home. The rickety sound of a buggy caught her attention. That had to be Amelia. Still a bit shaky, Heather watched from the doorway.

Amelia jumped from the buggy. "Have you been here long, Heather? I needed to find Cole before I left home." She stopped as she neared the door, carrying an armful of fabric. "What is wrong? You look so pale. Come sit down."

"'Tis my own fault." She told Amelia what happened.

"How awful. Are you hurt? You should not have started without me, especially with the baby—"

"Nay, I am not hurt, and the wee one is as active as ever."

"I am so sorry I am later than expected. I let you down."

"Please do not fret, Amelia. A gentleman happened to be passing by and came in and gave me assistance."

"A gentleman passing by? Who would be passing by here?"

"No one I have ever met before. A Mr. Cranford."

"This is not a thoroughfare to anywhere. What did he look like?"

"He had fair skin, reddish blond hair, blue eyes ... oh, and he had a scar on his right cheek. A well-mannered man and finely dressed."

"How long ago did this happen?"

"Perhaps ten minutes."

"He left you here alone, without escorting you home?"

"He offered to help me, but I assured him I needed no assistance. Why all the questions?"

"Why would anyone be riding by the schoolhouse, particularly someone who is not from around here? 'Tis well off the main path."

"He did not indicate his intent." Her headache had subsided a little, and she had no desire to come back to the schoolhouse another time. "Come inside, stop asking questions, and help me finish hanging these curtains. I told Polly I would not be gone long."

"Are you sure you are well enough?" A playful smile emerged on Amelia's face as they made their way to the bench. "Perhaps your mysterious stranger was an angel."

"Now you sound like you are the one who fell and hit her head."

Within a half hour, they were laughing and admiring their handiwork. They moved the bench back to its original spot.

Amelia laughed. "Why did we not think to do this before? The additional windows for added light, and now the curtains, make it look less like a barn."

"'Tis such an improvement. The wood stove took a long time to heat this large room in the colder months. I am certain Mr. Martin will be pleased."

"Do you want me to follow you home, Heather?"

"Nay. I am fine."

"Very well. Please promise me you will let us know if you need anything."

"I will. Matthew should be back within a fortnight."

Amelia grinned and climbed up on her buggy as Heather got in her cart to start the ride home.

"Be sure and tell me if your angel returns," Amelia called. "Mysterious strangers fascinate me."

The moment Heather walked through the door, Douglas ran into her outstretched arms.

Polly looked up and smiled from where she worked at the kitchen table.

"I planned to be home before this, Polly, but it took longer than expected. You would not believe what an improvement the curtains make to that large, drafty room." She kissed her son and through the window spotted Thomas and Todd near the barn.

Polly placed filled jugs to weigh down the vegetables soaking in the brine. "I will look forward to checking your handiwork at the schoolhouse on Sunday after services."

Heather set Douglas down. "When Todd took the horse and cart, he said a couple of guests arrived earlier, and another man came by but did not stay."

"The couple came about a half hour after you left. I put them upstairs in the blue room. The husband is not well, suffering from gout, I believe. I told them we would bring their supper up later if they wished."

"We can certainly do that." She smiled at Philip and made her way to where the boys had been playing on the floor. "What have we here?"

"I showed Douglas how to play marbles." Philip's contagious grin brought on a smile.

"It was kind of Philip to play with you, Douglas." She tousled her son's blond curls. The boy's attention was on Philip's next shot.

"It appears I did not get back in time to help you very much with the preserving, Polly. You are almost done. You have even boiled the jars."

"Laura slept, so I had little interruption. But I will go feed her now."

"By all means." She put on her apron and took a jug of cider off one of the larder shelves.

Thomas came through the door with Todd on his heels. He wiped his hands on a towel before tossing it to Todd. Thomas sat at the table and perused the *Gazette*. "We finished the roof over the well."

"Many thanks," Heather said. "I need to get a bucket of water, so I will go admire your handiwork." She set six cups on the table and filled them with cider. "Philip, Douglas, there is cider here for you."

"Todd," Thomas said, "go get the water for Mrs. Stewart. She does not need to be carrying heavy buckets."

"Yes, Pa." He walked back out the door.

Thomas took a long drink of the amber liquid. "I figure tomorrow the boys and I will get back to work on the stone wall. We might even get it done before Matthew returns. Polly tell you we have guests?"

"Aye." She cracked some eggs and measured flour and other ingredients into a bowl before stirring the batter.

"They brought a couple of *Gazettes*. Apparently, a mob broke into the magazine in Williamsburg and carried off a significant number of guns." Thomas went over to the sideboard and picked up another paper. "Governor Dunmore has abandoned the capitol. He has taken refuge on one of His Majesty's ships."

"Oh, my. And Lady Dunmore and their children, what has become of them?"

"They are all gone. Lord Dunmore remains anchored at Yorktown, but the article suggests his family has sailed for England. If Lord Dunmore has abandoned his post, the Royal government in Virginia has come to an end." Thomas put the paper down.

She stopped stirring, stunned. "Who will govern the colony?"

"The people, I imagine, unless we appoint our own governor."

Todd returned with the bucket, which he placed on a nearby counter.

"Son, you said another gent came by but chose not to stay. Did he say why?"

"He asked for Mr. Stewart."

She looked up from her preparations. "Who was it, Todd?"

"Never saw him before, and I would have remembered him. Sure had a big chestnut horse with the prettiest flaxen mane and tail."

Heather removed the wooden spoon from the batter and stared at the adolescent. "The man, what did he look like? How was he dressed?"

"Dressed like a gentleman, but I had my doubts about the fellow, 'cause he looked like he might have been in a fight some time back."

"Why do you say that?"

"Well, he walked strange, like his leg hurt. And he had a scar on his face."

A chill traveled up her spine. "And you say this man asked for Mr. Stewart by name?"

"Yes, ma'am."

She returned to stirring the batter for the corn fritters. He had to be the same man who'd rendered her assistance at the schoolhouse. What did John Cranford want with Matthew, and why had he not said something to her at the schoolhouse?

CHAPTER 10

Matthew brought the wagon around to the back of the Duncan home in Alexandria, and Adam came through the service yard waving. "You got here in good time. I can see to the horses after we let Maggie know you have arrived. The wagon and trunks will be secure in the barn overnight unless you need them."

Mark hopped off the wagon while Matthew assisted Mary down. When she was settled, he turned to shake Adam's hand. "Good to see you, my friend. We will not need the trunks, just the portmanteaus." He handed a crate of produce to Mark, lifted the bags, and preceded Adam into the house.

Inside, Maggie gave them each a hug. "You look grand, children. I know you must be excited about your summer in Philadelphia."

Mary looked around the kitchen and smiled when Jean entered. "Yes, we are."

Adam looked worn out. "I will be in shortly."

Matthew pointed to the crate that Mark had set on the table. "Something from the farm. Heather sends her love."

Maggie's eyes had dark circles underneath, and her ready smile was absent. "How kind, and is Heather faring well? I know you were worried about her fainting, but there's no need. 'Tis not that unusual in her condition."

"Aye, she's faring very well, though I'm certain she'll miss the children."

Maggie rummaged through the crate. "Bless her. Heather has included some herbs I don't grow. Go get settled, everyone. We will have dinner in about an hour."

Matthew glanced at the children as Cameron and William lured

Mark to the service yard. Jean and Mary disappeared upstairs. "I'm going out to see Adam."

In the barn, the men rubbed down the horses. Matthew didn't ask, but it was clear that something was troubling his old friend. After what Heather had told him, he feared he knew what it was.

After a few minutes, Adam said, "Donald joined the militia … He left a week ago. And Maggie is distraught."

"I'm sorry to hear that."

"The three of us quarreled when the boy first brought it up, but after listening to his reasoning, I could no longer argue with him."

Matthew put his hand on Adam's shoulder. "Donald is a fine young man and not one to act on impulse."

"Aye, he is a good boy, and I'm proud of him. But 'tis not setting right with Maggie."

"Women view these things differently, my friend. Maggie is a sensible woman. She may need some time to work through it, but I suspect she will come around."

"We shall see. But since she is not inclined to talk about it yet, the children keep quiet on the subject. Oh, Cameron will ask me questions, but only when we are alone."

"I won't bring it up."

When they gathered for dinner, Matthew sat beside Mark. He suspected that Cameron had filled Mark in on Donald's absence, but if he had not, Mark was likely to bring it up. Matthew looked around at the faces. The tension was discernible. What could he say or do to ease their distress?

After the blessing, food was passed around the table.

The boys' conversation was animated, quite a contrast to the serious look on Mary's face. No doubt the girls had also discussed Donald's departure.

Planting and the children's visit to Philadelphia dominated the discourse. Matthew watched Adam's eyes scan his family. Surely they would not get through the meal ignoring Donald's absence.

William addressed what no one else would. "Uncle Matt,

Donald left. He went away to fight the redcoats." Leave it to a five-year-old.

Silence as the young people's glances went from Maggie to Adam.

Maggie's eyes teared, and Adam cleared his throat.

When Mark's eyes widened, Matthew placed his hand on the boy's thigh.

Maggie got up. "I shall fetch the bread pudding." She stepped through the door and into the kitchen.

Silence settled on the group like a cloud until Cameron leaned toward Adam. "Does this mean we can talk about Donald now?"

"Aye." Maggie stood in the doorway holding a large bowl and looking like a ewe fending off a wolf from her young. "'Tis no secret, our Donald has joined the militia. He is off somewhere training."

Mark looked as if he was unsure how to react.

Jean and Mary were seated beside each other. Mary's eyes were cast down, and her arm extended toward Jean's lap, where he suspected they were holding hands.

"Donald has a good mind and heart," Matthew said. "I'm sure he gave this decision much thought. Our family will keep him and all the other young men who join him in the pursuit of liberty in our prayers."

Maggie sighed. She still wore her heartache like a veil. "We appreciate that." She set the pudding on the table and dished portions. With each spoonful, the tension eased.

Adam poured more water. "I'm going down to the wharf after dinner to do some work for William Ramsey."

Matthew nodded. "I will go part way with you. I have a couple of errands myself." At their earlier meeting, he had arranged to meet Stephens at a townhouse on Princess Street to work out some details regarding his initial meeting with the Ferguson family. He reached the house around four, but Stephens was not there, so he left a note with the housekeeper specifying where he was staying and telling the woman about his early departure the following morning. He returned to the Duncan home. Would Stephens get back to him in time, or would his time in Philadelphia be a lost opportunity? Part of him hoped for the latter, hoped to still avoid getting pulled into the conflict.

Shortly after eight o'clock, a stocky man came to the Duncan home asking for Matthew. When Adam asked him inside, the man declined. Matthew excused himself and walked out to where the man was pacing on the cobblestone street.

"Mr. Stewart?"

"Yes."

"Mr. Stephens is in a coach around the corner on Fairfax Street." The man headed off in the opposite direction and sat on a bench in the next block.

Matthew looked back at the Duncan home. Should he let them know he would be gone a while? No, questions might be asked. It was dusk by the time he got to the coach.

Stephens opened the door. "Glad I caught you before you left town."

"I presume that was your driver who came to the house."

"Yes. I will not take much of your time. Listen carefully. Go to Philadelphia, stay at the Davis Inn on Chestnut Street, and send a note to Henry Ferguson telling him that you are in Philadelphia for a week and that you want to make contact with him and his family while you are in town. Whatever reason you devise for your visit, make it one that will facilitate you returning later in the summer so you can tentatively make plans to meet again."

"A week? I had not planned to be gone that long."

"It may not take a week, but you need time to accommodate the Fergusons' social schedule. Ingratiate yourself with them. It may get you invited to a social function where their Tory or English officer friends will be present."

Matthew sighed. "Do you really think that British Regulars are going to share secrets at parties with strangers?"

"Of course not. But one never knows what might be useful." Stephens pulled a packet out of his coat pocket. "Deliver this to Henry Ferguson."

"And?"

"That is all. But as I indicated, try to set the stage for a meeting later in the summer. Then return to Alexandria and contact me at the house on Princess Street. We will assess your time in Philadelphia and determine what is next at that time. Take care to keep your plans to yourself."

CHAPTER 11

Matthew was amused at the stunned expressions on his children's faces as they entered the Philadelphia neighborhood of Society Hill.

Mary leaned toward him. "Papa, there are even more elegant houses here than there are in Alexandria."

"'Tis an affluent area, dear. But not all parts of the city are as fine as this."

Mark straightened his steenkirk. "Did you live near here, Papa?"

"No. My family's home was several blocks north, but it was sold and belongs to another family now."

Mary put her arm through his. "Did you know Grandmamma's cousin Susan, the lady whose home we are visiting?"

"'Tis Mrs. Brown to the two of you. And no, I never met the Browns. Your grandparents are more formal people than you are used to. Remember your table manners. I know I can trust you to be on your best behavior."

"We will," Mary said. "'Tis a good thing I have those new gowns. Mama was wise to prepare me for such a fashionable place."

"Remember what I said on the ride here, children. 'Twould be best if you refer to your mama as Heather. They know I remarried, but they still think of their daughter, Elizabeth, as your mother. We wouldn't want to hurt their feelings, right? And another thing, and this is important."

"What." Mary leaned back to study his face.

"Heather and I met … at the Duncans'. Your grandparents do not need to know that Heather was an indentured servant or that we met and married on the same day."

Mary's laughter was anything but ladylike. "Papa, I think I know better than to bring that subject up. But you." She turned to her brother. "You best heed what Papa's saying."

"Yes, sir."

Matthew pulled the carriage up to a large Georgian house on Cypress Street. "This is it. Now, remember, be very respectful to the Browns, the Moores, and anyone else you meet."

Mary nodded. "We will."

Mary's straw hat slipped off her head when she tipped it back to take in the three-story home. Matthew placed it back on her head and smiled. "I know you will have a wonderful time." They were good children, but this would be a unique experience for everyone.

A well-dressed doorman met them, bowed, and led them down a grand central hall to an arched doorway that led into a large square parlor. The scent of freshly brewed coffee permeated the room.

Louisa, Elizabeth's mother, sat beautifully dressed and coifed in an ivory damask wingback chair.

Across from her sat an aristocratic gentleman who appeared to be about Matthew's age. The gentleman stood and bowed.

Louisa smiled. "Matthew." She stood, curtsied, and walked over to him, studying the youngsters at his side with a reserved smile. "So these are Mary and Mark. We have looked forward to your arrival. Your grandpapa is away right now but will return later."

Matthew glanced at his children and puffed with pride. He observed his former mother-in-law. "'Tis good to see you again, Louisa." The woman was just as regal as he remembered.

She stepped back and focused on him. "And you, Matthew. Allow me to introduce you to Mr. John Hancock, the nephew of Thomas and Lydia Hancock, some very old friends of ours from Boston." She turned to her guest. "John, this is my late daughter's husband, Matthew Stewart, and my grandchildren, Mary and Mark. The children are visiting us from Virginia for the summer."

Matthew held out his hand to Louisa's guest. The man gripped his warmly. "'Tis an honor to meet you, sir."

Mark bowed, and Mary curtsied.

Mr. Hancock smiled warmly. "How delightful for all of you."

A butler entered the room carrying a sterling silver tray complete with coffee essentials and tea cakes.

Louisa waved toward the seating area, and the children sat on an ivory settee. Matthew took a nearby chair. So far, Mary and Mark had behaved admirably. His former mother-in-law was just as he remembered, elegant and formal. The children would certainly have a very different summer.

The children were captivated by their grandmother. Louisa demonstrated an artful precision as she poured them each coffee and passed a silver plate with some lemon tarts. The ritual reminded him of a musical conductor at a concert.

When she sat again, she addressed them all. "Mr. Hancock took time from his busy schedule to stop and visit us. He has been elected as President of the Continental Congress currently in session here in Philadelphia."

Matthew smiled. 'Twas good to know the Moores were on the right side of the issue. He had heard Hancock was a man of great wealth, but he seemed to be quite amiable and not the least bit condescending. Matthew had understood Peyton Randolph was serving as President of the Continental Congress. He had not learned of the change. "And what of Mr. Randolph?"

Mr. Hancock nodded. "Your confusion is understandable. Mr. Randolph stepped down and has returned to Williamsburg under the protection of the militia. The commander of British forces has been issued blank warrants for his and other rebel leaders' execution."

Matthew looked at his children and the fear that now etched their faces. Here only thirty minutes, and he was already gathering valuable information about those who supported the Patriot cause. Oh, that the rest of his time in Philadelphia would prove as fruitful amongst the opposition.

They spent the next half hour discussing the work of the Congress and Mr. Hancock's suggestions for the young people's activities while they were in the city. When Mr. Hancock left, Louisa rang a bell, and a woman hurried into the room. Louisa addressed Mary and Mark. "Children, you may be excused. The housekeeper will show you to your rooms and help you unpack."

Mary and Mark stood and were following the housekeeper when Louisa addressed him. "Matthew, I assume you will be staying with us tonight. What are your plans?"

Mary and Mark's heads swiveled to hear his response.

"I had planned to get a room at the Davis Inn on Chestnut Street."

"Nonsense. The Browns are gone until Friday, but I know I can speak for them. You are welcome to stay here while you are in town. It would be good for the children to have you around while they become more acquainted with us."

"That is very gracious of you." He had hoped she would offer to let him stay for the sake of the children. A day or two should be enough; then he would go to the Davis Inn.

Louisa issued instructions on what time to appear for supper before the three of them were escorted upstairs to their rooms.

Mark rubbed his hand along the polished curved banister and whispered, "I'm glad you are staying, Papa."

"As am I."

◉⚜❦⚜◉

Matthew, Mark, and Mary entered the dining room. The children's eyes grew large as they took in the massive table with six pieces of sterling flatware at each setting. The numerous silver candlesticks on the table and sideboard were striking and illuminated the large room. His children looked at him in awe. How could he have forgotten the way Elizabeth was raised? He should have done more to prepare them for the opulence they would see. From what he remembered, the Moores' home in Boston was of an equal status.

John and Louisa Moore entered the room, both elegantly dressed. Louisa introduced the children to their grandfather. John Moore's hair had greyed since Matthew had last seen him, but the tall man's jovial nature was still evident. John went out of his way to make them all feel welcome, enumerating the many places he wanted to show them in Philadelphia.

Servants entered the dining room with numerous trays and served a sumptuous meal of roast beef, Yorkshire pudding, and roasted vegetables, all on silver trays and dishes. The children would certainly be eating well while here. When Matthew picked up his fork, he noticed the children looking at the silverware in confusion. He cleared his throat, lifted the proper utensil, and waited until they'd followed suit. They caught his cues for the rest of the meal.

After everyone was finished, Louisa placed her napkin on the table, signaling the end of the meal.

"An invitation arrived today, John, for an assembly this Friday to be given in honor of some of the delegates. I suppose we were included because of our connections in Boston. Shall we accept?"

"Yes, my dear, we should probably attend."

She turned toward Matthew. "Be assured that the children will be well cared for whenever we are occupied elsewhere."

"That was never in doubt. I expect to leave Friday morning."

John Moore clapped his hands together. "Then we must make the most of tomorrow. Perhaps a visit to Carpenter's Hall."

Matthew motioned toward his children. "I had hoped to take Mark and Mary to Christ Church where my parents are buried. Perhaps we could walk there in the morning and enjoy an excursion to Carpenter's Hall in the afternoon."

"A fine plan."

The next morning, Matthew observed his children as they walked north on 3rd Street toward Christ Church. "I'm proud of the way you both have behaved around your grandparents, very grown up and polite."

Mary said, "You were not exaggerating when you said that our grandmamma was formal. So much silverware for a meal. How will we ever know which piece to use?"

Mark stopped to examine a set of pearl-handled knives in a shop window. "Who cares which fork or spoon we use as long as we get the food in our mouths?"

Matthew chuckled. "I suggest you watch your grandparents and use whichever piece they use."

Mark turned from the window and pointed to a spire down Church Street. "That is the tallest building I have ever seen."

"That, son, is Christ Church. If we have time, we can stop there after we visit the graveyard."

Mary looked amazed. "Is that where your parents' graves are?"

"No. but they are not far. Years ago, when the churchyard was filled, Christ Church bought acreage at the corner of 5th and Arch Streets."

Mark tugged on his sleeve. "We want to be sure to get back to Cypress Street in time for Grandpapa to take us to Carpenter's Hall."

"We will."

They reached the graveyard and wandered amongst the graves until they reached the Stewart headstones. Grass and weeds had grown up around them.

Matthew bent down and pulled them away until only grass remained. Then he stood silently for a couple of moments before turning to the children. "I say we visit Christ Church."

A few moments later as they entered the large Georgian structure, Mary whispered, "What a grand and beautiful church. It makes ours looks so humble."

Matthew placed his hand on her shoulder. "Both glorify God,

my dear. 'Tis not the building but the people who are the church."

There were others in the sanctuary, a couple standing to the side of the pulpit and a young man examining the baptismal font.

The Stewarts explored the church for a few minutes before they headed outside. Mark pointed to a bas-relief on the outside of the church. "Who is that?"

Matthew studied it for a moment. "His Majesty King George II."

"Maybe there are more on the other side." Mark turned and ran and nearly collided with a man in clerical garb. The minister reached out and stopped him before he tumbled into the lady walking beside him.

Mark's eyes were wide, his face crimson. "I apologize, sir, ma'am. Please forgive me."

The minister laughed. "Absolution granted." The lady smiled and patted Mark on the shoulder.

Matthew and Mary came alongside of Mark. "Please excuse us." He pointed in the direction of the newer graveyard. "We are visiting Philadelphia, and I wanted to show my children my parents' gravesite. We stopped to see the church while we were here."

"Welcome to Philadelphia and Christ Church. I'm Reverend William White, and this is my wife, Mary."

"A pleasure to meet you." The man was younger than he. "I'm Matthew Stewart, and these are my children, Mary and Mark."

Mary curtsied and Mark nodded.

Just then, the young man who had been studying the font approached the minister.

Mrs. White turned toward the children. "Where are you from?"

"Virginia. We are visiting with our grandparents for the summer."

"How delightful." She looked at Matthew. "I also come from Virginia. Are you in town for the Congress? We have met many Virginians who have arrived for it."

The Reverend reached out to the young man approaching

him. "Let me introduce our friend, Patrick O'Brian. He is a local cabinetmaker. I just commissioned him to build a desk for my office. Patrick, these are the Stewarts of Virginia."

The young man nodded. "More visitors from Virginia associated with the good work of the Congress? Just yesterday, I met a Mr. Thomas Nelson and a Mr. Benjamin Harrison from Virginia. I am pleased to make your acquaintance sir, miss. I hope you are enjoying our fine city."

Matthew extended his hand. "We are. We were about to return to the Browns' home, where we are expected."

Mrs. White smiled. "We hope to see you again, perhaps in church."

"Good day." The Stewarts turned and made their way back to Cypress Street.

❦

It wasn't until Friday after he'd checked in at the Davis Inn that Matthew had an opportunity to call at the Ferguson home on Chestnut Street. Since the family was away for the day, he left a note asking Henry to contact him.

Henry responded within hours and suggested they meet at City Tavern on Saturday. City Tavern had been built since Matthew was last in Philadelphia, but he'd heard it was a gathering spot for local businessmen and gentry to carry on business and eat. No wonder Henry would be comfortable here. Matthew entered the tavern from Second Street and looked down the long hallway. Henry said he would be in the dining room past the coffee room. When Matthew entered, Henry stood and greeted him. His friend had not changed much in the five years since they'd last met. At nearly six feet, Henry carried himself well, and his medium brown hair showed no traces of grey. Henry had selected a table in a corner of the room for their meal. Only three other tables had patrons, so they enjoyed some privacy. They ordered a venison stew and chatted about their lives and the different directions each had taken over the years. It would have been enjoyable under normal circumstances, but the sealed packet Matthew carried was never far from his mind. He needed to prudently turn the conversation to recent events and deliver the packet.

Henry finished the tankard of ale and set it down. "When Mother heard that you were in town, she asked if you might join us for dinner tomorrow. You will miss Frederick as he is in New York on Father's business, but Barbara will be there. She is married now to an officer in the Regulars." Henry leaned back and studied him through narrowed eyes.

Matthew laughed to himself. An opportunity had been presented, but he sensed Henry was also gauging his political leanings. "Good for Barbara. I would be delighted to join you and your family for dinner. These are troublesome times, with so many friends and neighbors at odds with each other. At the same time, Philadelphia is an interesting place to be with the Second Continental Congress meeting here."

"Philadelphia is becoming a less than friendly place for those with loyalties to the Crown."

Matthew took a deep breath. They were dancing around each other, and it was his move. "Having a British Army officer in the family must prove challenging in some circles."

"The Fergusons are not all in accord on recent events." Henry leaned forward and lowered his voice. "I have difficulty recognizing the authority of Parliament over our elected assemblies. Their Coercive Acts have made it impossible for moderates in the colonies to support Parliament."

Matthew nodded. "We agree." He pulled the packet from the inside of his jacket. "Which is why I was tasked to deliver this to you by some like-minded individuals." What would be next? Stephens' earlier remark suggested he would have another assignment during his next trip to Philadelphia to pick up the children.

Henry's eyes widened but only briefly as he slipped the packet into his jacket.

"Still want me to join your family for dinner tomorrow?"

"More than ever." There was a silent understanding in his smile.

The following afternoon, Matthew arrived at the Fergusons' Locust Street home. He was ushered into a parlor, where Henry's sister Barbara greeted him. Barbara was as lovely as he remembered. Henry and his parents joined them a few minutes later.

The house was elegant and tastefully furnished, and Henry's family acted genuinely pleased to see him. For a half hour, they shared memories and some of the changes in their lives that had occurred during the previous five years.

Barbara's voice was shrill and nervous. "I'm sorry you cannot meet my husband this visit. He is a captain in the Regulars and is currently near Boston. He's very well thought of by General Howe. Perhaps you will enjoy his acquaintance the next time you call."

He had forgotten how Barbara was so full of herself. "I would be honored."

When a liveried servant entered and announced dinner, they adjourned to the dining room. Matthew was seated across from Henry and next to Barbara.

Barbara took a sip of her claret and leaned in toward him. "Henry tells me that you remarried several years ago. I remember how devastated the Moores were when Elizabeth passed away. 'Tis good that you have someone to care for your children. Are you still on your Virginia farm or have you returned to city life?"

"Our family is still at our farm and ordinary."

"Oh, a farmer and in trade. How interesting. I suppose Henry told you he has been associating with the rebels. 'Tis such an embarrassment for my husband and the family."

Matthew smiled. How was he to respond to that kind of

comment? He took a bite of the aspic and was given a reprieve when Mrs. Ferguson asked Barbara a question which transferred her attention to her mother.

The easygoing exchange around the table while they dined on roast beef came to an abrupt end upon the arrival of a military messenger asking for Barbara. She left the room, and Matthew focused on Henry.

"Tell me more about those horses you mentioned purchasing. You are not still racing, are you?"

Henry's response was cut off by a scream.

Mrs. Ferguson's eyes widened, and Mr. Ferguson pushed back from the table. Henry stood as well, and Matthew followed suit. Before they could go see what happened, they heard footsteps rushing toward them.

Barbara pushed into the dining room, ashen, shaking, and waving a parchment. The stunned and furious look on her face made him cringe.

"Every rebel opposing the crown should be shot or hung!"

Mrs. Ferguson went to her daughter's side and put her arm around her. "What has happened?"

Barbara sobbed. "Alfred is dead. There was a battle on a peninsula in Boston Harbor." She looked at the parchment, which shook in her trembling hand. "He was shot ... and now he is dead."

A battle. Regulars dead. How many colonists would also be casualties?

Matthew offered his sympathy and left to give the family their privacy.

It mattered not what side of the argument one took. Suffering was the same when a loved one was lost. And more suffering would likely come.

CHAPTER 12

Heather walked alongside Douglas back from the blueberry grove. They were both carrying full baskets. "With the three baskets of blackberries we picked yesterday and these blueberries, how many total baskets of berries do we have?"

The towhead narrowed his eyes a moment before breaking out in a proud grin. "We have six baskets of berries."

"Aye, well done, laddie."

With his free hand, he brushed a fly from his face, leaving a blue streak across his cheek. "I keep thinking every day that Papa will get back from the city. I want to hear about Mark and Mary."

"It shan't be long, sweetie." Truth was, she was just as eager for Matthew to get home. What had delayed him?

They had not been back at the Green a half hour before the sound of the approaching carriage drew them out front. And there on the tall seat sat her husband, hale and healthy and smiling.

Douglas ran to greet his father and clasped onto him like a brier. "Papa, Papa, we missed you."

"I missed you, too." Matthew lifted the tot and swung him around, much to the boy's delight.

Heather laughed. "I will be satisfied with a hug and a kiss."

He settled Douglas on the ground and wrapped her in his arms, nuzzling her neck before meeting her waiting lips. "Good. I dare not twirl you around for fear of making the babe bilious. It is good to be home."

Good. So good to feel her husband's arms around her. She hadn't realized the anxiety she'd carried until it lifted away in that moment.

Philip ran from around the barn. "Mister Stewart, I will see to the horses, but tell me first, how is Mary ... oh, and Mark?" He began to unhitch the harnesses.

"They are doing very well. Mark said he hopes you will save some fish for him to catch when he gets home."

Philip grinned. "Mark is so silly. I could not catch all the fish in the pond or the Potomack."

Philip was still laughing as he led the horses toward the pasture.

At dinner, Matthew entertained everyone with stories of their outings in Philadelphia. When the meal was over, he motioned to Polly when she got up to help Heather clear the table. "Would you mind watching over Douglas for a bit while Heather and I talk?"

"Of course not. He can come back to the cottage and help me with Laura."

Heather took the tray Polly carried. "I will clean these if you take Douglas."

Polly nodded and motioned for Douglas to follow her outside.

When Thomas and the boys went back outside, Matthew picked up a tray of dishes and followed Heather to the kitchen. "You all said everything was fine in my absence, but is there anything I need to know about?"

Heather looked up from the dishes she washed. "Other than a couple of cows getting out of the pasture, some piglets being born, and Douglas letting a frog loose in the Green, it has been much as you left it."

He began wiping the dishes. "Please tell me the frog was removed and the cows returned."

"Aye, on both counts." She turned toward him. "Tell me now what you did not share with the others. How are the children doing at their grandparents? I expected you back sooner. Were there complications?"

"No complications. I stayed while they got the lay of the land." It wasn't a complete lie. He had stayed to do that. He'd also stayed for other reasons, though, and his conscience prickled. He had no choice but to deceive her, but he didn't have to like it. "They behaved admirably. You would be very proud of them."

"And what about the Duncans? Is Donald still threatening to join the militia?"

"He joined before we got there."

"Oh, my." Her face filled with concern. "How are Maggie and Adam dealing with that?"

"It was not very pleasant when we arrived on our way to Philadelphia, but they seemed more resigned by the time I stopped there on my way back, Adam more so than Maggie."

"I can imagine. We need to keep them all in prayer."

"Yes."

"What did Elizabeth's parents say about your remarriage?"

"They were genuinely happy for me and for the children."

"Did they express any disdain that you married an indentured servant or a Scot?"

"I told them I married a beautiful, educated, godly Scot, a wonderful cook and homemaker who loved the three of us."

"You kept the indentured servant part out, didn't you?" Her eyebrows rose.

"I saw no reason to bring it up."

"Well, let us hope it never comes out in Mary or Mark's conversations with them."

"It shan't."

"How do you know that?" She studied his expression. "You told the children not to tell them."

"I know the Moores. And I have learned over the years not to invite trouble."

She laughed and poked him in the stomach.

He took her in his arms. "And you were well in my absence? No problems?"

Heather pulled back with an odd expression on her face. "There was one occasion, but it was my own carelessness. I was hanging the new curtains at the schoolhouse with my arms raised too long. I fainted but was not injured, and the babe continued to be active. Thank God the babe has continued to be active since then."

"You assured me that Amelia and you were going to hang them together." He drew her close again as he fought the painful memories of losing Elizabeth and their babe.

Heather stroked his cheek. "Amelia was a bit late, and I foolishly did not wait for her. No harm was done. The curtains look fine and will truly help keep the cold out."

"I'm grateful you were not hurt."

"A stranger no one had ever seen before came to my aid."

He pulled away from her and searched her face.

"His name was Cranford. After leaving the schoolhouse, he came to the Green looking for you."

"I know no one by that name. Did he say what he wanted?"

"Nay. I thought it odd because I introduced myself to him, and he said nothing about coming to the Green to see you."

"It must not have been important." Was this man in any way associated with Stephens and Jones? They had never mentioned anyone else contacting him. "If we are finished here, I'm eager to get to work."

She reached up and kissed his cheek. "Then go. I have berries to preserve."

A couple of weeks later, Matthew was outside the barn when a rider on a large chestnut horse approached. The rider headed directly toward him. He had a scar on his cheek.

Matthew set down his hoe. "May I be of assistance?"

"Matthew Stewart?"

"Yes."

"My name is John Cranford. May I have a few minutes of your time?"

"Certainly. Shall we go inside?" Matthew pointed toward the Green. He was eager for a conversation with this man who'd helped his wife—and then disappeared.

Cranford dismounted and wrapped the reins around a fence post. "I hoped for a private conversation."

Matthew took a deep breath. Probably another chap involved with the Patriot scheme, but best to be wary in case it was a trap. "Follow me." They headed down the path that led to the pond.

Cranford cleared his throat. "You have quite a nice farm and ordinary. It supports two families, I believe."

"For a stranger to these parts, you seem to know a great deal about us."

"You are a well-respected member of the community."

"And your point?" He had better things to do than dodge verbally with this character.

"Virginia plays a pivotal role in the colonies' attitudes and actions toward the Crown. The colony will influence the outcome at the Philadelphia congress. While Virginia is largely populated by Scots and English, there are individuals being misled into joining the rebels."

Matthew stopped on the path and faced the man. "Why are you here, Mr. Cranford?"

"Anyone opposing the King will do so at great cost. There will be loss of life and property. We want you to encourage anyone who is being deceived by these rebels to be prudent, or at the least to let us know who the local leaders are so we can persuade them to return their loyalties to the Crown."

Matthew looked back toward the Green. While he had misjudged Cranford's intent, 'twas no surprise Loyalist acolytes would seek leverage or information. But how to respond?

"Who is this *we*?"

"Loyal Virginians."

"You overstate my ability to convince others who may hold differing views." Hopefully, that would satisfy the man.

Cranford pursed his lips. "I understand you have been to Philadelphia recently."

"I have." He was obviously being observed, but how closely?

"Be careful who you associate with."

"I will take that under advisement. And I must also thank you for coming to the aid of my wife last month at the school."

"I was happy to assist. None of us wants our loved ones injured." His expression left no doubt of his warning. "If you need to contact me, do so through Charles Whitney."

"I will do that." They walked back toward the Green, and Cranford left.

Matthew would need to alert Thomas and his neighbors to be mindful of what they said around the hot-tempered miller.

CHAPTER 13

They had returned home in the wagons from taking the corn to Whitney's Mill. Matthew lifted the hollow gourd from the bucket at the well and drank from it. "Many thanks, Thomas, for all the help."

"Of course." Thomas jumped from the wagon to the ground. "The boys and I will unload the bags and see to the horses."

Matthew wiped the sweat from his brow. There was little relief from the late August heat. "We got a fair price and enough meal to get through the winter. And we even managed to avoid political quarrels with the miller."

When he walked toward the back of the Green, he spotted Heather picking beans and squash in the garden.

She stood upright and waved. "I thought I heard the wagons return." She removed her hat and fanned herself then wiped her face with the handkerchief she pulled from her pocket.

"You look flushed. Go inside to rest a bit. I met the post rider on our way back, and there is a letter from Mary." He waved the post.

Heather removed her garden gloves and rushed toward him. "Finally."

He had told her about their trip to Philadelphia and the children's awe at the vibrant city and the formality of the Moores. Hardly a day passed when she wasn't speculating about what those two were up to. "Can you hold off, and we'll read it together later?"

"Of course," she said, though she looked at the letter eagerly.

He kissed her on the nose. "Go inside and rest. I worry you are overdoing it."

She scoffed but lifted her basket of produce and headed inside.

Matthew had just entered the barn when the sound of a horse's hooves drew him back outside. The rider on the lane spotted him and approached. The respite from his Patriot duty the past few weeks appeared to be over.

Lucas Stephens. He dismounted and reached into his bag, pulled out a packet, and handed it to him. "Your delivery for Ferguson in Philadelphia. You said you were returning soon."

Matthew took the packet and tucked it inside his shirt. "I leave in two days."

"Good."

"You should know, a man named Cranford showed up here a few weeks back. He wanted me to exert influence with any neighbors supporting the Patriot cause, or at the least be an informant. Do you know him?"

Stephens frowned. "No."

"He knew I had been to Philadelphia, and his tone was threatening. Can you find out who he is and why he is tracking me?"

"I can look into it." Stephens seemed rushed and not terribly concerned. "I need to get to Leesburg." He mounted his horse. "You know where you can reach me in Alexandria when you are finished in Philadelphia."

Matthew nodded and watched Stephens leave the way he had come.

Back in the barn, Matthew hid the packet for safekeeping. He doubted Heather had been aware of Cranford's earlier visit. She had never questioned him about it. But he would need an answer in case Heather had seen Stephens. She would recognize him.

Thirty minutes later, Matthew washed at the well and entered the Green. "We can read Mary's letter now or wait until after dinner."

"Read it now. Thomas and the boys are not here yet."

He unfolded the two pieces of parchment and began reading.

Dear Papa and Mama,

Mark and I are enjoying our time in Philadelphia with Grandmamma and Grandpapa. They have been very generous, taking us to many fine establishments like Carpenter's Hall and City Tavern. We have attended Sunday services at both Christ Church and St. Peter's.

The Browns have also been very kind to us, and very patient. I fear having young people in the house tires them. We are all invited to a reception at the State House in a few weeks. Grandmamma has given me two new gowns, but I have not made a decision which one I will wear. I shall write more later, before I post this. We miss all of you.

Mama and Papa,

Mary said I may add to her letter. Living in the city is so different than being at the Green. I do not miss the chores, but I miss the fishing, swimming, and days spent outside. The Browns have a room in their house full of books, and they allow us to select what we want to read. Tell Todd and Philip I look forward to going fishing when we return.

Your son, Mark

The handwriting shifted back to Mary's tidy script.

I meant to finish and post this letter sooner. Last week we went to a grand assembly where they served delicious food in a grand manner with fine china and silver. I wore the green damask gown Grandmamma gave me, which is quite fine, but nothing compared to the elegant gowns worn by the Philadelphia ladies.

Papa may have mentioned, we made the acquaintance of a nice young man, Patrick O'Brian. Papa, Mark and I first met him in the company of the clergyman at Christ Church. I enjoyed a conversation with him again at the assembly. Mr. O'Brian is a very respectable young man, and I hope he calls on us while we are at the Browns'. I believe Grandmamma is feeling poorly, as she often complains of a headache and even today has kept to her room.

One thing that is the same here in Philadelphia as at home is all the talk of war with England. It is hard to believe we have less than a month left here. I hope you are all well. Do give everyone our best wishes.
Your affectionate daughter,
Mary

Matthew laid the letter down. There was no doubt Heather would want to discuss it.

Todd and Philip came through the door, wiping their faces and necks off with damp cloths, and Thomas followed.

When everyone was at the table and the blessing said, Heather served the stew. "Matthew, who was the chap you were talking with by the barn? He looked familiar."

She had seen. Very little got past his wife. "Mr. Stephens. He came out from Alexandria on his way to Leesburg."

"I remember now. He stayed a while back and traveled with another gentleman."

"Mr. Jones." Matthew picked at the food on his plate.

"What was the packet he gave you?"

"Some news from town."

Thomas served himself a large helping of stew. "Did you get to read the letter from the children yet? How are they enjoying Philadelphia?"

Heather grinned. "It was full of news of their activities and impressions. They have been busy with all sorts of activities … and probably exhausting the Browns and Moores."

Matthew sent up a silent thank-you for Thomas' question and added the plea that Heather would forget to question him further about Stephens. He needed to keep his activities secret for her protection, but lying to her was as unnatural as speaking in a foreign language.

It was sunset, and the heat of the day along with the growing bairn added to Heather's fatigue. After putting Douglas to bed, she wandered to the back porch, pulled a crate over to raise her feet, and sank into the chair. The fragrant breeze and the evening sounds brought indescribable contentment. She leaned her head back and closed her eyes.

Matthew's hand on her shoulder and his voice roused her. "You look so at peace, my dear, but sleeping in bed might be more comfortable."

"I must have drifted off."

He pulled the other chair closer and sat. "Mind if I join you?"

"That would be delightful. Are you finished in the barn?"

"Yes." He took her hand, rubbing it gently. "'Tis very pleasant, just the two of us."

She wrapped her fingers through his. "What did you think of the children's letter?"

"I'm pleased they have opportunities to meet different people and do things they are not able to do here. It sounds like the visit is going well."

"Mark sounds like he misses being home." She brought his hand to her lips and kissed it. "Mary may have an adjustment when she returns home, with no assemblies, receptions, fascinating people, and elegant gowns."

"'Tis time for bed." Matthew rose and reached out to help her up from her chair.

They walked into the common room. The night sounds grew distant, and the dim light from the lantern lent it an intimate atmosphere. His arm around her waist was comforting. But his distant look suggested his mind was elsewhere.

"Is something wrong, Matthew?"

"No, my dear. Why do you ask?"

"You seem preoccupied. Please tell me if you are troubled about something."

He took her in his arms and held her close, and his gentle voice in her ear was a balm to her spirit. "Forgive me, I have much on my mind, but never want to give you cause to be anxious."

The following week, Matthew readied for his return trip to Pennsylvania. Bringing Mary and Mark home after all these weeks would be a relief. They had been missed, but he also wanted them closer to home during these uncertain times. As soon as he got to Philadelphia, he would take care of his business with Henry, then let the Moores know he had arrived.

Matthew had finished packing the evening before his departure. While Heather put Douglas to bed, he retrieved the gift he had purchased for her earlier in the week while in Leesburg on business. He opened the small velvet bag and held up the ribbon with the silver Celtic cross attached. It shimmered in the lamplight. A token of his love for her, but perhaps also to assuage the guilt he felt. Honesty was a personal attribute he valued, and deceiving Heather was a constant irritant. Even if the lies were for his family's protection. He returned it to its box at the sound of her footsteps in the hall.

The door opened, and Heather entered. She frowned, glancing at his travel bag resting on the floor. She approached him. "I have very mixed feelings. I'm eager to see the children, but I hate your being gone."

He took her in his arms, and she eased into him in one fluid movement. "We are of like mind, my dear." He bent down and smelled the fragrance of her freshly washed hair. There was a citrusy scent to it. "You know I will be back as soon as I can."

"Aye." She looked up at him with trusting light blue eyes and loving smile. "I will count the days," she whispered.

He kissed her nose. "I have something for you."

She scanned the room before noticing the green velvet bag on the bed. "What is that?" Her eyes glistened, and her smile broadened.

"Open it."

She pulled out the ribbon and held it up with one hand, then reached for the cross with the other. She rubbed the embossed knotted design. "I love it, Matthew. 'Tis precious." She went to where the mirror hung on the wall and tied the ribbon behind her neck. "What a sweet gesture."

"For my delightful lady." He came up behind her and turned her around to face him, touching his lips to hers, gently, then with more intensity as she returned his kisses. Her hands caressed his back. Then as if on cue, they both pulled back, looked at each other, and laughed.

Heather blushed. "I fear something ... well someone has come between us."

"That was a pretty healthy kick I felt." He laughed again. "Our child is already asserting his or her self. So much for passion."

"My love, in case you have forgotten, 'twas passion that initiated that kick."

Early the next morning after breakfasting, Matthew brought the wagon to the front of the Green. He placed his bag and a basket of food into it before returning to the porch where Heather stood.

He caressed her cheek. "Do not exert yourself, and no climbing. 'Tis not too many weeks before our little one will join us. The Gordons will help you with anything you need done."

"Aye, dear." She opened her arms, and he pulled her close.

His kiss, only meant to be a farewell, met with hers, was difficult to walk away from. "Baiting the hook to reel me back?"

"'Tis true."

"I shall come back for more." He smiled and climbed onto the wagon and made his way down the lane. When he turned to wave, she was doing likewise.

CHAPTER 14

Matthew left Henry a note at the Ferguson residence when he arrived in Philadelphia. From there he went to Chestnut Street and checked into the Davis Inn. He would complete his business with Henry before announcing his arrival at the Browns' home to pick up the children. An hour later, a courier arrived at the inn with a note from Henry requesting a meeting at Tun Tavern near the waterfront at six that evening.

When he entered the tavern, Henry waved him back to a table. Matthew searched the dark room. Quite a few patrons but no uniforms in sight. "Henry." Matthew shook his hand and sat down across from him.

Henry scanned the room before directing his gaze back at him. "Any issues?"

A server came to the table, took their orders for drinks, and left.

"No." Matthew handed the packet to Henry, which he placed inside his jacket. "How are your parents and sister?"

"As well as can be expected. Barbara has moved back home but rarely speaks to me."

"Is she hostile because of your Patriot associations?"

"She blames 'my kind' for her loss, and she is very bitter."

The server returned with their order, picked up Henry's coins, and departed.

Henry continued. "Since I also cause my parents anxiety, I'm usually occupied elsewhere, thereby facilitating a more tranquil atmosphere at Ferguson House."

Matthew drank some cider. "'Tis unfortunate when families are at odds with one another."

"Agreed. 'Twill be easier once I leave the Locust Street residence."

"You are leaving Philadelphia?"

Henry laughed. "I'm getting married next month and will establish my own residence."

Matthew tipped his head. "Congratulations, my friend. And she is?"

"Her name is Constance." Henry gave him a knowing grin. "The daughter of one of the delegates to the Convention. Does that answer your question?"

"Yes." Henry was as astute as ever. "I wish you both a happy and long life together."

"You can meet her Saturday at the State House reception. I want you to be my guest."

Matthew took another drink and set the tankard down. "I have some other business to attend to while I'm here. Not sure I will be available." Henry did not know he was in town to pick up his children, and Matthew saw no reason to address that with him.

"Please consider it. Seven o'clock at the State House. You will not only be able to meet Constance and her father but also many other gentlemen who are our friends."

"I appreciate the invitation, but do not be disappointed if I cannot come."

"If not Saturday, then next month. Stephens will give you an address where we can meet."

"I shan't be back next month. My wife and I expect a child in October."

"Then you are to be congratulated also."

"Many thanks. Now I need to go and contact some of my family in town."

The men both stood, and Henry picked up his hat. "Saturday or November."

Matthew pushed his shoulders back. Why had he not asked Stephens or Jones how many trips to Philadelphia he would be expected to make? "I suppose so."

Matthew sent a courier with a note to the Moores informing them he was in town and asking when it would be convenient for him to call.

Their response arrived at the inn early the next morning. The Moores extended the Browns' invitation to stay at their home and attend the State House reception with them and his children. He looked out the window. Interesting. Two invitations to the same event.

When Matthew arrived later that day at Cypress Street, Mary and Mark flew into his arms. At dinner, the children shared stories of their excursions, all the sites they had visited and calls they had made. It would seem there had not been any major problems during the children's visit.

Louisa leaned toward him. "Your arrival could not have come at a better time. You can attend the reception with us and meet some of the delegates to the Convention who are still in town."

"I appreciate your invitation, but I only brought clothes suitable for Sunday services."

Mary's amber eyes cajoled. "You must come, Papa. 'Twill be exciting."

Mark's eyes rolled. "Please, Papa, I need you to come. Who else will I talk to?

He chuckled. It was going to be difficult to reject such coaxing.

John Moore settled the question. "I assure you, Sunday clothes will be very acceptable."

That Saturday, two coaches, one for the Browns and their daughter and son-in-law and the other for the Stewarts and the Moores, arrived at six-forty-five to take them to the State House.

Mary came down the stairway to the center hall dressed in a stunning amber damask gown with her hair worn high and adorned with ribbons. She took his breath away. Where had his little girl gone?

Her eyes sparkled. She pulled him near. "Papa, do you like my new gown? And look. Grandmamma gave me these pearl earrings and pendant to wear and this beautiful fan." Her gloved hand flicked it open and waved it before her face as if she had exercised the skill her entire life.

Dressed equally well but enjoying it far less, Mark sat reading on a heavily embroidered bench along the parlor wall. When the Moores entered the room, they all exchanged compliments before heading out to the coaches.

The setting sun cast a beautiful glow on the warm evening.

Inside the State House, the group entered a large, elegant room decorated for the reception. Well-dressed men and women milled about everywhere. Chairs were set against the walls for those who preferred to sit. Liveried servants carried trays with drinks.

Louisa drew Mary and Mark toward a gathering of women while John introduced Matthew to the Reverend White.

The cleric reached for Matthew's hand. "'Tis good to see you again, Mr. Stewart. We have enjoyed getting better acquainted with your children this summer at church."

"I'm glad to hear it."

"From what the children have told me, their time here has been well spent."

The young man they met on their walk to the church approached and greeted them. "Patrick O'Brian. We met at Christ Church."

"Yes, Mr. O'Brian, I remember you well, the cabinetmaker." Matthew took a shrub glass from a liveried server. "You were constructing a desk for Reverend White. Have you finished it yet?"

"No, but it will be completed within the month." The young man's manner was engaging.

John Moore stood nearby and introduced himself. "Have you an establishment?"

"Not yet, sir. One day, I hope to have my own shop. I have been working for Thomas Affleck the past two years."

John nodded. "I have heard good things of Mr. Affleck's work.

A fine profession and one that will keep you well employed here, I think."

"Yes, sir. I have learned much from him about the craft and the administrative side of the business."

Matthew set his glass on a table and listened as John spoke of some prized furniture he had. Matthew scanned the room for Henry Ferguson and his intended but could not locate them. But it was impossible to miss Patrick O' Brian's gaze across the room to Mary.

She stood with some young ladies, deep in conversation, but her eyes were on Patrick.

Matthew felt John's hand on his arm. "If you and Mr. O'Brian will excuse me, I must return to the discussion of the Olive Branch Petition Mr. Penn will take to London." He turned and rejoined a group of gentlemen in a heated discussion in the far corner of the room.

Matthew turned to Patrick. "Do politics interest you, Mr. O'Brian?"

"The current events force one to take an interest. Soon 'twill be more than talk."

John called out to him. "Matthew, come here. You need to meet these gentlemen."

"Excuse me, Mr. O'Brian." Matthew bowed and made his way over to the group. Matthew was introduced and listened to those gathered. Among the group of eight were three delegates to the convention still in town. Matthew listened as the men discussed General Washington's appointment as Commander in Chief of the Continental forces.

One of the younger men present shook his head. "The vote was ultimately unanimous. General Washington has a commanding presence, and with his military experience, he is the right man for the job."

The man to Matthew's right added, "With all the insurrection taking place up north, a southerner like Washington will be a unifier and bring support from the southern colonies."

Another man bellowed, "We must enlist the Canadian provinces. All along the waterways, the colonials and Canadians have forts. We cannot afford to let the English get a stronger foothold than they already have. I understand General Schuyler is organizing the Continental forces in New York,"

"Gentlemen, gentlemen." John Moore raised his hands. "Shall we put aside our strategies for this evening and join the ladies?"

Matthew returned to searching the room for Henry while also distracted by the visual exchange between Patrick and his daughter. Mary was fiddling awkwardly with her fan. The coy smile she wore implied she wasn't nervous but flirting, and Patrick appeared receptive.

Matthew noticed John Moore also observing the flirtation, and the old gent could hardly contain his laughter. Mary was definitely maturing at a rate Matthew wasn't prepared to acknowledge.

He looked around the room for Mark. There he was, in a corner playing a game of cards with some of the other young guests. He walked over for a closer look. The boys were absorbed in a game of Lanterloo.

An hour later, the Stewarts and Moores made their way back to Cypress Street. Matthew was seated in the coach between Mark and Mary. Louisa and John sat across from them.

"'Twas a lovely evening," Matthew said, "and kind of you to include me."

"We are glad you joined us." John grinned.

Louisa's eyes were trained on Mary like a hawk. "Was that young man you were speaking with the Mr. O'Brian we spoke of a few weeks ago?"

"Yes. Papa and Grandpapa spoke with him also." Mary's blissful expression became apprehensive.

Matthew took her hand. "He seems like a fine young man."

"And Grandpapa," Mary said, "did you not find Patrick O'Brian cordial?"

John smirked. "Very pleasant and well mannered … and quite restrained when you messaged him with the language of the fan."

Mary's jaw dropped.

John continued. "You wished him to speak with you, then indicated you were married before asking him if he loved you. Finally, you informed him you were engaged, yet wished to speak with him and wanted to be friends."

Matthew bit his lip. Poor Mary. The look of mortification on her face and the look of horror on Louisa's would be etched in his mind forever.

CHAPTER 15

Heather rubbed her swollen hands against her lower back. September arrived with a violent storm that brought howling, driving winds and torrential rain. Wringing out saturated towels and cloths was taking its toll, but they had stemmed the flooding around the windows and doors. She glanced out the kitchen window. Tree branches waved, and leaves blew everywhere. The wind's sound increased to a deafening pitch as Polly carried in another bucket of soaked towels and cloths.

Heather handed her bucket to Polly. "We shall need these again. The storm seems to be getting worse."

"Let me take over for a while. You sit for a bit."

Heather nodded. "I'm worried about Matthew and the children traveling back from Philadelphia in all of this."

"The storm's path is unknown. Who knows if 'tis raining where they are? They may be in Baltimore or Alexandria with friends or taking refuge at an ordinary along the way."

A loud crash made them both jump. Heather screamed, "The children!"

They ran to the public room. Douglas was under a table, and Laura was in her cradle.

Douglas ran up to Heather and nestled into her skirts. "What was that noise?"

"'Tis all right, laddie." She turned to Polly. "We need to check upstairs. Where are Thomas and the boys?"

Polly nodded. "In the barn. I will check upstairs."

Douglas followed Heather to the kitchen still holding on to her skirt. From the window, she spotted Philip opening the large barn door. She waved. Philip and Todd were looking toward the Green. Todd looked anxious. "Polly," she yelled. "I think the sound came from the barn."

Polly ran into the kitchen. "Upstairs is fine." She ran out the back door.

Heather looked down on Douglas, still hovering at her skirt. She leaned down and put her arms around him. "Dear God in heaven, please let no one be hurt. Please protect us."

Thomas, drenched, came through the back door. "Polly said everyone was safe here."

"Aye." Heather nodded. "We have been dealing with the rain coming in, but 'twas the sound that frightened us. How are Todd and Philip?"

Thomas leaned against a wall. "Polly is with them. They are fine and seeing to the animals in the barn. The horses were shaken when the tree fell. We will have a job cutting up all that wood and repairing the barn roof."

Heather poured him some coffee. "We can deal with that once the storm passes.

❦❧

Twenty-four hours later, the sun was shining, and the common room was the gathering place for its exhausted residents. Thomas and the boys had spent hours cutting the tree and moving the wood.

Heather set a large tray of bread, ham, cheese, and apples on one of the tables. "That tree did a lot of damage."

Thomas, his legs spread out in front of him, looked out a window and rubbed one of his shoulders. "We can get started on the repairs as soon as we get all of the wood out of the way. 'Tis amazing the difference a day can make. It could not be sunnier outside."

Heather set the plates around another table. "You all have been working constantly. Polly, Douglas, and I can gather the branches and put them in a pile."

Polly got up to help serve. "We have so much to be thankful for. No one was hurt."

Heather nodded. "And the Green and the cottage are not damaged."

Thomas stood and stretched. "The animals and chickens were panicked, but they have all settled back into their normal routine."

The summer had come to an end, and the children would be home soon. On Sunday morning, Heather got Douglas ready for church. Hearing an encouraging sermon and spending the day in the company of so many friends would be a blessing.

Seated in their pew, Douglas slipped his hand into hers as she listened to Reverend Grayson speak on the Book of Job and God's faithfulness to this godly man who endured such suffering yet remained steadfast in his faith. *I hope, Lord, if I ever am faced with such severe trials, You will find me faithful and able to endure.*

Douglas interrupted her silent prayer when he nudged her in the side. She bent close to him, hoping not to disturb others nearby. "What is it?"

"Why is Mrs. Whitcomb crying?" He pointed to their neighbor seated across the aisle.

She reached for his extended hand and held it. "Do not point, dear."

A tear streamed down Hannah's cheek that she dabbed with her handkerchief.

After the service, the congregation gathered for a shared meal. Polly sat with Laura and Douglas under the large oak tree while the Gordon boys brought chairs out from the schoolhouse. Heather retrieved the baskets with their food from the wagons. She turned when she heard Hannah's raspy voice.

"The curtains you and Amelia made look nice."

Heather smiled. "Many thanks." Hannah looked tired but appeared sincere.

"Here, let me help you with that." Hannah reached for the basket Heather was lifting.

She handed Hannah the basket with the vegetables and looked for any sign of her earlier melancholy. "The window coverings should keep the room warmer in the winter months, so Mr. Martin can get by with less firewood." They walked back to where the others were gathered. The silence was odd. Hannah always had something to say. "We have not spoken since Matthew left. How are you and your family? Will Martha be back from Williamsburg soon?"

Hannah came to an abrupt stop and faced her. "Did you notice Tobias is not with us?"

"Why, I ... Is he ill?"

"He has joined the militia, the First Regiment."

"Oh, Hannah."

"I fear this fight will spread, and Tobias will never come home again."

"Do not say that."

"We have no business going against our king and country."

Heather juggled the basket of oatcakes and cheese and put her arm around Hannah. "I am so sorry. I can only imagine the worry this causes you."

"Worry. I can hardly sleep thinking about my boy getting shot."

"Perhaps things will settle down and there will be reconciliation with England now that the Continental Congress has sent the King the petition."

"George says this Olive Branch Petition won't accomplish anything. He believes the current hostilities will mean outright war is certain and soon."

"I hope not." Her stomach tightened at the thought of it.

She joined Amelia in the shade of a large tree beside the creek.

Emily, Ellen, and Douglas splashed in the edge of the shallow c.

Thomas and Betsy Edwards walked by the little group. "Good day, ladies," Doctor Edwards said. "It must be only about another month for you, Heather, until you add to your clan."

"Aye, Doctor Edwards, I believe this wee bairn is longing to join us."

"And Matthew will be returning with the children soon?"

"They are expected back later this week."

"If you need assistance or anything else before they return, let Betsy or me know."

"You are both so kind, but I am fine and in no immediate need of help. I have Polly and Thomas. I am not concerned about Matthew's absence, yet."

"Very well, we will look forward to seeing you next Sunday."

Amelia stood, picked up the blanket, and stretched. "I saw you with Hannah earlier. Did she tell you about Tobias?"

"Aye, she did. I fear my attempt to reassure her that war is not inevitable brought little comfort, but I understand her anxiety."

"Our Cole has made comments about joining the militia. 'Tis no wonder, with the men constantly talking of war."

"Perhaps the petition to England will settle the dispute. These boys are young and inexperienced. How are they to fight against the Crown's army?"

Amelia frowned. "None of us knows how this conflict will end, but the siege of Boston and the recent battle at Breed's Hill makes me think we are closer to becoming part of it."

"All I think about is Matthew and the children coming home." She rubbed the small silver Celtic cross that hung from a pale blue ribbon around her neck. It had brought tears to her eyes then and brought warmth to her cheeks now. She got up and signaled Douglas to join her on the creek bank.

"Douglas, we must gather our things and be on our way. The Gordons have already headed back to the Green."

CHAPTER 16

Heather looked up from the sheet she and Polly were draping over the privet hedge. The approaching wagon on the drive caught her attention. "They are back." Her heart raced. Having her family reunited brought tears to her eyes. There would surely be no reason for them to be parted again.

"What is all the commotion?" Todd came from behind the Green where he, Philip, and their father had been working on the stone fence. Douglas followed right behind him.

Mary and Mark were waving from the wagon as it neared the house.

Matthew reined in the horses and smiled. "This is a nice welcome home."

Philip ran to the carriage and helped Mary down.

Thomas approached. "Todd, Philip, help me get these trunks and things inside. Let the Stewarts catch up a bit." He took the reins while the boys saw to the unloading.

Heather embraced Matthew. Then she went to Mark and Mary for hugs before they headed inside.

Heather peeled Douglas off Mark. "Let Mary and Mark settle in, laddie. 'Twill be plenty of opportunities for you to spend time with them."

Over the next hour, they reported on the activities around the Green and the surrounding neighborhood. Mark and Mary shared their impressions of the people and places in Philadelphia.

At three, Heather got up to prepare dinner. "Mary, would you help set the table?"

Mary uttered a long sigh. "Yes, ma'am. My brief respite appears to be over."

Heather took a deep breath. "Holidays end and life with its responsibilities resumes." She tried to muster sympathy. *Lord, help us all to extend patience and grace to one another.*

When they sat down to dinner, Matthew had no sooner finished the blessing when Mark began chattering. "Grandpapa took me to the Port of Philadelphia. I read *The Life of Robinson Crusoe* and *Gulliver's Travels*."

Heather smiled. "Impressive. Mr. Martin will be gratified to know he is motivating his young charges to further their education even when they are not in school."

Heather turned to Mary. "It sounded like you were busy making calls, shopping, and attending assemblies. What delighted you the most?"

"All of it. We met interesting people, even some members of the Continental Congress. Grandmamma and Grandpapa said they enjoyed our visit, even if sometimes we might have tired them and taxed their patience."

"I know they enjoyed your visit." Matthew's secretive grin at his daughter and the sheepish glance Mary returned sparked her curiosity. Hopefully, he would explain later.

Later that evening, Heather sat on Mary's bed holding one of the frocks they had unpacked. "These are lovely gowns your grandparents gave you. 'Twas generous of them. I hope it was not because they did not approve of your clothes."

"Oh no, Grandmamma liked the dresses, but she enjoyed taking me shopping. I think she wanted me to have some gowns that were more elegant for the social engagements we attended."

"I suppose life in the city would require finer clothes. And she probably had pleasure in having a young lady to shop for as she once did for your mother." She ran her hand over the ivory dress richly embroidered with a variety of colored silk threads.

"I wore the yellow dress often, and I received multiple compliments on it."

It touched her that Mary appreciated the dress she'd remade for her. "I have no doubt you were stunning in all of the gowns. You sound as though you genuinely enjoyed yourself."

"Yes, but I was ill at ease at times. Grandmamma suggested I should work on my deportment. I fear I embarrassed her on more than one occasion. There is so much to learn about serving coffee, which silverware to use for each part of the meal, or handling one's fan, when and how to address someone, correct conversation, oh, and so much more."

"Your grandmother is sure to understand that away from the city, you would have little occasion to learn or use these social graces. Perhaps I focused too much on getting your wardrobe ready. I did not even consider you might benefit from reviewing society's manners."

"'Tis not your fault. I have no recollection of my mother being as refined in her behavior as Grandmamma, though she must have been before she came to Virginia."

"I'm sure your grandmother brought your mother up to be a genteel lady, but it may have not been something your mother viewed as essential here."

Mary hung gowns in the wardrobe, pressing the skirts out with her hands. "I wonder if I will ever have occasion to wear these again."

"Oh, I suspect you will, my dear, and I will look forward to seeing you in them. Tomorrow, I want to hear all about the people you met and about your visit with the Duncans."

The frown on Mary's brow suggested she had some tales to tell, but it would need to wait until later. Heather made her way downstairs.

From his seat in the common area, Matthew smiled at her and turned to Mark. "Well, young man, if you wish to go fishing tomorrow morning, you must complete your chores first. Head off to bed with Douglas."

"Chores?"

"You have not been gone so long to forget that you *still* have responsibilities." Matthew carried the drowsy Douglas upstairs with Mark following.

Less than an hour later, Matthew came into the kitchen, put his arms around her, and nuzzled her neck.

"I got the bread started for tomorrow," she said. Why did she allow anything to trouble her when this wonderful husband made her life so complete?

She turned and drew her arms up, wrapping them around his broad shoulders. "I'm so glad you and the children are home."

He gently caressed her cheek and neck and then held up two of his fingers with a dusting of flour on them. "You have immersed yourself in your work, my dear."

"Well, I am exhausted and ready for bed. Are you ready to go up?"

"After I make the rounds outside. Thomas and I will need to get started on repairing the barn. I'm thankful none of you were hurt in the storm."

Upstairs, she checked on the children before going to their room, pausing to take in the sights of Mary and Mark in their beds. How she'd missed them when they were gone. But now, her family was all gathered close again.

She left the children to sleep and went to her own bedroom. She had braided her hair by the time Matthew came through the door.

"Now tell me," she said, "what was your impression of Mary and Mark's visit with their grandparents? Do you believe it went well?"

"John and Louisa were very grateful to spend time with them." His mischievous smile intrigued her.

"What else?"

"I suspect they were also pleased when I came to retrieve them. Who would blame them? It has been a long time since they had youngsters around."

"Of course. Were there problems? Mary had rather a coy look about her at dinner."

"Having an attractive, maturing young lady around may have posed challenges they had not anticipated."

"Oh, Matthew, please explain that."

"Mary caught the attention of the young Irish cabinetmaker she mentioned in her letter, and I doubt John and Louisa were prepared for some of the flirtation between the two of them."

"Oh, my. Mary and I will need to chat about that," Heather said.

"You are much more equipped to guide her through some of these areas than I am, my love. God blessed me when you showed up on the *Providence*."

"I think we both agree the Lord worked in mysterious ways that day. Good night, my love."

CHAPTER 17

Heather walked around the side of the Green, dragging the small wagon filled with squash and root vegetables. She approached Mary. "Polly and I picked these, but she needed to see to Laura. When you can, please take these down to the cellar."

The girl's eyes narrowed. "Where is Mark? I have been finishing the laundry."

"He went fishing after helping the Gordon boys split wood this morning. 'Tis been over a month since the two of you returned from Philadelphia, yet you seem to be having a hard time adjusting to the work involved in a farm and ordinary."

Polly returned with Laura.

Mary's shoulders sagged. "I apologize and will take them down as soon as I finish spreading the laundry."

Polly handed Laura to Heather. "I will help Mary."

"I appreciate you both. Once this wee one is born, I will be back to my old self."

The sound came of a horse and rider rapidly approaching on the lane leading to the Green. Heather shaded her eyes from the sun as she peered down the drive "'Tis George Whitcomb. I wonder what brings him here at such a pace."

Polly wiped her hands. "He is not coming from his farm."

Matthew jogged from the barn and joined the women as George pulled the horse to a stop. "What is it?"

"Word came ..." George caught his breath. "The King issued a proclamation in August declaring the colonials are 'engaged in open and avowed rebellion.'"

Still holding Laura, Heather turned to Matthew. "What does

that mean? Surely the King has known of the events occurring throughout the colonies."

Matthew removed his hat and wiped the perspiration from his brow. His focus shifted from George to her. "'Tis a formality that will serve as a precursor to whatever actions result. The British, particularly those loyal to the Crown already on this side of the Atlantic, will direct more aggression toward us." Matthew waved at George. "Come inside and have a cool drink."

George pulled the reins of his horse. "No. I got the news at the Falls Church and have stopped several places already. I need to get home. We can talk at church tomorrow."

Matthew nodded. "Tomorrow it is."

George turned his horse's head in the direction of his farm and rode off.

Mary walked over from the hedgerow, frowning. "Will the fighting with the English get worse, Papa?"

"'Tis likely to, and we need to be prepared."

Heather and Matthew looked into each other's eyes. His face was a picture of resolve.

She had prayed that an agreement could be worked out, but it sounded now as if all hope was gone.

Later that day, Matthew sat on a bench in the barn cleaning another hunting rifle when he heard Mary calling him. "What is it, poppet?"

"Two gentlemen just rode up looking for you. Do you want me to send them in here?"

He walked to the door. Stephens and Jones again. "Yes, ask them to come over here."

"Do you think they will be staying? I can go and tell Mama."

"No need. They shan't be staying."

She tilted her head. "How do you know that?"

"I just know. Go inside and help your mother. She is near her time and needs rest."

From the barn door, he watched Mary return and deliver his instructions, then wander inside.

Stephens reached the door first and whispered, "You alone?"

"Yes, come over here ... out of sight." Matthew pointed toward one of the stalls, which was out of view from outside but a good spot from which he could keep an eye on the door in case anyone approached.

Jones thrust a packet at him.

Stephens looked nervous. "'Tis for Ferguson in Philadelphia."

Matthew looked briefly at the sealed packet. He could not leave Heather now, not this close to the child's arrival. He had been just as anxious as when Douglas and John were born. Did this packet have anything to do with the King's proclamation? The danger was increasing in this venture. "You find out anything about that chap, Cranford?"

"Not yet."

"What is the reaction in Philadelphia and Alexandria to the King's proclamation?"

"The Convention reconvened mid-September. The announcement did not catch the Patriots by surprise and will only embolden Loyalists. Be careful, in case you are being observed or followed."

Matthew wiped the perspiration from his brow. "I'm not leaving for a few weeks."

Jones' brow furrowed. "Why not?"

"I'm not leaving my wife until after the baby is born and I know she is well.

Stephens and Jones looked at each other.

"'Twill either wait until next month, or you may find someone else to make the delivery."

Stephens grimaced. "Just get it to him as soon as you can."

"I will." He was torn, but as long as Heather and the baby were doing well, he would honor this commitment. After this trip, he would need to determine whether to continue.

CHAPTER 18

The late October air was crisp, and the amber and red leaves on the trees were bright in the morning sunlight as the Stewarts made their way to church the following day. Heather put her arm through Matthew's. "I love the sound of the horse and wheels driving over the fallen leaves and the musty fragrance they release."

Matthew glanced at her each time the carriage jostled on the rut-filled road. She tried to hide her cringing, but by the concerned look on his face, he wasn't convinced. In back, Douglas quizzed Mark about the number of rabbits he'd trapped. Mary sat in silence.

When they got out of the carriage and started walking toward the chapel, Heather took a deep breath. She had felt odd since breakfast had ended.

Sitting through the long service didn't help. After, Mary pointed to a bench Philip had brought out from the school. "Mama, go sit down. I can get the baskets from the carriage."

"I think I will."

Heather rubbed her lower back to relieve the pressure and cramping and sat on the bench. Ten minutes later, Martha returned with Mary, each carrying a basket.

Heather only half listened to the women's conversation around her while they ate. The children were in gaggles enjoying themselves, and the men were standing by the creek in an animated conversation. Discussing the Crown's proclamation, no doubt.

An hour later, after bidding their farewells, most of the neighbors, laden with pots and baskets, made their way back to their wagons and buggies.

Heather smiled up at Matthew when he reached for her arm.

"'Twill be good to get home." He had been very solicitous the past week, checking on her numerous times each day. Was he thinking about Elizabeth and their baby and how they'd both passed away so quickly after she'd given birth?

The cramping had intensified by the time they reached the wagon. Mary lifted Douglas up to Mark, who was already seated.

A sharp pain left Heather breathless. She gasped and leaned against the front wheel. "Your father, Mary. Where is your father?"

Mary came to her side and held her. "He was speaking to Doctor Edwards. I will help you up."

Matthew hurried to the wagon.

Heather gripped Matthew's arm like a vise while he and Mary lifted her into the carriage. "We need to get home. 'Tis time."

"I know." Matthew kissed her cheek after getting her settled. "The Gordons and Betsy Edwards are coming right behind us. Everything will be fine."

She looked over at him, trying to steady her breathing. "God willing."

They headed down the lane at a rapid pace.

The older children were silent, but Douglas sounded excited and oblivious to her circumstances. "Go faster, Papa. Who are we racing?"

Mary nudged her brother. "Quiet, Douglas,"

In their bedroom back at the Green, Heather struggled to catch her breath between cramps. How long had she been there? Polly Gordon and Betsy Edwards were at her bedside. "I'm glad you came."

Betsy squeezed her hand. "I wouldn't be anyplace else."

They appeared to have the situation well in hand. Matthew had come to the door a couple of times. Heather arched her back as the last pain seared through her body. Her eyes closed tight, and her teeth clenched. She reached for Betsy's hand. "How long has it been ... the time?" She squeezed it as the pain reached its peak.

"I believe it is five or a little after." Betsy's easy smile held no concern.

She took another deep breath as the pain subsided.

"'Twill not be long now. Polly went downstairs to let Matthew and the children know how you are."

"Oh." *Another pain, so soon.* She bit her lip.

Polly entered the bedroom carrying a large bowl. "How is she doing?"

"The pains are getting closer. I believe Heather will be holding her baby very soon." Polly set the bowl down on the stand nearby and rubbed a cool, damp cloth across her face.

The pressure to bear down intensified. *Aye, it must be soon.* Her friends at the foot of the bed sprang into action.

Minutes later, Heather held her swaddled baby girl close. Tears ran down her cheeks as she kissed the tiny face. A wee lass to love.

Polly asked, "Shall we get Matthew so he can meet his new little daughter?"

"Aye, please do. Would you prop me up first?"

Polly stepped out while Betsy placed some pillows behind her and brushed the damp strands of hair that had worked free from the rest.

Heather gazed down at the sleeping child in her arms. Tears flowed. *Each life is a miraculous gift from God. I'm so grateful, Lord.* She looked up at the sound of the door opening.

Matthew entered, smiling, and Betsy departed.

"My love, you look lovely holding our daughter." He sat on the side of the bed and pulled back the cloth. "She is beautiful, just like her mother."

She reached up and caressed his cheek. "She is precious, and I'm so thankful." With his kiss, her tears returned. "Oh, dearest, I'm so overwhelmed with emotion."

"You have every right to be after the sorrows you have known.

Tell me, my sweet, do you think she looks like a Sara Stewart, or do you want a different name for her now that you have met her? She looks fair like you."

Her mind raced back to her days on the *Providence* and her short but treasured friendship with Sara Macmillan, who perished on their journey from Scotland. *You will be named Sara just like my wise and loving friend.* "Sara Stewart she is, if that meets your approval."

"It does." He placed one arm under the swaddling cloth and lifted the quiet child, holding her close to him.

"We dedicate this child, this girl, and the woman she will grow to be to You, Lord. Please guide us as we raise her to know, love, and serve You all the days of her life." Matthew bent over their sleeping daughter and kissed her delicate fair head.

He placed Sara back in her arms and stood. "I will bring the other children up if you wish. They are eager to meet their sister."

"Aye, let them come and meet Sara."

CHAPTER 19

Matthew washed at the well before heading inside, leaving Thomas and the boys still at work on the other side of the barn. It had been a fortnight since Sara's birth, and he needed to talk with Heather alone. The trip to Philadelphia had to be done now, and he could no longer put off telling her. Since Sara had been safely delivered and Heather was recovering, he had been at odds with himself on how soon to leave, but he needed to be back before hog-killing time. More than once, the family had chided him about his distracted state. He'd take Heather for a walk since challenging topics were best addressed when they were free from distractions. Mary was inside and could watch over Sara.

Upon entering the kitchen and spotting a kettle boiling over, Matthew picked up a hook and swung the trammel, removing it from the heat. Heather must have left it to tend the baby and forgotten it.

He walked to the common room. Heather was seated and mending near a sunny window, tapping on one of the cradle legs to make it rock. What a look of pure joy she had watching the sleeping infant. "I was hoping we could have some time together, maybe take a walk to the pond. I can ask Mary to watch over Sara while we are gone."

She looked at him and smiled. "I would like that. We need to talk. Mary is in the kitchen making soup."

"Mary was not there when I came through. I shifted the boiling kettle away from the fire."

"Oh, my," Heather got up and walked toward the kitchen. He followed.

Just as they both got there, Mary came through the back door and rushed to the kettle. "I went to the garden to pick herbs for the soup. I did not think it would boil that fast." Her lips pressed together and brow furrowed.

Heather stifled a grin. "No harm done. You are not the first young woman to let a pot boil over or even burn a meal. We have all done it, and more than once."

"What about the soup?" Mary asked.

Matthew came alongside Mary. "Add some more water and 'twill be fine."

Mary sighed. "In Philadelphia, my biggest concern was what to wear to an assembly or which fork to use with the chilled crab."

Matthew put an arm around her. "Unless you marry a wealthy man, you need to know how to cook and keep a house."

Mary returned his hug. "Marrying a wealthy man sounds more to my liking."

Heather laughed. "Running a fine household has its own troublesome tasks. Such a lady must manage and care for servants, budget funds, allocate purchases, plan meals, and perform other chores you might find disagreeable. Nobody's life is as carefree as you might think."

Mary poured water into the kettle and began chopping the herbs. "'Tis not likely I would meet, much less marry, a man of means."

Matthew returned the trammel holding the kettle to its spot over the fire. "Our hope for you children is that you marry a person of godly character whom you respect and love. Since you are not yet sixteen, you have plenty of time. Heather was near thirty when we married."

"How dreadful to still be unmarried by—" Mary's eyes widened, and her hand went to her crimson cheek. "I did not mean ..."

Laughing, Heather put her arm around the girl. "Marriage for me came past the age when most girls marry, but waiting turned out to be a blessing." Heather approached Matthew and put her arm through his.

"'Twill happen in God's timing, poppet," Matthew said. "Would you mind caring for Sara while your mother and I take a walk?"

"Of course." Mary nodded. "And I will make sure the kettle is moved before it boils again."

Polly came in the kitchen door. "A coach is approaching."

Heather placed her hand on Polly's back. "Matthew and I were just about to take a walk."

"Go ahead. I will see to the guests."

As Polly headed to the door, Matthew said, "We shan't be long."

A minute later, Polly returned to the kitchen. "'Tis the Duncans."

Matthew looked at Heather. The disappointment in her eyes matched his feelings. "Our walk will have to wait." He would have to tell her later.

Todd, Mark, and Philip approached the Duncans' carriage when it came to a stop in front of the Green. Matthew and Heather drew near, smiling and waving.

"First things first." Maggie climbed down. "Looking at you, I know a baby has been born who I long to meet."

Adam helped the children step down from the coach. The Duncan boys took off in Mark's direction. Jean grinned when she spotted Mary coming out the front door.

As hugs were passed around, Heather waved to Adam and the others. "You must be hungry. We will have plenty for supper. Come inside and meet Sara."

Heather ushered them to the cradle in the common room. "Meet Sara Stewart."

Maggie leaned over the sleeping babe. "She is beautiful."

Douglas stood near the cradle. Maggie squatted and opened her arms to him. "What do you think of your baby sister?"

"She is small, very noisy, and sometimes smells."

Everyone laughed.

A Heart for Freedom

Later, Matthew took Adam aside near the well. "How is your family? Maggie seems less anxious."

"We are well and adjusting to Donald's absence. Heather looks besotted with Sara."

"She is a charmer. I'm grateful both Heather and Sara are doing well." Matthew looked around. No one else was in sight. "I will be gone for a while to purchase some Devon cattle and other things for the farm. I put it off long enough. I have not mentioned it to Heather yet, but I wanted you to know." His life was becoming a series of half-truths, but there was no other way. Confiding in his friend would bring a measure of peace, but it wasn't worth the risk. "We should join the others."

"We are on our way to Leesburg. Are there spare rooms for us to stay here tonight?"

"Certainly, we have no other guests."

They joined the others in the common room. Matthew poured cider into two tankards and handed one to Adam.

After supper while they were still seated around the table, Matthew leaned toward Mary. "The soup was quite good."

"Thank you, Papa." She winked at him and turned to Maggie. "What do you hear from Donald?"

Maggie's expression grew solemn as she studied her bowl.

Adam cleared his throat. "We understand he was in the Hampton area with Colonel Woodford and the militia."

Heather glanced at Maggie. "Is trouble expected there?"

Matthew got up and added a couple of pieces of wood to the fire. "With the Royal Navy and Lord Dunmore still in the area, a confrontation is expected."

Adam's eyes met his. "A ship left Alexandria full of Tories headed to England. I suspect more will follow. Last week, two ships left from the port of Norfolk."

Matthew rejoined the group. "Events are moving fast. We are praying for Donald's safety, as well as that of the other soldiers."

He could no longer put off telling Heather of his intended

departure. She would need a couple of days to adjust to the idea. He did not want to leave her upset. He hated the idea of leaving her at all.

The next day after the Duncans' departure, Heather watched Matthew as he strode toward the barn. What was bothering him? Perhaps they could go for their walk now. She sighed and placed her hand on Mark's shoulder. "Please take Douglas inside and watch over him. I want to speak with your papa. Sara should sleep for a while."

"Yes, ma'am."

Shivering in the crisp fall air, she wrapped her shawl tighter around herself and entered the barn. As her eyes adjusted to the diminished light, she looked around the large expanse. Sounds from one of the stalls directed her path.

Matthew was brushing down the mare but stopped when she approached.

For a moment she stood silently. His brown eyes, so penetrating, caught hers. "Are the boys inside?"

"Aye." She looked around until she located an old crate, which she moved closer to him and sat upon. The sounds of the animals were pleasant, but they would not answer her questions. "Matthew."

"What is on your mind?"

"That is the question I have for you. What has you so unsettled? You are not yourself."

He returned to brushing the mare, slowly and deliberately. "I need to go away for a time, around two weeks, maybe more." His eyes met hers only briefly. "Some farm business. I am looking into purchasing some equipment and some Devon cattle."

"This is the first time you said anything about a trip. How long have you been planning this?"

"I wanted to wait until after the baby came. I need to get this done before hog-killing time."

She studied him. Something didn't feel right. "Purchasing farm equipment and animals has you troubled?" She got up and walked to where he stood on the opposite side of the mare. She reached up and stroked Tillie's smooth chestnut neck. "You seem so distant lately." She tried to make eye contact with him.

He avoided her gaze. "Please forgive me if I have not been myself of late. My thoughts have been on the farm and all the talk of separating from England." He put the brush down, walked over to her, and opened his arms. She stepped into them.

He gently brushed the loose hair from her face and held her close. "You are dearer to me than you will ever know."

His kiss reassured her, but as he pulled back, something in his face still begged questions. He took her hand and led her to a bench against the wall. "Winter is coming. We will have more time together then."

"Gone a fortnight?"

"Possibly more."

"We will—" His warm mouth on hers made it difficult to think straight. His kisses always made her lose her train of thought.

As they walked hand in hand back to the Green, she listened to his instructions on what to anticipate during his absence.

He glanced toward the cottage. "Thomas and the boys can take care of anything that might occur."

She took a deep breath as they approached the door. "When will you be leaving?"

"Day after tomorrow."

"Where are you going?"

The door opened, and Mary stormed outside. "Oh, good, you are back. Where were you?"

Mark was right behind her, scowling. "I told you, they were in the barn."

"Please tell Mark to leave me alone. He keeps pestering me."

"Shall we discuss this inside and not annoy the Gordons?"

Matthew steered them back into the common room. "Now, what is the problem?"

Mark looked defensive. "There is no problem."

Douglas, seated at the far end of the room near Sara's cradle, looked confused.

Heather picked Sara up and sat on a bench, shaking her head. "You two need to work out whatever petty quarrel you are having. What upset you so, Mary?"

Mary shook her head. "'Tis not worth all the fuss. Forget about it."

"Philip and Mary were kissing." Douglas's words brought silence to the room, and everyone's focus shifted to him.

Like speeding bullets, Matthew's eyes met Heather's before turning to their daughter.

Mary's face turned crimson. "'Tis not as Douglas says."

Heather placed her hand on Mary's shoulder. "I am going upstairs to feed Sara. Perhaps you should come with me and tell me what happened."

Mark held up his hands. "I did not tell them."

Mary scowled at him before she headed upstairs.

Heather followed. *Lord, please help me to listen and to advise with the right words.*

Mary, still blushing, reached the upper hallway. "Your room?"

"Aye, 'twill give us some privacy." They sat on the large bed. She began feeding Sara while Mary's eyes filled with tears.

"It did not happen as Douglas suggested, *exactly*. I went for a walk after the Duncans left, but I soon headed back. I cried, thinking about Donald being in the militia, and Philip came over and asked me what had troubled me. I explained and ... he held me ... like a brother. You know how tenderhearted Philip is."

It all sounded believable. She looked into Mary's amber eyes and waited.

"He comforted me, and when I looked up at him to thank him ... he sort of ... kissed me. I certainly did not expect it to happen. Mark and Douglas were in the garden and started squealing like pigs. I pulled away and came inside. It was so awkward."

"Philip is a very compassionate young man. I can well understand how something like that might happen."

"Philip is like a brother to me. What should I do?"

"You are a young lady now, and the boys you have grown up with, as well as some of your newer acquaintances, are young men. Young women your age need to be more circumspect about conversations and behavior so as not to be misunderstood. I am not faulting you at all, dear, because I can imagine myself as a young woman getting into such a situation."

"What must Philip be thinking?" Mary's face showed her distress. "Should I say something to him? I do not want to hurt his feelings."

Heather shifted Sara in her arms. "'Tis possible the kiss took Philip by surprise also, and he may be as embarrassed as you are. Were it me, I would not bring it up but continue to treat him with kindness. If he approaches you again in such a personal way or says something about it, you may need to tell him you consider him a very special friend, like a brother. He is a sensitive person, and you must be sure not to hurt him."

⊚⧉⧉⊚

Heather had little time to dwell on Mary's plight. Matthew's preparations for his journey took most of the next day. He told the children of his travel plans, and he spent time with Thomas and the boys in the morning and early afternoon going over the details of the farm chores that would need addressing in his absence.

Later, after the children had gone to bed, Heather reached up and stroked Matthew's cheek. "I love you, and I will miss you. We all will."

He held her close, looking into her eyes. "You know how deeply I love you, more with every passing day. You and the children are always in my thoughts and prayers."

Matthew's kiss warmed her. They always did. She never doubted his love for her and the family, and he seemed in good health, yet something weighed him down that he had not addressed.

When Matthew pulled away, his smile brought tears to her eyes. He caressed her face and reached for the Celtic cross at her neck. He rubbed his finger across the raised knotted design.

"You are a good man, Matthew Stewart. I'm forever grateful 'twas you who bought my indenture and then married me."

He laughed. "Best investment I ever made, and I never doubted for a minute the Lord orchestrated the timing and outcome of that endeavor." He kissed her forehead before moving to her waiting lips.

"Matthew, tell me we will not go to war with England. I love our life."

"I wish I could, but that would be giving you false hope. We must each follow the path God has set before us, no matter the cost."

She backed off at the intensity of his remark. "I need to see to Sara." As she picked Sara up and began feeding her, heaviness engulfed her. Was she partially responsible for Matthew's evasiveness? Had her bristling each time the escalating tension and violence in the colonies was brought up made him less than candid? She needed to make more of an effort to accept what she could not change.

When he returned from his trip, she would endeavor to do just that.

Somehow, the decision did not ease her worry.

Early dawn the next morning, Heather stood on the front porch as Matthew loaded his pack behind the saddle. "Are the others still sleeping?

"Aye."

The glance Matthew gave her reminded her of the tenderness and passion they had shared the night before. She must not weep and make leaving more difficult for him. Why was she so emotional? Was it because she had just borne a child or was it something else? She felt a churning in her gut, and the peace she had felt in recent days had vanished. Her fingers brushed the cross that hung from the blue ribbon around her neck, a recent habit she had developed whenever under stress. Slowly, she untied the ribbon at the back of her neck. She held the cross in her hand and brought it to her lips. Kissing it, she looked into the face of the giver of the gift.

"Here, Matthew, I want you to take this with you. Bring it back to me when you come home." She handed it to him as he leaned down from the roan mount. They kissed, and once more, she looked into those brown eyes that melted her like butter.

"I will keep it close to my heart, beloved, until I return." He pulled back on the reins before turning the horse down the drive.

She wrapped her shawl tightly across her and watched as Matthew and his horse disappeared down the lane in the early morning fog. A sick feeling filled her, and tears ran down her cheeks. Was it his leaving or her fear of an impending war she wanted to ignore? Perhaps both. *"There is no fear in love; but perfect love casteth out fear: because fear hath torment. He that feareth is not made perfect in love."* She reminded herself of verses she'd known all her life. *"Thou shalt not be afraid for the terror by night; nor for the arrow that flieth by day."*

I must combat my fears with prayer. Lord, watch over Matthew and keep him safe while he is apart from us.

CHAPTER 20

Matthew arrived in Philadelphia the second week of November. He wasn't surprised when the doorman at the Ferguson home said that Henry was no longer in residence. Before mounting his horse, he opened the folded note Henry had left for him.

Sorry to have missed you, Matthew. Travel across the Delaware River to Pomona Hall in Camden, New Jersey. I look forward to seeing you and introducing you to Constance. Henry

Matthew looked down Locust Street. He would need to find a ferry crossing nearby to reach the New Jersey side of the river.

Upon arrival at Pomona Hall, a doorman ushered him into a small room.

A stocky and stern-looking woman entered the parlor a few minutes later. "I'm the housekeeper, sir. May I be of assistance?"

"Mr. Henry Ferguson left a message that I was to contact him here."

The woman studied him for a moment. "Mr. Ferguson was here but left five days past. He said he was going to Swedesboro."

"Swedesboro? And where is that from here?"

She studied his less than formal riding attire. "Swedesboro's around twenty-five miles southwest. I was born and raised near there."

Another twenty-five miles? It would be impossible to complete his task and be home within a fortnight.

The woman continued. "The village is beyond Mickleton near Raccoon Creek in Greenwich Township."

"Much appreciated." He nodded and left. There was nothing to be gained from wallowing in frustration. Best to get the packet to Henry so he could get home.

After traveling a couple of hours, Matthew stopped at a creek to rest. He dismounted and rubbed the mare's neck. "You thirsty, Bonny?" He had to be about halfway to his destination. Something moved in the fallen leaves behind him while his horse drank from the creek. Was it another rider or a deer? He scanned the area around him but saw nothing in the dense woods.

When the horse was satisfied, Matthew tied the reins to the branch of a nearby tree. Sitting on the trunk of a fallen oak, he ate the bread and cheese purchased earlier in Philadelphia.

Stephens' reminder to be careful in case he was being watched flashed through his mind. Ever since he left Pomona Hall, he had felt an uneasiness he could not explain. Perhaps it was guilt over his deception that was gnawing at him. When he'd finished his meal, he pulled the small silver cross attached to the blue ribbon from his waistcoat. As he rubbed the raised surface, he pictured Heather standing on the porch shivering the morning he left, her expression one of trust, love, and hope. It tore him apart that he was hiding his mission from her. Someday, he would tell her and hoped she would understand that it was his way to provide aid in securing their future. He looked around but heard no further sound. Must have been deer. They probably watered here also.

He continued south until he came to another creek, probably Raccoon Creek. He must be near Swedesboro by now. If Bonny was as thirsty as he was, they best stop to get a drink.

The cool water was refreshing. Just as Matthew raised his eyes, leaves behind him rustled, and he felt a sharp blow to the back of his head. He jerked forward and collapsed. He heard the loud report of a musket, followed by intense pain.

His world turned black.

Matthew winced at the pain in his side and head. Struggling to remember what had happened, he fought to open his eyes, and when he did, everything looked blurry. He shifted to get his face, now nearly numb, out of the icy water. The pain in his side was like a knife stabbing. If only that were numb.

What had happened? There were no sounds, and no one seemed to be around. It was getting dark. How long had he been there? How would he get help?

He pushed himself up and moved slowly away from the creek. He could do no more, though. The work robbed him of what little strength he had. His eyes closed. He was going to die if help did not come soon. Was this how it would end? He forced himself to take a deep breath, to feel the life fill his lungs. The effort brought more pain than relief. *Please let me live, Father. Let me get back to my family.*

Pictures flitted through his mind. Heather walking back from the pond, smiling and waving at him. Her hair like golden wheat, loose and blowing in the breeze. Mark and Mary chasing each other in the apple orchard. Douglas lifting his chubby arms, his baby face bright with joy. Sara in her mother's arms.

A noise pulled him back from the memories.

Was that Bonny neighing? Was she still nearby?

Your will be done, Father.

Heather stood over the kettle stirring the chowder and glanced out the window. It was dusk. Mary should be returning from the Whitcombs' soon. She shivered as the chilly wind howled outside.

Mark came through the kitchen door. "Douglas, where are you? I need you to man the door while we bring the wood in."

A big grin appeared on his face as Douglas came running to the door and held it open. "I'm manning the door."

Heather chuckled. It felt good to laugh, a rarity the last few weeks. Why had Matthew not sent word? He had been due back over a week ago.

Douglas shivered as he opened the door each time one of the boys approached. "Hurry, Mark, 'tis cold in here."

Mark and Todd carried wood inside for the hearth and fireplaces.

Mark brushed by Douglas and sneered. "'Tis a lot colder outside. Do you want to carry the wood while I hold the door?" His eyes were no more than slits as he carried an armful of wood into the kitchen and placed it in the wood box near the hearth.

Todd entered with his arms full. "Where do you want these, Mrs. Stewart?"

"The common room."

Todd stopped near the kettle. "Smells good."

"Ham and corn chowder. Let your family know supper will be served about seven."

"Yes, ma'am." When he returned to the kitchen and reached the door, he leaned down and patted Douglas on the head. "You can close the door now, little man; we are finished." Todd turned to leave just as Mary came through the door. Philip entered behind her with a basket of kindling and set it by the kitchen hearth. "Todd left this by the door." He grinned at Mary while she hung her cape on a peg, then continued out the door.

Heather pulled some bread from the oven. "I'm glad you are back. Would you set the large table for supper? The Gordons will join us."

As Mary hurried to complete the request, Douglas came alongside her. "Why does Philip always have that silly smile when he looks at you?"

She scowled. "Douglas, you need to go and sweep up the wood chips."

Heather stopped slicing the bread and peered at Mary. Everyone's short temper in recent days only aggravated her own worries about Matthew. "What is wrong? Did you see the dejected look on the tyke's face when he left the kitchen?"

"I'm sorry, but I have had a bad afternoon. First 'twas Mrs. Whitcomb's strange behavior and then Philip pursuing me."

Heather took off her apron. "The chowder is simmering. Shall we go upstairs? 'Tis near time to feed Sara. You can tell me what happened."

With Sara in her arms, Heather closed the bedroom door once Mary entered.

"I passed the boys herding the sheep on my way to Martha's, and Philip came running over, questioning me about where I was going. I was clearly on the path to the Whitcomb home, and I probably was a bit curt with him. 'Tis just that lately, since he … kissed me, I'm worried he may try it again."

Heather placed Sara to feed. "Perhaps he was just being friendly. Be patient with him. Philip has a kind heart."

"I know. Then, when I got to Martha's, her mother was sitting in a chair, staring out the window. She did not move or acknowledge either Martha or me when we entered the room, so we went upstairs to work on our needlework. Poor Martha was so embarrassed she began apologizing and tried to explain that her mother was sad."

"Hannah is overwrought by Tobias leaving to join the fight."

"I know that. When I asked Martha if she had heard from James, she told me he had written to her and was also thinking of joining the Patriot cause."

"Oh no, not James, too."

"James said his father has business in Fairfax, so they may come here before the end of the year."

"'Twould be nice."

"Martha asked me where Papa was and when he was coming home."

A lump formed in Heather's throat. The same anxious feeling kept returning. "What did you tell her?"

"I could not answer her because I do not know."

"I'm sorry I did not get more information from him before he left."

Mary reached for Sara's hand, caressing the tiny fingers. "'Tis not like Papa to be gone over a fortnight and not tell us where he was going."

Heather bit her lip. "I asked George Whitcomb and all our neighbors if your father mentioned to any of them where he planned to purchase the Devon cattle. I thought if we could trace him there, we might get some answers, but no one knew anything about his plans. I am at a loss as to where to turn next." She shook her head and rubbed her temples.

"My afternoon did not end with that," Mary continued. "On my way back to the Green, Philip was waiting on the path. He said he wanted to make sure I got home safely. I told him I could take care of getting home by myself. Oh, Mama, the hurt look on his face stung."

Heather shook her head as she changed Sara's wet clothing.

"Philip took my hand and told me I was special. So, I told him he was special too and that he was like the older brother every girl wants."

"What did he say?"

"He looked confused and said he was Todd's older brother. So I told him I could not imagine a better older brother." Mary handed Heather the baby's blanket.

"Very artfully done. For being caught off guard, I think you handled it quite well. You assured him you valued him and cared for him in a special, yet sisterly way."

"Do not credit me for being so nimble. For days I have mulled over in my mind how to respond if the situation arose. And if I did well, why is my heart so heavy?"

"You were gracious to Philip. We can only pray he will receive it well, though he may feel confused or bruised for a while. Now, we need to get downstairs and get supper on the table."

Both families gathered in the common room for the meal.

Heather fought back tears when Thomas offered the blessing and again asked for Matthew's safe return. Where could he be? What could have delayed him? The questions were never far from her mind. And the answers kept getting darker, scarier. Yet, she must remain strong and hopeful for the sake of the children. And for her own sake as well. She must believe he would return to her.

She ladled chowder into everyone's bowl and observed Philip watching Mary, who was ignoring him. How was that situation to be solved?

Thomas looked at her. "'Tis hog-killing time."

She nodded. "Aye, we cannot put it off any longer. You and the boys can start on that, and we—"

"I will care for Laura and Sara to free you and Miss Polly to assist them," Mary offered. "And of course, I will help if we have any guests."

Heather looked at Mary and chuckled. "How generous of you, dear."

<hr/>

Matthew pried his eyes open. He turned his head to the side as he took in the savory scent of roasting meat, which made his stomach roil. He retched until nothing more came up. Wincing from the pain in his side and stomach, he rolled his head back to the softness of his resting place. His eyes closed briefly as he caught his breath and tried to ignore the bitter taste in his mouth. He opened his eyes again at the sound of a voice.

"*Herr?* Mister?"

Was the cloudy vision of a woman's face above him an apparition? He closed his eyes.

A cold hand touched his forehead.

Du är feberisk, herrn ... Ahh! You are feverish." She walked away and soon returned with a bowl. "*Jag kommer att ha en tendens till dig.*"

"Ma'am?"

She wrung out a cloth and placed it on his forehead. "I will tend to you. Talk *engelska* ... You should rest. 'Tis good you are conscious."

Was he conscious? He felt in a fog. His eyes closed, and he drifted to sleep again.

When he awoke, he scanned the small room. Everything still appeared foggy. A couple sat muttering by a hearth.

"Ma'am?"

They walked to his side. "I am Anna Fleming." She nodded to the man. "Husband is Oden Fleming." The woman spoke slowly and enunciated each word melodically.

Matthew stared up at the tall and lean couple, perhaps in their fifties. "Where am I?"

The woman placed the damp cool rag on his brow. "Swedesboro. You injured."

"Yes." That much he knew.

She pointed. "Your head hurt, and you shot in the … side."

Matthew closed his eyes. Yes, he had a vague memory. He'd been at the creek. Then felt the sharp pains. When he opened his eyes again, the woman had a cup in her hand.

She reached behind his head with one hand and gently lifted it while bringing the cup to his mouth. "Drink slow." Grey curls crowned the front of her cap. Her blue eyes were kind.

He sipped the water. *Please let it stay down.*

The man, who could pass for her brother, leaned over him. "*Vem är du och var bor du?*"

The woman swatted him on the arm. "*Prata engelska*, Oden."

"*You* speak English, wife." Oden turned back to him and spoke with a heavy accent. "Who are you? Where do you live?"

Matthew studied the man. Could he be trusted? "Matthew … from Virginia."

She motioned for her husband to leave before turning back to him. "You tired. We talk tomorrow. Maybe you eat. *God natt.*"

He nodded and drifted off to sleep.

CHAPTER 21

It had started to snow by the time Heather got near enough to see the Turner farm. Early for mid-December, but pretty. Smoke was coming from the chimneys. A welcome sight. She had hoped to talk with Amelia and Aaron yesterday after services, but this conversation needed privacy.

When she reached the stone dwelling, she got down from Tillie and tied the reins to a fence rail. "'Twill not be long, girl." She walked up the steps of the porch and knocked on the door. A minute later Amelia, smiling, opened it and drew her inside.

"Come in, come in." Amelia looked to where Tillie was tied. "Cole, please put Mrs. Stewart's horse in the barn."

Cole came to the door. "Good day, Mrs. Stewart."

"Tillie and I appreciate it."

Heather scanned the hall and large front room. Where were the others? "I needed to talk with you and Aaron … but privately."

Amelia helped her off with her cape. "I think I sensed that yesterday. In fact, Aaron intended to ride to your place later today. Go sit by the fire while I get us some hot cider." Amelia took the cape and walked toward her kitchen. "Logan, would you tell your father Mrs. Stewart is here to see us."

"Yes, Ma."

Heather walked into the room and sat in a chair by the large fireplace. The warmth was welcoming, particularly for her chilled hands.

Amelia returned with a tray with three steaming cups, followed by Emily and Ellen, both grinning and curtsying. "Mrs. Stewart," they said, almost in unison.

Amelia set the tray down and placed an arm around each of the twins. "Girls, you may go up to your room. Logan will be up soon to read to you."

Heather tried to hide a smile watching Amelia dispatching each of her children when Aaron and the boys entered the room. Did her friend realize she had been Heather's mentor ever since she'd married Matthew?

Aaron and Amelia sat on the couch across from her. Aaron leaned forward. "I was going to come by today. I know you have been waiting to hear."

"Please forgive me if I took you away from your work, but I could not wait any longer. Did you learn anything about Matthew on your trip to Leesburg?"

Aaron shook his head. "No. The folks I spoke with have not seen or heard anything of him. The good thing is that they are aware he is missing and will be mindful of letting us know if they hear of or see anything."

"What about Alexandria?" Heather asked. "Will you go and speak with Adam Duncan ... and anyone else you think might be able to shed some light on his whereabouts. Between you and Adam, I'm hoping you can learn something ... anything. 'Tis been nearly six weeks. He just cannot have disappeared. Matthew may be ill or injured. Why else would he not come home or let us know why?"

"I will go this week," Aaron said.

The concern on Amelia and Aaron's faces was a mirror into her own heart. She put her hand to her lips, and the tears she had fought came.

Amelia came and kneeled beside her. She placed her arm around her. "We are praying for his safe return ... and for you and your family."

Heather just nodded and smiled through her tears. "I know." She took a deep breath. "I cannot tell you enough how much your help means to me." She glanced out the window. The snow was continuing to fall. "I should get back now."

Aaron looked at Amelia and stood. "I will get your horse and ride with you. I need to go see George." He walked out the door.

Amelia went for her cape, returned, and helped her on with it.

Heather smiled. "Aaron does not really need to see George, does he?"

"No."

"I thought not." Heather hugged Amelia. "My precious friends."

Heather stepped back from the table, dusting the flour from her hands. How many times waiting for Matthew's return had she kneaded dough to relieve the tension? Best let it rest and rise, or it would only be fit for pudding. She placed the ball of dough in the wooden bowl, covered it with a cloth, and set it near the hearth. She needed to have hope that Adam or Aaron would discover news of Matthew.

Stirring the soup steaming in the kettle, she glanced out the window to the dusky sky. Mary and Mark should have been home from the Whitcombs' by now. Hopefully, they found Hannah less melancholy. The snow had stopped hours ago, but the wind blew so much it sounded like a wail and— Todd Gordon burst through the kitchen door, his face almost scarlet from the cold. "Mrs. Stewart, Mark has been hurt. They are bringing him here."

She dropped the ladle and ran to the door. "What happened?"

George Whitcomb and Philip carried Mark inside. Mary followed, carrying her brother's hat. Blood dripped from Mark's nose onto his shirt.

Heather peered at George and Mary. "What happened? Why is he unable to walk?"

The expression on George's face alarmed her. "A fight, and he fell down the stairs. His leg is hurt, and possibly his head. After we set him down, I will fetch Dr. Edwards."

She stood back, stunned. "Take him upstairs, George. I will be right up." Heather poured water into a bowl and gathered some clean cloths.

Douglas ran into the room, his eyes wide as he reached for her skirt and cried.

She stooped and held him close to her. "Mark is hurt. I need to go and take care of him."

Mary stood still as a statue, staring at her.

Heather poured water into a bowl and gathered some rags. "Please take Douglas to the cottage and ask Polly if she can keep him for a bit."

George came down the stairs as Heather entered the central hall. "Before you go for Dr. Edwards, tell me what happened."

Their neighbor glanced at Mary as she bundled up Douglas. "Todd and Philip are getting him settled. Mary can tell you what happened. I need to find the doctor."

"I'm obliged to you for bringing Mark home." As George rushed out the door, Heather turned her attention to Mary. "As soon as you have him settled with Polly, please come back."

"Yes, ma'am."

About ten minutes later, Mary came into Mark's room and sat on the bench at the end of the bed. She focused on her brother. "I'm sorry you are hurting, Mark."

Heather studied her son's face and rinsed the blood-soaked cloth in the bowl. "His nose has stopped bleeding, but he will probably have some bruising and this nasty bump on his head. His leg does not appear to be broken, but Dr. Edwards will know."

Mary reached for her brother's hand.

Heather watched the two. The tender sight stilled her. Better that than the pounding her heart had been doing. "Could Polly see to Douglas?"

"She said yes, and if you needed help with Sara ..."

"I fed her not a half hour before you came home. She is sleeping.

Come with me."

Heather headed toward her room. Mary followed.

Once they were both in the room, Heather shut the door. "Tell me what brought all this about?"

Mary took her cape off. The look on her face and her reluctance to talk about the incident was troubling.

"Tell me everything. Who did this to Mark and why?"

"Teddy Whitcomb. Mark hit him, they got in a scuffle, and Mark fell down the stairs."

"Teddy? Why would those two fight? They are best friends."

"Teddy provoked Mark." Tears formed in Mary's eyes. "He said Papa left because he sided with the Tories."

"What? Why would he suggest such a thing?"

A pained look remained on Mary's face. She knew more than she had disclosed. Teddy would never make such an accusation, unless ...

"How is Han ... Mrs. Whitcomb? Does she still keep to herself?"

"Mama, I wonder if Mrs. Whitcomb had something to do with Teddy's comments. She has been so withdrawn. A few days ago, Teddy told Mark that his mother took a strap to him for no reason. And a week ago, Mrs. Whitcomb attacked Martha, calling her all sorts of vile names."

"The Whitcomb children told you these things?"

"Yes. When I pressed Martha about her cheek being red and swollen, she cried and said her mother flew into rages. She is still upset about Timothy's death years ago, and Tobias joining the militia seems to have made things worse."

Heather sat back and took a deep breath. "Something must be amiss with Mrs. Whitcomb. What happened to Mark today is proof of the harm gossip brings. It is a false suggestion that your father left home because he is associated with the Loyalists."

Mary pulled back. "What should we say when people ask us where Papa is? He has been gone for six weeks. He would never choose to be gone so long."

"'Tis true." Heather rubbed the knot in the back of her neck. There was no faulting the children for being confused and anxious. She must remain strong and set a good example for them. "I need to look in on Mark."

When Heather reached Mark's room, he was on his side, leaning close to the lantern and reading. He looked up when she entered.

"Are you in pain? Does your head ache?"

"My whole face hurts."

"Let me put this cloth back on. You can read later. Can you move your leg?"

"Yes. But it hurts. May I have something to eat? I'm starving."

"Mr. Whitcomb went for Dr. Edwards to make sure nothing serious is wrong with you. There is soup downstairs, and I will bring you some if the doctor agrees." She left him and was walking downstairs when she heard men at the door.

Dr. Edwards entered with his black bag. "How is the boy?"

Mary took the doctor's coat.

"Bless you for coming," Heather said. "He is hungry, so I believe he is better, but he has some bad bruises and a bump on his head. Mary, please take the doctor upstairs."

George Whitcomb, his hat in his hand, stood in the center hall. He watched the two as they left the room.

Heather stared at her neighbor. "I asked Mary what caused this fracas. She told me Teddy said Matthew left our family to support the Loyalist cause. Where would he hear such rubbish?"

George looked embarrassed. "Teddy should not have said that. He will be rebuked and apologize for this."

"But why he would believe such a thing? Is the community sharing this falsehood?"

"No. I have never heard any neighbors question Matthew's loyalty to the Patriot cause."

"You make it sound as if he has joined that group. He is a farmer and a businessman. While he believes as strongly as anyone we should not be subject to British tyranny, he has not joined the

Patriots or the Loyalists."

"Then where is he?" George said. "'Tis what folks are wondering."

She threw the towel on the table. "I do not know. Day and night, I question why he has not returned. I fear he may be lying in a ditch somewhere, hurt and without help."

George bent his head.

She took a deep breath. "Matthew was only to be gone a fortnight. Aaron Turner went to Leesburg and is going to Alexandria to make inquiries ... get some answers. If something detained Matthew, he would write or send word to us. Where do I go for help to find my husband?" She shook but felt relieved voicing her concerns to another human being.

"We all are concerned for Matthew's safety, and for you and the children."

"Where did Teddy come up with such a far-fetched story?"

George looked down for a moment. When he looked back up, his cheeks had reddened, and his eyes looked sad. "Hannah has not been well since Tobias joined the militia. She has strange imaginings. At times she makes outrageous comments and has fits of rage. I fear for her safety."

Heather relaxed. George was in the midst of his own agonizing situation. She was not the only suffering spouse. "I'm so sorry, George. What can I do to help?"

His eyes grew moist. "What can any of us do to help her? I think her outburst about Matthew comes from her fear that Tobias and the rest of us are in danger."

"If your children knew Hannah was ill, it might be easier for them to cope with her outbursts."

"You are right. Hannah's odd behavior has been difficult. Having it known outside of the family ... well, 'tis not hidden anymore."

"Feel free to send the children here for a break. We will pray for your family."

George nodded. "You are a good friend."

Footsteps sounded on the stairs. The smile on Dr. Edward's face relieved her.

"I believe Mark will recover very well. I wrapped his ankle and suspect 'tis only a sprain. His face will heal, and the nose does not appear broken. Put cold compresses on the goose egg. Some birch bark tea or a little lemon balm for the headache. His eyes look clear. Keep him quiet for a few days. He says he is hungry, so that is good, but I advise only clear broth today."

"I appreciate your coming, doctor. May I offer you some soup?"

"Not for me. Betsy has supper waiting."

She bundled up some of the scones she had made earlier in the day along with some of her apple butter and handed it to Doctor Edwards, who received the gift with a smile.

George put his hat on. "I will get you home to your supper, doctor. Goodnight, Heather. Teddy will be by tomorrow if that is acceptable to you."

"Of course. Good night, gentlemen."

CHAPTER 22

Matthew's head still ached. He reached up and touched his face. Quite a growth. His fingers traveled higher to his forehead. A bandage was wrapped around it. He moaned when he turned to scan the room.

Anna stood by a steaming pot and turned toward him. "You wake."

She brought him some broth, which he managed to retain. When he finished it, she returned with some cloth, a blue bowl, and a cup. "I clean and dress wounds."

Matthew bit his lip. "Much obliged."

She smiled and lifted his head again to drink. "Drink slow."

He choked as the burning liquid went down his throat. "'Tis not water."

"Brandy. Helps when I take dressing off."

His throat burned less with each swallow. He winced as she began to peel off the bandage. She jammed a roll of cloth into his mouth and poured some of the brandy on the wound.

His muffled scream brought Oden back to the bed. Her husband held his arms down while she executed her ministrations. His head throbbed with pain. Was it the head injury, a reaction to the side wound, or the kindly woman's aid?

Sleep finally came, and along with it, dreams. Something hitting his head, the sound of musket fire, and his face in the mud. His head ached something fierce, and his side was in excruciating pain. He lay in the mud and touched the back of his head. He felt wetness and looked at his fingertips. Bright red blood covered his hand. Blood oozed from his side. He could not rise, and he was alone. He would die there. "I'm so sorry, Heather."

Within two days, Mark improved not only in how he felt but also in how he looked. As promised, Teddy Whitcomb came to the Green and apologized. Mark and Teddy's longstanding friendship did not appear altered by their fight.

Heather poured hot chocolate for the boys and for Martha, who accompanied him. The unspoken topic of their mother's health and behavior was as much a guest at the table as any of them. Had George relayed to his children their conversation about Hannah's condition? She needed to address it with care.

Heather brought a plate of sliced gingerbread to the table. "Your papa told me about your mother's melancholy and how hard it has been for you. I am praying for her and all of you. Losing a loved one can change a person's attitude and affect everyone in the family. Please come here whenever you wish."

Martha wiped away a tear. "None of us is free from worries."

"True, and the Lord tells us, 'Peace I leave with you, my peace I give unto you: not as the world giveth, give I unto you. Let not your heart be troubled, neither let it be afraid.'"

Early the next morning, Heather tucked Sara into the cradle in the common room. She added kindling and a few logs to the embers still glowing from the previous evening. The dark morning ensured the children would sleep a while longer. She wrapped her woolen shawl tightly for warmth and sat in a favorite chair. Gazing out the window, she watched the sunrise.

Lord, You know where Matthew is. Please tell me how to find him. You assure us You will instruct us and teach us in the way we should go, and that You will guide us. I need Your guidance now. To whom shall I turn, and where do I go to seek the answers we need?

She wandered into the kitchen. Sunrise made the lane leading up to the Green visible, although a mist still covered the path that led to the pond. It had been five days with no guests at the Green. The diminished workload allowed her more time to tend to Sara and to Mark as he healed, but the addition of guests added vitality and information to their lives, not to mention the additional funds. If only someone would come with news of Matthew. She must focus on her blessings.

Lord, You protected Mark. You have provided for our financial needs and an abundance of crops. You have given us good neighbors and friends so we are not without resources. A tear rolled down her cheek. *Please protect Matthew wherever he is. If injured, supply him help and healing. Give him the ability to communicate with us. Bring hope, restoration, and comfort for Hannah and her family.*

Later at dinner, the Stewarts and Gordons enjoyed banter and laughter, which were lately in short supply.

Mary sat at the table, rocking Sara. "'Tis Yuletide. We should gather some greens and decorate. Mark, I can cut some holly if you will bring some pine boughs."

Heather smiled. The children's spirits were improving. "That is an excellent idea. We may yet have patrons this season. I will heat some spiced cider."

Polly got up and gathered the dishes. "You make your plans while I wash these."

Thomas put some more logs on the fire before rejoining the others at the table. "George Whitcomb spotted a five-point yesterday. We plan to go hunting in the morning. You boys want to join us?"

They all responded with enthusiasm.

Polly stood in the doorway, animated and grinning. "We have guests riding up the path."

The guests might be friends, or perhaps—Matthew.

Heather rushed from the common room to the kitchen window to see. Though she was disappointed the horse didn't carry her beloved, she was pleased at who was coming. "Andrew and James—how wonderful. I had forgotten they planned to come in December."

Polly squeezed her hand, her eyes conveying understanding. "I shall go tell the children."

An hour later, Polly served their guests spiced cider and hot chocolate while they gathered around the fire, relaying all their activities since they were last together. Most of the tales were of Mary and Mark's visit to Philadelphia.

Heather motioned Andrew to join her in the front parlor. Closing the door behind them, she steadied herself. "I did not want to say anything in front of the children when you asked about Matthew. We all are frightened and confused about his absence."

"I received your letter and would have been here sooner, but I wanted to wait for James to join me. Have you learned anything?"

She sat on the settee. "Nay, and none of this makes sense. Matthew would have gotten word to us if something kept him from returning."

He sat beside her. "I made inquiries in Fredericksburg and every town and village around, but I learned nothing."

"Bless you for all your help."

"And your neighbors had no knowledge of his plans?"

"Nay, no one knows anything." She bit her lip.

"What is it?"

"Some people have asked if he was involved with the Patriot cause, and others wonder if he is aligned with the Tories."

Andrew stood by the hearth and leaned his back against the brickwork. "We should not be surprised people would speculate during these times, but Matthew steers clear of politics. The suggestion he would leave his family to support the Crown is laughable. You mentioned he might have had some business in Alexandria or possibly Annapolis. I will go there and learn if any of my acquaintances have any leads."

She stood and paced. "Our neighbor, Aaron Turner, went to

Leesburg and learned nothing. He is going to Alexandria and will meet with Adam Duncan, who has also made inquiries." She looked up into Andrew's gentle eyes. His sad expression broke her heart. He was well acquainted with loss. Her tears flowed. Weeks of strain, exhaustion, and trying to be strong left her emotions raw. Sobs from deep inside burst forth, and her whole body shook.

Andrew walked to her and put his hand on her shoulder. "Take heart, Heather." He had a helpless expression as he shook his head. "A man does not just disappear. We will find him. Try not to fear, and do not lose faith. There may be an explanation we have not yet considered."

She reached into her pocket for her handkerchief and dabbed her cheeks and nose before looking up. She was thankful for his friendship, encouraged by his offer of aid, and hopeful he would provide some answers. Standing back, she rubbed her neck. "I am so grateful for your help. We'd better join the others, or they may wonder whether you are providing information I'm not sharing with them."

Later that night after everyone bid their good-nights, she went upstairs to her bedroom. She fed Sara and then pulled out her Bible for encouragement and guidance. The bayberry candles in the mirrored sconces on the wall beside the bed provided ample light, but she sat several minutes, staring at the words. *Lord, I sense You are telling me to search the Scriptures. Where do I start?* The Psalms always brought great comfort. As she turned the pages to the Psalms, they opened to Psalm 119, and her eyes fell on the 130th verse, which both stunned her and brought a giggle.

"The entrance of thy words giveth light; it giveth understanding unto the simple."

Well, I need light and understanding. Are You also reminding me I am simple?

She continued reading where she'd left off the previous night. Turning to her ribbon located in the Gospel of Luke, she began reading but kept stopping, finding it difficult to concentrate. The earlier verse she'd read in Psalm 119 kept playing through her head.

"The entrance of thy words giveth light; it giveth understanding."

The next morning, Heather brought hoecakes and ham to the table in the common room. Mary announced that the boys had agreed to stay and decorate the Green rather than join George hunting.

Heather looked across the table at them. "'Twill bring some much-needed joy to the Yule season."

Andrew smiled at the young people. As nice as it was seeing him enjoying the children, it was a painful reminder of how empty their home was without Matthew.

After they finished eating and clearing the dishes, Mary and James left to cut holly. Mark, Todd, and Philip planned to cut pine boughs later.

Douglas tugged at Heather's skirt. "What can I do, Mama?"

She smiled. "We should gather some pine cones. Would you like that?"

"Yes, can we go now?"

"Later, my sweet."

Mary and James returned a short while later with armloads of holly loaded with bright red berries. Mary searched through the hutch drawers at the end of the room. "Have we any ribbon?"

"I believe we have some left from our sewing preparations for Philadelphia. I will look." The children's enthusiasm over their project delighted her. Now to keep the youngster's spirits buoyed in the days to come.

Andrew, James, and the children were seated at a table. James looked first to Mary as she rummaged through a wooden box, then to Andrew. He appeared to be searching for words. "I want to call at the Whitcombs' home while we are here. It would be courteous since I spent time with Martha in Williamsburg this past summer." His cheeks were flushed.

Mary's head bobbed up from her search for ribbon. "You should call on them after we finish the decorations."

Mary's arched eyebrow and expression suggested she might not have completely accepted James and Martha's growing rapport. *Dear Lord, please protect their friendships.* Heather focused on her other guest. "Andrew, may I get you anything else?"

"More coffee would be appreciated. Have you a recent copy of the *Gazette?*"

"I believe there's one on the sideboard."

"Aye." He stood and located the newspaper. "Now that Congress has established an American Navy, I am wondering if they will go after Dunmore. Did you know he has issued a call to slaves to rebel against their masters? He is making them all sorts of grand promises."

"I did read that. Very troubling indeed."

Philip came into the common room. "Todd is outside. We can go get the pine boughs now."

Mark got up from the table. "The saws are in the barn." He grabbed several of the warm biscuits on his way to the door. "We will need these in case we get hungry while we are working."

CHAPTER 23

A loud crack woke Matthew. Was that gunfire? He glanced around the cabin, but no one was in sight. He tried to lift his head. The dizziness returned. Water, he needed water.

The door opened, and Anna came in wrapped in her heavy shawl and carrying a basket. She gave him a broad smile. "*Du är vaken*. Pardon. You are awake."

"I'm thirsty, Anna."

"I get you water."

Matthew turned his head toward the window beside his pallet. Ice hung on the branches of the tree. Why was he so hot if it was freezing outside?

"Here, take sip."

He turned back to the woman sitting on the stool by his pallet. She held a pewter cup out to him.

Matthew closed his eyes. He hardly had strength to lift his head. Anna's hand on the back of his head felt cold, but she had been outside.

"You burning up. Must have fever." Her eyes had a gentleness about them, but her expression was one of worry. She lifted his head so he could drink.

The cool water felt good on his lips and relieved his dry mouth and throat.

"Slowly, or you get sick again." Anna eased his head back on the drenched pillow and set the cup on the table beside the pallet.

"Did I hear gunfire a while ago?"

"*Ja. Sköt en hjort. Engelsk.*" Her pale blue eyes squinted. "Oden shot deer."

Matthew sighed. Better a deer shot than him, again. He closed his eyes. When he opened them, Anna had a cold damp rag she was patting all over his face.

"I make you some bark tea and a poultice for wound."

Matthew drifted off and woke to the sound of voices. It was dark. How long had he slept?

"Oden, *komma*," Anna said.

Oden and Anna approached him. "Drink this tea for fever. Oden hold you; I put poultice on."

He was shaking and cold when he sipped the odd concoction. There was the brandy bottle again. His body tensed. He knew what was coming.

Oden held his arms down as Matthew bit down on the cloth and Anna peeled back the dressing on his side. He nearly passed out from the intense pain as she cleaned his wound with brandy. It continued to sting long after she had dressed it and covered him up with a blanket.

He struggled to stay awake, but Anna's ministrations had drained him of what little strength he had. *Bless them, Lord, for caring for me. Help me heal and get stronger.*

It was light when Matthew next awoke. The smell of something cooking made him hungry. He scanned the room. Anna was seated at the table.

"May I have some water?"

"*Ja.*" She was smiling when she brought the cup. Gently, she drew his head up to drink.

He took a sip. "How long have I been here. What day is it?"

She looked away for a minute. "Hmm. *Jultid*—Yuletide."

He closed his eyes. The end of December? Had to be about six weeks he had been gone. What to do? He would need to think this through.

"How you feel?"

"A bit better. Not hot or cold."

"*Bra, bra.*"

"What?"

"Good. Today, I bathe you. You smell."

Laughing hurt, but she amused him—when she wasn't torturing him.

The door opened and Heather glanced at the clock. One o'clock. Mark and the Gordon boys returned with plenty of pine boughs.

Mary was separating the holly into piles. "I still have not found the ribbon."

"Mary, I'm going upstairs to feed Sara. I will look for some. We will need the bowls for the cock-a-leekie, and there is bread pudding prepared. You can assemble the decorations after dinner."

Heather's mind wandered as she fed Sara. Andrew and James' visit had brought distraction and cheer back into their home, but thoughts of Matthew robbed her of her momentary joy. As she caressed Sara's cheek, a tear fell onto the bairn's forehead. *Nay, concentrate on all the blessings.*

God is faithful. He will provide everything we need, even answers, in His time. "The entrance of thy words giveth light; it giveth understanding."

She glanced over at the chest-on-chest. She must remember to look in the drawer for ribbon.

After Sara was settled in the cradle, Heather went to the chest. When she tried to pull open the drawer, it jammed. She pulled Matthew's drawer out above it to clear the jam. After placing his drawer on the bench at the foot of the bed, she searched the notion drawer, pulling out various ribbons the young folks might use.

What? She looked to where she had set Matthew's drawer. How odd. His Bible was in the drawer. Why had he left his Bible? He usually took it with him when he was gone for several days. She set the ribbons down and picked up the well-worn Bible and thought of the Scripture she'd read the night before. *"The entrance of thy words giveth light; it giveth understanding."*

Why had he not taken his Bible? She sat on the bed next to the drawer and stared at the worn leather cover. That he had left it behind was unsettling. She closed her eyes and held it to her chest. It was as close as she had felt to him for so long.

She placed it on her lap and rubbed her hand across the leather cover before opening it. There at the beginning of the Book of Joshua were two folded pieces of paper, one larger than the other. It gave her a start as she unfolded them. Matthew's handwriting. She read the larger page.

Dearest Heather,

In the event something interferes with my return, you need to know that nothing in my power would keep me from being with you and the children, the people I love most in this world. Hopefully, my absence is only a delay, and if I have an opportunity, I will get word to you. If I do not come home, you are to go on with your life and find as much joy as possible.

Still holding the letter, her hand dropped to her lap. Her other hand went to her throat. Trying to catch her breath, she continued.

You are a strong and capable woman, and I have every confidence you will make wise decisions when it comes to the children, our farm, the ordinary, and your future. You should be able to operate the ordinary for many years to come. Keep the farm for Mark and Douglas if you can. Should you need to sell some of it, or all of it, do what you think is wise.

I am comforted knowing we have fine friends and neighbors who will aid you in any way you may require. I hope Thomas and his family will remain. I know the Duncans, the Turners, and Andrew Macmillan will do anything they can to offer assistance. They are good people.

God is faithful, Heather, never lose sight of that. You are a woman of faith, and I know our Lord will be with you, guiding you, and providing all you need.

Your loving husband,
Matthew

Her breathing grew labored, and her hand trembled holding the rough parchment. Setting it aside, she unfolded the smaller paper.

I know you may keep my letter, so I am providing you with this information—and then you must destroy it.

There are some extra funds buried in a jar halfway between the Green and the well. Use them as needed. You may remember Mr. Martin Jones and Mr. Lucas Stephens, who were guests at the Green earlier this year. If they return, they may have helpful insights or information regarding my mission. You can trust them.

I remain loyal to you, our children, and the colonies.
Matthew

Her head throbbed as she tried to process all Matthew had revealed. What did this mean? He had anticipated something might keep him from coming home. But what? She must show these notes to Andrew. What should she tell the children?

She refolded the letters and put them back in Matthew's Bible. What if she had never gotten into his drawer and found them?

"The entrance of thy words giveth light; it giveth understanding." She clutched the Bible to her chest. *Lord, You did this. You led me to open the Scriptures. How many other times have You answered my questions and I have been unaware?*

Heather studied the group gathered with their greenery in the common room. Douglas beamed with pride at his bucket full of pinecones. Mary was setting the table for dinner. The savory aroma of the cock-a-leekie wafted in from the kitchen, so she wandered back there to find out if it needed attention. Mary joined her to help.

Andrew came in from outside. "Something smells wonderful." His face was red and damp from sweating as he removed his coat and rubbed his hands together in front of the hearth.

Heather's heart ached as she studied the man. He reminded her of Matthew when he came inside after working.

"Got some of the wood split," he said.

"You do not need to cut wood. Thomas and the boys do that."

"I know, but I want to help. Is there anything else I can do for you?"

Mary slammed the wooden trencher onto the work table. "Find our father, Mr. Macmillan. Papa's inexplicable absence is breaking our hearts."

Andrew stopped abruptly and turned toward her, his eyes full of empathy.

Heather went to her daughter's side. "Mary, you needn't ..."

Andrew held up his hand. "'Tis a justifiable request."

Mary looked down at the bread in front of her. "I'm sorry. We are all so anxious for Papa to come home, and we do not know what to do or where to turn."

He came over to the table where Mary stood. "I have already started making inquiries on my way here, and I will go to Alexandria and Annapolis and look for answers there also. Do not lose heart. There has to be a reason for his delay, and as soon as I learn anything, I will get word to all of you."

Mary ducked her head and swiped at a stray tear. "We are so grateful."

When they were seated and had given thanks, they began their meal. Heather looked at her soup, but her mind kept wandering back to Matthew's letters. She was overjoyed to have gotten them, but they raised so many questions. She glanced at Andrew. He and James were listening to Mark's animated retelling of his visit to Carpenter's Hall and the shipyard. She would show him Matthew's letters and find out what he thought.

When the meal was over, she and Mary gathered the dishes and took them to the kitchen.

"What is wrong, Mama? You are so quiet."

"I'm fine. I have a lot on my mind."

"Papa?"

When tears formed in her eyes, she quickly glanced away.

"Do not cry. Mr. Macmillan said he will try to find Papa. What more can we do?" Mary put her arms around her, and for a moment they held each other in silence.

"You are right. I'm certain 'tis no accident the Macmillans are here now. The Lord may be orchestrating events so we will learn of your father's whereabouts. We must continue to trust the Lord will be with us. And, God willing, we shall be provided with the answers we need."

Mary tilted her head toward the common room. "I can clean these. You go in and visit with Mr. Macmillan. James is going to see Martha for a while before we all work on the decorations. He mentioned they are leaving in the morning."

Heather removed her apron and went upstairs to retrieve the letters before joining the others. She caught Andrew's eye and signaled him to follow her.

Once in the parlor, she closed the door behind them. "I found two letters Matthew left." She drew them from her pocket and handed them to him. She pointed to the longer missive. "Read this one first."

She watched his expression change as he read them and then looked at her. "This is welcoming and troubling at the same time."

"My thoughts also. What do you think it means?"

"That his trip had little to do with buying farm equipment and cattle, but what he is involved in is puzzling. Matthew would not be secretive about his activities, but it clearly sounds like he was concerned that ..."

When he didn't finish, she said, "Go ahead and say it ... that he might be in some danger and possibly would not come home."

Andrew stared at the floor.

She took the letters from his hand. "Where do we go from here?"

"I will keep this in mind as I search for answers."

They returned to the common room as James left for the Whitcombs' and the others worked on their crafts.

The afternoon passed quickly as the young people assembled and hung the wreaths and pine boughs. With the decorating completed, the group settled into a variety of activities.

At half past five, Heather looked up from her mending. "'Tis dark out, Mary. What are you doing by the window?"

"James has been gone for hours. I wonder if he will have trouble finding his way back in the dark."

Philip jumped up from where he was playing with Douglas. "I will get a lantern and wait for him."

Mary rolled her eyes and sat next to Heather on the settee.

Andrew rose from his seat. "No need, Philip, I can go out with a lantern."

Mark smirked at his sister. "The Whitcombs will give James a lantern to light the way."

Mary picked up the embroidery and glared at her brother.

It was almost six when Andrew and James returned.

Mary helped to serve the tankards of warm cider Polly brought to the room. "How were Martha and her family, James?"

James' expression turned pensive as he took a sip from the steamy cup. "Martha's mother appeared ... upset. I wonder if my call troubled her."

Heather approached him. "Mrs. Whitcomb's demeanor has nothing to do with you. She has been suffering from melancholy ever since Tobias joined the militia."

"Martha said as much when I expressed my concern to her."

Mary cocked her head. "Martha said you spent a lot of time together in Williamsburg."

James shrugged and smiled. "We ran into each other one day, and she encouraged me to visit at her aunt and uncle's home. They were all very gracious and invited me to return several times. I think Martha enjoyed having someone she already knew in town."

Mary smiled. "You were generous to make her feel less lonely while she was there." James was a nice young man. 'Twas no wonder Martha had taken a shine to him.

CHAPTER 24

Matthew woke to the aroma of baking bread. Could he eat something solid today and keep it down? The headaches and nausea continued, but the head injury was better. His gunshot wound was another matter. It had festered, leaving him weak and feverish. Anna alternately cleaned the wound with brandy or a concoction of vinegar and balsam apple leaves before dressing it again. God willing, one day he would be able to pay back the Flemings' kindness.

Matthew glanced out the window to the blowing snow. Driving off questions that plagued him day and night was impossible. How were Heather and the children? What must they be thinking about his absence? Had Heather found his letters? Who had attacked him? Did it have anything to do with the packet he carried for Henry Ferguson? If it did, getting word of his whereabouts to Heather and the family could endanger them and the Flemings. Oden and Anna seemed trustworthy, but revealing anything to them might place them—or him—in additional danger. They must know nothing of his activities.

Matthew rested against the pillow on the narrow pallet and surveyed the cabin. It was modest but had some well-crafted pieces of furniture. A door at the far end led to what he assumed was a bedroom.

This was a home, a lovely home filled with love. But it wasn't his.

He must figure a way to get back to Heather and the children as soon as he could travel.

Heather pulled back on the reins as their wagon approached the front of the Green. Church that morning had been a balm to her spirit. The pastor's message encouraged her, and the dinner in the school with their neighbors had been the respite they all needed. On this blustery February day, it had warmed her heart and helped dispel the ever-present cloud of anxiety over Matthew's absence.

"Mark, please take care of the horse. The Gordons have not yet returned from church."

Mary handed Sara to her before helping Douglas out of the wagon.

Heather shifted Sara in her arms and led Douglas and Mary to the front door. Once inside, Douglas headed toward the common room.

Heather stopped abruptly. Something was wrong.

The drawer from the hall table lay on the floor, its contents spread everywhere. She looked to the left. The parlor looked like a storm had blown through it.

"Stop!" she screamed.

The children froze and stared at the mess.

"Mary, take Sara and Douglas back outside, now."

"What happened here?" Mary's shrill cry did nothing to ease Heather's nerves.

"Now! Take them outside right now."

Mark ran to the door and peeked inside. "What happened?"

"Mark, stay out front with the mare. Do not go in the barn." She placed Sara into Mary's arms. "Go, now!"

"Mama, what is wrong?" Douglas wailed.

Mark grabbed his little brother's hand. "Everything is scattered everywhere."

"The Green has been ransacked," Heather said. "Take the others and run up the lane and wait for the Gordons to return." Heather picked up the poker by the hearth in the parlor and walked to the common room. Everywhere she looked was a mess. The contents of the bookcase had been strewn on the floor, and the kitchen was in total disarray. Broken pottery was scattered all over the floor. Her heart raced, and beads of perspiration formed on her brow.

She climbed the stairs avoiding the spots she knew to creak. She first went to the right, down the hallway to the patrons' rooms. Each room was in shambles. Why had she not gotten the gun from the parlor?

Then she headed in the other direction. In Mary's room, clothes had been tossed on the floor. Heather tightened her grip on the poker and crossed the hall. The boys' room was in the same state. Back in the hallway, she glanced down the hall to Matthew's and her bedroom. She inched down the hallway, the poker raised above her head and the taste of bile in her throat. Opening the door, she swallowed the bad taste that came up in her mouth. Clothes had been pulled from the wardrobe. The thought of some stranger handling her garments was disgusting. Everything would need to be washed. Even the mattress had been pulled from the bedstead and cut open. The chaos was stunning. Who would do this ... and why? What could they possibly have been looking for?

She glanced at the chest-on-chest with its drawers pulled out and askew. *The letters, Matthew's letters.* She caught her breath. She had taken Matthew's Bible and the letters tucked inside with her to church since Mary had asked to use hers. *Praise you, Lord.*

She climbed over her things to get to the window. Mary stood in front of the Green holding Sara and Douglas by his hand. Heather didn't see Mark. She made her way to the stairs.

Mark stood at the foot of the stairs with the gun readied. "I'm here ... and ready."

"Aye, we need to get the children inside. I'm warning you, this is distressing, but we will put it back in order."

Heather began picking up items from the floor. "Why would someone do this? And who ... who would do such a thing?"

She could hear Mark, still holding the gun, wandering from

room to room.

He came into the kitchen with a look of fury she had never before witnessed. "Who did this, Mama? The only people who come this way are boarders, and they rarely come by till afternoon."

She glanced at the hutch where some pieces of silver and pewter appeared untouched. "Put the gun back. Everything is not destroyed, just scattered about. Whoever did this is gone."

Mark headed for the parlor as Mary and the children came in. Douglas ran across the debris-laden floor and latched onto Heather's skirts. She rubbed his soft hair. "Everybody is well."

Mary's face had broken out with blotches. "Who would rob us while we were at church?"

Douglas held on to Heather's skirt, following her as she tried to put their home in order.

"I'm not certain, but I question the intruder's motive. The gun, the silver, and the pewter are still here, as are other things of value. Had it been robbers, they would have taken those." She walked over to Mary and caressed Sara's cheek. "Please put her down for a nap and watch Douglas. Mark, come with me to the barn to see what that looks like. We will see that this mess is made right."

She headed to the barn only to find more disorder. They had their work cut out for them. Nothing seemed to be missing except a small amount of money in the hutch drawer. Could any of this have to do with Matthew's situation? She needed to tell the children about the letters, but this wasn't the time.

When the Gordons returned from church, they found their own cottage in disarray. Mark rode over to the Whitcombs' to see if their home had also been targeted. George and Martha Whitcomb had not been at church and had seen nothing unusual. They came back to the Green with him to assist them in restoring their home.

George's mouth dropped open at the sight of the chaos. "Leave the heavier items to me."

"Did you notice any riders or activity around here this morning?"

"I saw no one coming from this direction."

It took the remainder of the day to put their homes and barn back in order. Exhausted, everyone readied for bed by nine. As she was, sleep eluded her. Every noise made her jump. Would the intruder return? How could she trust boarders after this?

CHAPTER 25

Matthew sat on the side of the pallet with Oden on one side and Anna on the other. Mid-February and he was finally making progress in his recovery. "Try again. If I could just stand."

Oden took one of his arms and put it over his shoulder. "*Han är för svag.*"

Anna took his other arm. "*Engelsk*, Oden."

"He is too weak, woman!"

"I can do this," Matthew choked. "Just help me."

They got him on his feet.

His breathing was rapid, but Anna's big grin was contagious.

Oden put his free arm behind Matthew's back. "*Bra, bra.*"

Matthew took a step forward, then another, breathing hard and working up a sweat.

"Rest now. Enough for today." Anna signaled Oden with a nod of her head back toward the pallet.

They turned him gently and got him back to a seating position.

"Thank you. Let me rest a few minutes, and then I want to try again."

His caretakers looked at each other with raised brows.

"'Tis the only way I will get stronger."

Over the next couple of hours, he made two more attempts to stand and walk.

Anna brought him some broth. "You doing good. We try again tomorrow."

Matthew looked at Anna, then Oden. "Have you told anyone that I'm here?"

"No." Anna gazed at Oden. "You say anything, Oden?"

"*Nej.*" He shook his head.

Matthew took a deep breath. "Good. I may still be in danger, and I would not want to put you in peril for taking care of me."

"You said you not criminal," Oden said, "and we believe you. Why you not want family know you here?"

"It might put them in danger or allow people to trace me here. My horse. Do you still have my horse?"

"*Ja.*" Oden nodded. "In barn most of time, just take out after dark, like you said."

"I need to get strong enough to go home, for your protection, mine, and my family's." He lay back on the pallet, spent. Tomorrow, he would try again to walk to build up his strength. Bless this dear couple for all their aid.

Anna bent over him. "You hungry?"

"Too tired right now ... later."

⊚⅋⅊⅊⊚

The day after the break-in was bitterly cold. As Heather walked back toward the Green from the barn, she spotted a coach in the distance. Mark and Todd were not home yet from the schoolhouse, so Thomas or Philip would need to mind the horses.

Thomas came alongside her. "It looks like we have guests. Philip is hunting a couple of deer he spotted earlier. I can see to the horses."

She strained to make out the party approaching. "I think it might be the Duncans."

Mary came out the door, putting her cape on as she hurried down the steps.

As the Duncans arrived and began to unload the wagon, unexpected tears filled Heather's eyes. She hugged Maggie. "You are an answer to prayer."

Maggie's eyes were filled with compassion. "We would have been here sooner, but between the weather and some illness, we had to postpone the trip. We are finally beginning to be ourselves again."

She held on to Maggie as if she were clinging to life itself. "I'm so glad you came." She wiped tears from her cheeks.

"Have you received any word at all from Matthew? We were shocked when Aaron Turner brought your letter and told us Matthew had not returned."

"Nay, we have heard nothing."

They went inside to the kitchen, the children to the common room.

With her head up and shoulders back, Heather fought to keep her emotions under control.

Adam removed his coat. "I made some inquiries about Matt in town, but to no avail. If that is coffee, I will have some." He rubbed his hands together before the hearth.

Heather reached for the kettle and motioned to Adam and Maggie. "Please stay in here a few minutes … away from the children." Heather poured them each some of the steamy brew and then detailed the events of the previous day's disturbing home breach. Talking about it made her shake again.

Adam looked drawn. "I will get some new hardware for the Green with a better locking function. Maggie's brother-in-law in Leesburg is a gunsmith and locksmith."

"That sounds like a good idea," Heather said. "Some money was stolen, but as near as I can tell, nothing else is missing. We have no idea what they were seeking. Nothing else of value is gone."

Maggie held her hand. "I cannot imagine how frightening it must have been to come home and find the house in such a state."

"I hardly slept at all last night. Every sound made me jump." She shuddered, wanting to put the whole event behind her. "Now, tell me how all of you are."

Adam poured more coffee. "I suppose you know Andrew Macmillan came by and stayed with us an evening before traveling on to Annapolis. He mentioned a letter Matthew left you. What is that all about?"

Heather looked around. "We need to speak softly. I have not yet mentioned the letters to the children. Let me fetch them and see what you make of them." She went upstairs, leaving Adam and Maggie at the table in the kitchen. When she returned, she put on a shawl. "Bring your coffee to the barn so we can speak privately."

Maggie and Adam followed her into the chilly confines of the barn.

She motioned for them to sit on some wooden crates. "'Twas uncanny and providential that I found the letters in Matthew's Bible while Andrew and James were still here. But I fear they raise more questions than answers." She handed them to Adam.

Adam rubbed his forehead as he read. "'Tis as Andrew said, and I do not like how it sounds."

Heather stood near the barn door. "It suggests Matthew anticipated something might ... delay or prevent his returning home. What might he be involved in that could place him in danger?"

"You had no inkling of anything amiss before he left?"

"He said he would be away about a fortnight to purchase farm equipment and some cattle. He never mentioned his destination, and now, I feel foolish for not having asked more questions."

Maggie got up and placed an arm around her. "'Tis odd Matthew did not mention his destination."

Maggie and Adam exchanged glances.

Heather fought back tears. "Matthew had been distracted for a while. He dismissed it whenever I asked him what troubled him." She paced back and forth, glancing occasionally out the open door.

Adam got up and motioned for her to sit with Maggie. "Who are these Jones and Stephens chaps he mentions? This sounds like they might have knowledge about his whereabouts."

She sat on the crate next to Maggie and locked eyes with Adam. "I went back to the log we keep of our guests. The men were patrons here in June. One of them returned in August. I have been asking myself these same questions since I found the letters."

Maggie and Adam shook their heads.

Heather gazed out the door in the direction of the Green. "We best get back inside. The children may be wondering where we are. We should refrain from discussing Matthew's absence during dinner as 'tis distressing for the children."

"Of course."

When they entered the kitchen, Sara's cries were coming from the common room. Mary looked relieved when they entered the room.

Maggie reached for the baby. "Let me hold that precious girl. Heather, she has your fair coloring, same as Douglas."

An hour later, seated around the large table sharing their meal, Heather passed a platter to Adam. "What have you learned of Donald? Is he still in Hampton?"

"We received a letter from him." Maggie reached into her pocket and pulled out a post and handed it to Adam. He unfolded it.

"This first part is dated mid-December."

My Dear Family,

I'm sorry I have not written in a while. I miss all of you, and especially your cooking, Ma. I'm still serving under Colonel Woodford.

Our detachment of the 2nd Virginia Regiment arrived near a bridge south of Norfolk December 4th. The area is surrounded by water and marsh and some islands and joined to the mainland by causeways. Governor Dunmore's detachments of the 14th Regiment of Foot, which includes some runaway slaves and Norfolk Tories, were in a wooden fort on the north island. We erected a breast-work opposite their fort and were encamped in front of a church near some houses not far from the southern causeway.

The British were well entrenched on the other side of the bridge. We were under continual fire but, unlike the enemy, we had no casualties. Most of the bridge was destroyed, and some of the British made their way across it. They burned houses. A contingent of men from Carolina with armaments joined us.

It is cold and muddy, and we are short of blankets, shoes, and ammunition. How I miss your cooking, Ma, and being home with all of you.

Later December.
We took the British fort after they abandoned it, and they suffered numerous losses.

When they crossed the bridge in the early morning, we took them on. We killed a significant number and did not lose a man.

January 15th
I will finally be able to post this. Our forces have been occupying Norfolk with little resistance since most of the Tory merchants have fled. On the first day of the year, British ships in the harbor began shelling Norfolk. I cannot even describe the sound of the continual cannon fire. When the British landed, they began burning what they believed were Whig establishments. We did nothing to stop the flames, and, in truth, contributed by burning what had been Tory properties.

I miss you all and pray you are well. If we are ever near Alexandria, I hope to be able to visit you.
Donald

Heather shuddered. "He sounds so grown up. What happened to the boy?" She handed Sara to Maggie while she took the dishes from the table.

Adam cleared his throat, his face a mix of pride and emotion. "Donald is eighteen years old now and very much a man. One does not go into battle and come away unchanged."

A tear rolled down Maggie's cheek.

Mary shifted in her seat. She looked moved by Donald's letter. "May we be excused, Mama?"

"Of course, but first, please make sure all is well with the boys."

Once Mary and Jean were gone, Maggie came alongside of

Heather, leaned over, and gave her a hug. It felt like food to a starving dog. She struggled to hold back the tears always waiting to burst forth. "What should I do to find Matthew?"

Maggie reached for her hand and gave it a squeeze. "Pray, my dear, as we are. Perhaps Matthew has fallen ill and is recovering someplace."

Adam stood, walked to the hearth, and lit his pipe. "If we find one or both of these men, Stephens or Jones, we might get some answers."

She wiped a tear from her cheek. "When I asked Matthew where he met them, he indicated Alexandria, though he suggested they may come from Philadelphia. I have searched my memory to try and remember if Matthew told me anything else about them."

Adam sat down and shook his head. "I will ask around. Perhaps someone can provide some helpful information. I will notify you if I learn anything. I will also inquire in Leesburg while we are there."

At the end of the day when they went upstairs, Maggie approached Heather. "Might we go into your room a minute? I have an idea."

Heather nodded, led her inside her bedroom, and closed the door behind them. "What is it?"

Maggie sat in the chair. "What would you think about Mary coming back to Alexandria with us for a visit? We can pick her up on our way back from Leesburg. The girls enjoy each other, and a few weeks in Alexandria might do her good. Can you do without her for that long?"

Heather sat on the edge of the bed and considered Maggie's suggestion.

"No need to give an answer tonight," Maggie said. "Think and pray about it. There are assemblies and activities she might enjoy. And it might help her through this time while Matthew is absent."

Heather wandered to the window. Winter tended to isolate all of them. With Mary's wounded friendship with Martha, Matthew's unexplained absence, and the invasion of their home, Mary's nerves were as frayed as hers. "Let me speak with her, and I will let you know."

The next morning, Heather spotted Mary alone in the kitchen. "Sit with me a moment. Maggie had a suggestion."

A radiant smile blossomed across the girl's face when she relayed Maggie's offer.

"Mama, please, I would love to go with them if you can do without me."

"Between Polly and me, we can spare you a few weeks." When Mary threw her arms around Heather, it warmed her heart and removed any doubt about Maggie's plan. "We have a couple of days to get you ready before the Duncans return from Leesburg."

"Do you think Mark will be disappointed to not be included?"

"That is sweet of you to think of him, but Mark has school, so he will understand. Perhaps there will be another time for him to visit."

"May I say something to Jean now?"

"Let me tell Maggie before you say anything. She will want to tell her family first."

"Of course."

That night, after rereading Matthew's letters, Heather wrapped up in a blanket in the chair opposite her bed, took his Bible, and held it close to her. For too many nights she avoided the lonely bed and chose to sleep in the chair. Tears she held back all day were released, often a nightly ritual. She needed to be strong for the children as well as herself.

Closing her eyes, she grasped Matthew's Bible. *Lord, I cannot do this without You. I need Your strength. Please help me.*

Leaning back in the chair, she relaxed her grip. Where were those notes? She fingered through the Bible and came to some verses she had written out that she found encouraging.

"Peace I leave with you, my peace I give unto you: not as the world giveth, give I unto you. Let not your heart be troubled, neither let it be

afraid." John 14:27

"In all thy ways acknowledge him, and he shall direct thy paths." Proverbs 3:6

"I will instruct thee and teach thee in the way which thou shalt go: I will guide thee with mine eye." Psalms 32:8

Those words brought peace. Matthew had reminded her in his letter that God is faithful. She reminded herself of all the Lord had done. She needed to have faith and believe God. She needed to trust that whatever the circumstances, He had a plan, and He would direct her path.

She would continue to find verses that encouraged her. It would keep her focus where it needed to be—on the Lord. With His help, she would respond in a manner that honored God and do exactly as she needed to do.

CHAPTER 26

Three weeks after Mary left with the Duncans for Alexandria, Heather and the boys were sitting at the table after dinner when she heard the sound of an approaching horse. Mark stood and went to the window, and she joined him, her heart skipping a beat. Every day she looked for a rider, one specific rider—Matthew. A coach was headed toward the Green. "'Tis the Duncans and Mary."

Mark and Douglas followed her outside.

"What a welcome sight. Mark, please run and ask Philip and Todd to mind the horses."

Mary got down from the wagon. "Any news of Papa?"

"Nay. 'Tis so good to have you home."

Mary hugged her. "'Tis good to be home." Once greetings and hugs were exchanged, they went inside.

Heather took Maggie's cape. "We have beef-and-barley stew, so please sit down."

Maggie set a couple of baskets on the floor near the table. "Some salt and staples I thought you might use."

"Many thanks. Tell me what we owe you."

"Some more of your smoked pork, but only if you have some to spare."

"We have plenty. Thomas and the boys replenished our stock at hog-killing time."

The mention of it reminded her again of Matthew, as if he were ever far from her mind. She looked at Adam. Did he have any news?

Adam looked out the back window. "I have something for

Thomas. Is he here?"

"Aye, he is most likely at the cottage unless he has gone back to work after dinner." She ladled stew into bowls.

"I shall find him after dinner."

Maggie sliced some bread and took it to the table. "We are going to Leesburg tomorrow to visit my sister and her family. May we stop back in a couple of days?"

"Certainly. We have had few guests lately, so there should be plenty of room." She set bowls around the table.

Mary sat at the table bouncing Sara on her lap. "I should help, but I cannot bear putting Sara down. I missed you so, sweet girl."

Heather smiled at Mary. "I'm eager to hear about your visit."

Mark tugged at some loose strands of his sister's hair as he passed by her. "I am glad you are home so I no longer have to get the eggs in the morning."

"So nice to be appreciated. I missed you, too."

When the meal ended, Sara napped in her cradle. Cameron followed Mark outside to complete his chores while Mary and Jean were persuaded to read to Douglas and William in the common room. Maggie and Adam remained at the kitchen table.

Heather glanced out the window while she cleaned the dishes. "Adam, Thomas just left the cottage and went to the barn."

Adam headed toward the door. "Perhaps we can talk a little later, Heather."

"Aye, hurry back. I am eager to hear what you have learned." From the window, she watched him go first to the carriage and pull out a long, wrapped package before walking toward the barn.

Maggie brought the last of the dinner dishes to the counter beside her. "How are you? I have been so concerned."

"I have good days and difficult days. I must do more to find Matthew."

"What more can you do? The word is out and friends are searching for any possible leads."

"I know." She stowed the plates and approached Maggie. "How

did Mary do? She had grown so moody here worrying about her father."

"I believe her time in Alexandria, with all its distractions, helped her. The girls enjoyed being together and attended an assembly at Carlyle House and a party at the Lamonts.'"

"It was kind of you to invite her. Has Adam learned anything of Matthew or the two men, Mr. Jones or Mr. Stephens?"

"Not much, but he will tell you all about it." Maggie wrapped her arms around Heather.

The welcome embrace brought on the tears she had hoped to quell. "I pray every day for Matthew's safety. Mary and Mark know nothing of the two letters he left, but I must tell them something now that Mary is home. I have tried preparing a notice of inquiry to place in the *Gazette*, but I have felt something holding me back from advertising Matthew's absence."

"Perhaps 'tis wise not to advertise his absence, given the comments in his letters. Adam may have some suggestions when he comes inside. Donald came home for a couple of days as a courier. He was carrying correspondence to someone in Alexandria."

"How wonderful that you got to see him, Maggie. How is he?"

"Older. He is now a man. And ..." She looked around the room. "I believe Donald declared himself to Mary."

"Oh, my. I had no idea."

"He has been smitten with her for a long time. He told us that when he returns after the hostilities, he plans to court her. I believe he also told her."

"I wonder how she responded. I cannot imagine a nicer young man for her, but they are so young."

"They are, but they have time to be sure."

"I'm grateful you told me so I will be prepared for what Mary may share with me. My heart goes out to them, dealing with such an uncertain future."

Heather glanced to the door. Adam must have still been with Thomas. "What was in the package Adam brought for Thomas?"

Maggie brushed crumbs from her skirt. "Ask Adam."

Why was Maggie being evasive?

A few minutes later, Adam came through the door, removed his jacket, and hung it on one of the pegs. "It has started to rain. We got here none too soon. God willing, 'twill clear by the time we leave tomorrow." He sat next to Maggie, thumped his fingers on the table, and looked at Heather, his face unreadable.

"Please tell me what you have learned of Matthew," Heather said. "And what did you bring in that large bag for Thomas, if you do not mind my asking?"

"The bag for Thomas has a rifle and a musket in it." He glanced at Maggie.

"We have two hunting rifles. Did Thomas ask you for them?"

"No." Adam's perplexing expression answered nothing. "I brought them in the event that there is ... trouble."

"What kind of trouble? What do you know?"

Maggie placed her hand on Heather's. "There is unrest all about. Fights have broken out between neighbors. We wanted you to be more prepared should the Loyalists make trouble, or if the British army returns to Virginia."

"Oh. Do you think that's possible? I had not considered it. Tell me, Adam, have you learned anything about Matthew?"

Maggie got up from the table. "I'm going to see what the children are about, so you can talk privately."

Adam rubbed his hand along the top of the oak table. "I asked around about those two chaps, Martin Jones and Lucas Stephens. They have both been observed at Whig gatherings."

"Where are they?" Her heart beat faster.

"Ethan Campbell noticed the two at tavern meetings where discussions can get heated. He said they are sympathetic to the Patriot movement. I went with Ethan to the tavern a couple of evenings hoping one or both would show up again. The second time we went, Jones and Stephens were both there."

"Did you ask them about Matthew?"

"I introduced myself and mentioned our friendship and that Matt had spoken well of them. My comment startled Jones. He looked at Stephens and then eyed some of the others in the room. I had the sense Jones wanted to say something, but before we continued the conversation, a couple of suspected Loyalists came over. They were surprised I attended one of these 'quarrelsome gatherings.'"

"Is that all you know?" Heather asked. "Surely you pursued the men."

"While Stephens and Jones were reserved in their comments, I am convinced they are sympathetic to the Whig cause. I excused myself from the group and approached them when they got up to leave. They were dismissive and suggested they had little contact with Matt. They knew him only as the proprietor of Stewart's Green. Thinking they might be reluctant to say anything in a public place, I asked to meet with them privately."

"Did you meet with them?"

"Outside of Brady's shop the next day. I told them about Matt's unexplained absence and his remark that they were trustworthy. I mentioned his note suggesting they might have information."

"What did they say?" *Please give me reason to hope.*

"When I told them Matt never returned after his trip in November, and no one had received any word from him or about him, they said nothing for the longest time. But then Stephens said he had been near the Green and had heard from one of your neighbors that Matthew had been absent for many weeks." Adam's expression turned quizzical. "We talked for quite a while. Virginia has a fair share of people loyal to England, though fewer in Alexandria. I think Stephens and Jones, not knowing my leanings, were initially reluctant to be forthright with me about Matt's efforts on their behalf, but trust between us built. One does not know who informers might be." Adam poured himself some water and drank it. "It sounds like Matt was getting involved with the Patriot cause."

"What do you mean?" Why had not he told her?

"Apparently, he had been meeting with folks of a like mind to separate from England."

Heather let those words sink in. "He suggested the time was drawing closer and we must choose whether to align ourselves with the Crown or the Patriots. But what does this have to do with Matthew's not returning home?"

"Stephens suggested Matt had Patriot connections in Philadelphia and passed information to someone there. 'Tis possible he was intercepted by Loyalists."

Her throat tightened, and her heart raced. "He may have been captured. What would they do with him? Imprison him?"

"Not sure. And not knowing Matt's location or who he met with, we have no way of knowing if he has been captured or injured or what."

Maggie returned to the room, sat beside Heather, and held her hand. "All we can do is pray and hope for some word."

"Nay, there must be more. We can go to Philadelphia, ask people what they may know of Matthew, or find out who we should contact."

Adam held up his hand. "That might put Matt in greater danger. We are unacquainted with the circumstances surrounding his activities, what he might have been carrying, who is involved, and who might be an adversary."

Heather sat back in the chair. Tears filled her eyes as she gazed across the table at Maggie and Adam. They loved Matthew like a brother and would never do anything to put him in more danger, but surely there was some way to learn more. What Adam had told her so far was based only on suppositions.

Adam's smile was compassionate. "We all want to find out what happened to Matt. I think our best option is to have one or more people not closely associated with him go to Philadelphia and try to learn more surreptitiously. Someone who already lived there would raise less suspicion."

What Adam said made sense. "We must not place Matthew in increased peril, but who can we trust? We do not even know for sure if he got to Philadelphia."

Adam drew his chair closer to hers. "Are Mary and Mark's grandparents sympathetic to the Loyalists or Whigs? If they are aligned with us and are trustworthy, they might be able to suggest some people to contact."

"I can ask Mary. She might have some insight into their attitudes. I need to tell Mary and Mark about their father's letters, too."

Later that evening, Heather pulled Mary aside. "Please come upstairs with me while I feed Sara. I'm eager to hear about your time in Alexandria."

Mary looked over her shoulder at Jean. "There is too much to share tonight. Perhaps after the Duncans leave."

"Just a bit tonight then, and we will talk more tomorrow."

While she fed the baby, Heather observed Mary. How to ask her about her grandparents' loyalties without raising her curiosity as to her motives?

Mary sat next to her on the bed, watching her sister. "Sara is changing so quickly and smiling more."

"Aye." She let the comment pass and the silence settle, then changed the subject. "Maggie mentioned you attended an assembly at Carlyle House and a party at the Lamont home."

"Yes, and all the social skills I learned in Philadelphia prepared me well."

Just the opening Heather needed. "And the trip to Philadelphia was a good chance to get to know your grandparents better. There must have been talk of the crisis with England while you were in Philadelphia. Did your grandparents discuss it? Did you get any sense of what their attitudes are regarding the colonies and Britain?"

Mary tilted her head to the side and narrowed her eyes. "I thought you wanted to hear about my visit to Alexandria."

"I was curious about your grandparents' attitudes."

"I believe they support the Patriot cause. A nephew of friends of theirs from Boston called on Grandmamma the day we arrived. Mr. Hancock was in Philadelphia with the Continental Congress. Grandmamma said he was the president of the Congress."

"You never mentioned him before."

"There were so many interesting things going on in Philadelphia. When Papa returned for us, we all went to an assembly given in honor of some of the delegates."

Heather laughed.

"Why are you laughing?"

"I am not laughing at you, Mary. But, to many people, the activities at the Continental Congress are significant, and many would relish the chance to meet its president. If your grandparents had Tory sympathies, they would not be entertaining or mixing with members of the Continental Congress."

"Were you thinking of contacting our grandparents to help us locate Papa?"

"Aye. Your grandparents could have connections in Philadelphia who might assist us."

"What about Patrick O'Brian, the man I told you I met in Philadelphia?"

"Do you know him well enough to trust where his sympathies lie?"

"He is most assuredly aligned with the Whigs. I was surprised to see him at the Carlyle House assembly since he lives in Philadelphia. But he had come to Alexandria to visit his brother, Peter, who is also a cabinetmaker. Patrick spoke very well of the pamphlet *Common Sense*. He said that the author makes a strong case for immediate independence from British rule. 'Twas only published this year, and already so many people have read it."

Heather placed Sara in her cradle. "Perhaps he could be of

assistance. We should get back to our guests. We can talk tomorrow about Alexandria. I want to hear about Donald's visit."

CHAPTER 27

Heather joined Polly in the kitchen the morning after the Duncans departed. She made bread while Polly worked the dasher at the butter churn in a corner.

"Could one of your boys take Douglas to your cottage for a while after dinner? I need to address something with Mark, Mary, Thomas, and you. Hopefully, the girls will nap."

Polly set the paddle down and wiped her brow. "Todd can take Douglas and work on the hornbook. Philip is repairing tools."

At dinner, Heather partially listened to Mary's tales of her time in Alexandria while she worried over how to broach the subject of Matthew's letters and explain why she had not told them before.

Mary detailed the many social functions she had attended. After several minutes, Mark rolled his eyes. "We need not know *everything* about the grand homes and parties."

Mary smirked at her brother. "I do have one bit of news you would be interested in, Mark. Owen Lamont joined the Continental Army."

"Oh, my," Heather said. "Not him, too."

"Remember how rude Mrs. Blakemore was to Mrs. Lamont, Mama?"

"Aye. If she had not left for England, I suspect she would have given her an earful now."

Todd added, "The Whitney boys left home to join the Continentals, and their pa had a fit."

Thomas reached for the plate of ham. "That must have been a blow to Charles. He is a Tory sympathizer."

Mary turned toward Todd. "How long ago did they join? Jean

and I saw Mr. Whitney in Alexandria near Brady's Shop. He acted odd at the time, but we thought his behavior must have been related to the conversation he was having at that time. He was in a deep discussion with his friend, Mr. Cranford."

Heather looked up from her plate. "Did you say Cranford?"

"Yes," Mary continued. "It was awkward when Mr. Whitney introduced us to him. Jean was introduced as Adam Duncan's daughter, and I was identified as Matthew Stewart's daughter. He even mentioned Stewart's Green. Does Papa know Mr. Cranford? Did he stay at the Green? I surely would have remembered him, given his unusual appearance."

Douglas' eyes grew wide. "Was he scary looking?"

Mary smiled. "Not scary. He had an ugly scar on his face and walked with a limp."

Heather nodded. The same man who'd helped her after her fall. The same man who had come to the Green looking for Matthew shortly afterward. "Mary, did either man mention your father's absence?"

"They did not mention it, and I remembered that you'd said not to mention Papa being gone to anyone we did not know."

Thomas got up from the table. "I think 'tis time we got back to work."

Heather put her hand up. "Please stay a few minutes, Thomas. Philip can go back and work a while until you get there."

Polly looked toward her youngest son. "And Todd, would you please take Douglas to the cottage and work with his hornbook or read with him until I come for Laura."

After Philip, Todd, and Douglas had gone, Heather cleared her throat. "I need to tell you something."

Mary frowned. "Is it about Papa?"

"Aye, 'tis."

Heather spent the next few minutes telling them about finding Matthew's letters while the Macmillans were with them. She pulled them from her pocket and read them aloud.

They listened silently. When Heather was finished, Mary pushed back from the table and stood. "You should have shared this with us in December."

"Perhaps," Heather said. "I tried to make sense of what your father had written. 'Twas very confusing and upsetting that he had an inkling of being delayed or not returning. I wanted more answers before saying anything to any of you. The Macmillans were here at the time, so I enlisted Andrew to find out what he could learn about your father's absence. I also asked Adam Duncan to pursue any leads he could find. While you were in Alexandria, Adam tracked down the two gentlemen mentioned in the letter."

Heather shared about Adam's meeting with Mr. Stephens and Mr. Jones. "That is everything Adam told me. 'Tis not much, I know. I was not trying to keep anything from you, only to protect you from information that would only distress you further."

Thomas, stunned, leaned back in the chair. "None of us knew anything about this. 'Tis not like Matthew to be secretive."

Heather leaned back. "I suspect Matthew didn't tell us what he was up to for our protection."

Mary sat down, looking resigned. "I still cannot imagine how you kept this to yourself."

"'Twas not easy."

⊛⁂⊛

Matthew walked haltingly with Anna's and Oden's assistance all the way to the door leading to the bedroom. The pain in his side was bad, but his legs were stronger. "Help me back to the table. Then I will walk on my own." He gauged the distance between the table and the door. About ten feet. He could do that.

"You better every day," Anna said, "but you ready to walk alone?"

"I need to try."

They had just reached the table when the sound of horses

neighing stopped them.

Oden took a firmer grip around him. "Anna, quick, go check window."

After darting to the window, she turned back toward them. "Two riders. We get you to room." Anna came alongside him, and they all but carried him to the bedroom.

Inside, Matthew collapsed on the bed. His fatigue competed with the pain coming from the wound.

Anna ran into the room with his clothing and bedding. "*Tyst!* ... No sound." She jammed the things into a wardrobe. "On floor ... *glida* ... slide under bed!"

He rolled off the bed and managed to push himself under.

Anna got on the bed.

From the cold wood floor, his view of the room was suddenly blocked by a quilt. Oden and some other voices drifted in from the other room, but it was difficult to make out what was being said. He was sweating and his heart raced. Was it someone looking for him? Surely they would not come in their bedroom. *Please, Lord, protect this dear couple ... and me.*

Anna moaned.

Hard to guess how much time elapsed before the quilt was removed. It seemed like forever.

Oden's face appeared. He extended an arm to pull Matthew out from under the bed. That was a painful exercise he never wanted repeated.

The couple assisted him back to his pallet. The curtains at the windows were closed.

Oden lit another lantern. "Some men from town." Oden looked out a window and had a grim look when he turned around. "Ask if we see any strangers."

Sitting on the pallet, Matthew leaned back against the wall and caught his breath. He was exhausted. The troubled expression on Oden's face settled it. He must leave as soon as he could ride. "Oden, did the men go near the barn? Might they have seen my horse?"

"*Nej* … I watched them go. Told them wife sick, so not been to town."

Matthew gazed at Anna working at the kitchen table. "'Twas a canny plan to hide me that way with the quilt blocking a view of under the bed."

The Flemings grinned, and Anna laughed. "We planned it many days ago."

Matthew shifted on the pallet to take the pressure off his side. "I am grateful for how you both trusted me, cared for me, and protected me. I need to leave soon. You may be at risk if I'm found."

Anna came over to the pallet with her bowl of water. "I clean wound now."

He lay back and stared up at her face. *Please protect this dear couple, Lord.*

He raised his shirt, and she gently unbound his wrapped torso.

"It opened and seeping." She dabbed it first with warm water, then with some concoction before she put a poultice on it. "You good man. Heard you pray. Have family?"

He shook his head and looked toward the wall. The less they knew about him, the better. Deceiving people had become a way of life and not one he wanted to continue. But for now, it was the only way.

❧❧❧

After supper, Heather was upstairs feeding Sara when someone knocked on the door.

"'Tis me." Mary opened the door a crack. "May I come in?"

"Certainly." Heather motioned for her to sit on the bed.

"I apologize for being short with you for not telling us about Papa's letters earlier."

"I understand. Now, tell me about seeing Patrick O'Brian again."

Mary smoothed her skirt as she positioned herself on the bed. "He was friendly, well mannered, and very engaging. Peter O'Brian's shop is only four blocks from the Duncan home. Patrick and Peter called at the Duncan home two times, and we saw them again at Sally Lamont's birthday party. I believe Peter O'Brian is partial to Jean. He may continue to call on Jean and her family."

Heather held Sara to her shoulder. "Courting Jean? She is but fourteen."

Mary had a sly grin. "Do you think fifteen too young for courting?"

Heather set Sara on the bed. She must tread gently. "Why do you ask?"

"I saw Donald while I was there."

"Aye, Maggie mentioned it."

Mary picked at the quilt. "When the Duncans were here visiting, before he joined the militia, Donald said he cared for me."

Heather tilted her head. "What did you think of that?"

"I was surprised by his comment. He kissed me." Her face reddened.

"*Oh tha mi!*" Oh, my. Mary was a bonny young woman. Why was she surprised?

"No Gaelic, Mama."

"What I mean to say is, how do you feel about Donald?"

The blush was replaced by a bold look in her eyes. "I care a great deal for him. I always have, and I'm realizing that 'tis different than it was when we were younger. When Donald was home, he said he believes this fight with England will get far worse. He wants to court me when the war is over and said that my waiting for him would give him great hope."

She needed Matthew's insights. What would he advise? More waiting and less kissing, no doubt.

"Is this what you want?"

"I'm not sure yet, but I think I will know better by the time the war ends."

"Aye." *And none of us knows when that will be.*

The next day, Heather sat sewing in the common room. Mary came in with her sewing basket and sat across from her on one of the settees. "What if I contacted Patrick O'Brian and asked him to help us find out more about Papa?"

Heather looked up. Mary's thoughts seemed to be tracking her own since she now knew more about the Irishman. "Given the nature of the work your father was involved in, I'm uncertain how to proceed."

"We could travel to Philadelphia. I think Patrick would assist us in any way he could."

"We cannot raise suspicions which might endanger your father even more."

Mary groaned. "What should we do now?"

"If Peter O'Brian calls on the Duncan family, perhaps it would not appear as unusual if Adam and he traveled to Philadelphia to meet with his brother. Once in Philadelphia, Adam might be able to learn more about your father's connections. Mr. Stephens said your father carried information to someone there."

"Shall I write to Patrick O'Brian?"

"Not yet. Adam will know what to do. Meanwhile, we can pray for an answer."

Mary got up. "At least we are doing something instead of sitting here waiting."

"Aye." She gave Mary a strong hug. "I am glad you are back. I missed you."

CHAPTER 28

Matthew walked haltingly toward the table and took a seat. "Whatever you are cooking smells good."

Anna stirred the kettle at the hearth. "You doing good, Matthew."

"Better every day."

Oden, grinning, placed more logs on the fire before joining them. "*Sjömansbiffgryta.*"

Matthew's mouth watered. Anna's fisherman's beef stew was a favorite.

She ladled some of the crusty, savory stew into bowls and carried them to the table, where she sat.

After a short prayer, Oden passed him the plate of dark bread. "'Tis all set up for day after tomorrow, but you sure you strong enough for trip?"

"I have to get home." Matthew gazed at these two who had come to mean so much to him. "'Twas a godsend that you were deer hunting near Raccoon Creek, Oden, when I was lying in the mud. If I had not frozen to death, I would have bled to death by that creek." He focused on Anna. "And all you did, with your sometimes tortuous ministrations and miraculous herbs and brews, probably saved me. I can never thank the two of you enough for all the weeks of care you have given me."

"You good man," Anna said. "We get you home. But first *Sjömansbiffgryta.*"

They had just finished their meal when the sound of loud voices and gunfire ended the evening's peace.

Several British Regulars burst into the cabin, their firearms aimed.

Matthew's heart raced. He stood, light-headed, pushing away the wave of fear.

Anna and Oden stood and clung to each other.

A man in civilian clothes, the same one who had been to see him at the Green, Cranford, pointed at him. "That is the man, Matthew Stewart, Patriot courier. Arrest him."

Anna put her hand up in front of one of the soldiers. "He hurt …"

Matthew cut in. "I do not know what you are talking about. I was badly injured and have been laid up for many weeks. These kind folks found me when I was nearly dead and have been nursing me back to health." He looked at Anna and Oden. *Please let them discern my motives.* "I cannot even remember my surname, just Matthew."

The soldiers looked back and forth between the man in civilian dress and each other.

Oden came forward and placed his arm around Anna. "What man says is true. He never tell us his last name, or where he from. He *galen*."

Anna turned and stared at her husband. "*Prata engelska*, Oden!." She faced Cranford. "Husband says, man crazy in head."

Matthew looked back at Cranford with as blank a stare as he could muster. Sure, Cranford knew who he was, but the truth was that the Flemings were ignorant of his identity and the purpose of his mission.

"I know who you are. Take him," Cranford said.

Anna stepped in front of Matthew and pointed at Cranford. "You Christian?"

"I … ah." Cranford grimaced and looked around at the soldiers gathered. "Of course."

"Good. Then you would do like we do."

Matthew swallowed. Anna was quick-witted, but judging from the annoyed expression on Cranford's face, her comment had embarrassed him.

"Out of the way, woman!" Cranford turned to the soldiers. "I said, take him. These people are no use to us."

Two soldiers yanked Matthew away and tied his hands behind his back. "'Tis prison or execution for you."

The soldiers dragged him into the cold night.

The next morning, Heather woke early. She went to the cradle where Sara still slept. *Sweet child, when will your father get to know what a precious little girl you are?*

Taking Matthew's Bible, she crept downstairs to the common room. The quiet, early morning hours when she could reflect and pray always energized her. And spring, with all the new life around, encouraged her. She caressed the leather cover.

Adam had agreed to travel to Philadelphia with or without Peter O'Brian. Hopefully, he had found out what Matthew had carried and whom he'd intended to meet there. Would Patrick O'Brian be of any help? Surely, Adam would contact her soon with the details of his trip.

She opened Matthew's Bible to the Psalms and read for a bit. She looked up and smiled when she spotted the bowl of flowers Polly had arranged for her. The Gordon family had blessed her in so many ways, helping with the farm and ordinary as well as providing friendship and encouragement. She would have been lost without them the past six months.

You have provided so much, Lord. The Gordons and we have not gone without food or anything else we needed. Guests continue to come to the Green, and we have sufficient funds and no serious illnesses or injuries. She wiped tears from her cheeks and glanced again at the Bible.

Please protect Matthew and bring him safely home. Help us find him. Give Adam wisdom, discernment, and success in any discovery he might make. Lord, You never leave us without hope.

She turned to the pages where she'd placed Matthew's letters and began reading the first chapter of Joshua. Taking a deep breath, a sensation of heat coursed through her body, and fresh tears fill her eyes. There were no words to express the way the ninth verse of the first chapter spoke to her heart. It confirmed that the Lord carried this burden with them.

"Have not I commanded thee? Be strong and of a good courage; be not afraid, neither be thou dismayed: for the Lord thy God is with thee whithersoever thou goest."

Lord God, I am in awe of Your presence, provision, and faithfulness.

Sounds coming from upstairs as well as the kitchen were heralding in the day. She set the Bible on the table beside her and got up. "'Tis the day which the Lord hath made; I will rejoice and be glad in it."

Matthew rode between two of the soldiers. They had stolen Bonny and his saddle from the Flemings' barn right after one of the brutes had roughed him up. What kind of coward beats a shackled man?

Dazed and dizzy, Matthew looked at the landscape around them. Where were they taking him? Were they heading back toward the ferry and Philadelphia? He eyed Cranford riding ahead, remembering the man's earlier threats as they began the journey. Imprisonment or execution. At least they'd left the Flemings in peace, a reason to be thankful. Fear and worry dogged him. Fear? Fear of torture … fear of execution … fear of imprisonment, which often resulted in death. Worry? Leaving those he loved and how they would fare. Heather was a strong woman. She would carry on and do the best for the children. Regrets? Being caught, certainly, but not of aiding his countrymen in pursuit of liberty. His only regret was having left Heather and the children. *Lord, please watch over them, and in Your time, bring them peace.*

Heather had finished tidying the rooms after all the guests departed. She opened windows, letting the fresh April air diffuse the cooking smells. Thomas came back into the kitchen and poured himself a cup of water. "Another week and 'twill be planting time. Do we want to plant as much this year? We could let one field lie fallow." He lifted the tankard to his lips without taking his eyes off her.

His expression suggested he thought that without Matthew's help, the crop size should be reduced. "I trust your judgment."

"If circumstances change, we can always plant additional crops later." His easy smile encouraged her.

"Mark and Todd will be out of school soon, so they will have more time to help you and Philip. Anything else?"

"No. I'm off to get the cows out to pasture."

After dinner, Heather went out to the garden.

Mary came running outside within minutes. "A carriage is approaching, and I think it may be the Duncans."

It had been over a month since Adam had offered to go to Philadelphia. *Please let it be good news.* "Douglas, come with me to clean our hands at the well." She picked him up and sped toward the side of the house.

The carriage pulled up to the Green. Todd and Philip stood with Mary. Philip reached for the harness as soon as the carriage pulled in front of the ordinary.

Heather took the basket Maggie handed her and helped her friend descend while Adam assisted the children. "We have been so eager for your visit."

"I am sorry it took us this long to get here." Maggie held her close.

Heather allowed herself the comfort of her friend's arms. "No matter. Come inside so we can catch up." She was ushering the group inside when Adam came alongside of her.

"Might we take a walk while Maggie gets the young ones

settled?" His hand rested on her back. He looked serious. Perhaps he'd learned something about Matthew. No doubt that was why he wanted to speak with her privately.

"Certainly." She called to Mary, who was speaking with Jean. "Please see that everyone has what they need and listen for Sara." She turned back to Adam.

"We can walk to the pond."

They walked a minute in silence, Adam staring straight ahead.

"What is it? What have you learned?"

"I went to Philadelphia and met with Patrick O'Brian. Nice chap and very helpful."

"And?"

Adam pointed to the bench now in sight. "Shall we sit?"

"Very well." Normally, this was a place of peace for her, but now she felt a knot in her gut. She sat on the bench and faced him.

"'Tis not good news." His eyes filled with tears.

She dug her fingers into the oak bench and tried to brace herself. The breath went out of her.

"Matthew attempted to deliver a packet, but the man he planned to meet had traveled elsewhere. Matthew never arrived at the prearranged location. Concerned their system of passing messages might be compromised, the man dared not wait for him."

She sat silent, stunned, heart racing. "What? Did anyone search for him? What about questioning those where he stayed in Philadelphia?"

"Yes, they went to the Davis Inn, but the proprietor said that Matt had not been seen since the morning he was to make his delivery. He expected to stay another evening but never returned, and he left nothing in the room. 'Tis not unusual that he would have taken his belongings with him."

He reached for her hand and held it. "Your husband carried secrets, so if the intended recipient did not get the package, the man would not have been eager to let anyone know."

"Why did Matthew do this?"

"We can only guess. Come back to the Green. Maggie will be worrying about you."

As they headed back up the path, she rubbed the stiffness at the back of her neck. She still had no answers.

Maggie spoke as she approached them on the path. "I wanted to get the children occupied."

Adam stopped and faced her. "Heather, there is more."

She only had to look into his eyes to guess what he might say. *Hope—hope—my hope is in the Lord. The Psalms ... think. "Be of good courage, and he shall strengthen your heart, all ye that hope in the Lord."*

Maggie came alongside her and placed her arm around her waist. Adam reached for her hand again. "A couple of weeks later, someone found a body in the woods on the outskirts of Philadelphia and reported it to the authorities. Stephens and Jones were in Philadelphia, evidently trying to trace Matthew. When they heard about the body, they went to see it, not an easy task since it had been badly ... They identified it as Matt."

She pulled her hand away from him, wrenched away from Maggie's arms. "If the body had deteriorated, they cannot be sure." She clenched her hands.

Adam reached into his jacket and pulled out a small linen packet and handed it to her.

"Nay!" She took it and slowly peeled back the fabric. The Celtic cross with the pale blue ribbon Matthew had given her, the same one she had given him and asked him to carry until he returned home, rested in her hand. A cold chill ran through her body, and she shook uncontrollably. The linen fabric dropped to the ground. Her eyes filled with tears.

Adam's voice cracked. "I did not want to believe it either, but when they showed it to us, I recognized it as the one you used to wear."

Maggie put her arms around her and held her.

"I ... there might be a mistake. I cannot believe he is ... gone. I would know if he—"

"My dear, you have had a shock," Adam said. "You will need time to work through this."

Tears ran down Maggie's face. "You are not alone. You have friends."

She pulled back, her head pounding. "There must be some mistake. I would know it." She searched Adam's tear-filled eyes. "The children. This will devastate the children."

"Heather, you and the children are like family. We will help in any way we can."

She wiped the tears from her face. "I appreciate all you have done." She gazed toward the Green. How would she tell the children?

Heather pushed her shoulders back and shook her head. She would need to be strong, now more than ever. "I must tell them."

"They will have questions, and I will try to answer them as best as I can."

"Where is he? Where is Matthew?"

"Christ Church," he said, "buried in the graveyard alongside his parents."

"'Tis not here, but 'twill do. How did he die, is it known?"

He took a deep breath and seemed to have to force himself not to look away. "He was shot, several times."

She gasped. Shot? Someone murdered him? "Why? Who would do this?" A terrible taste filled her throat.

"I'm not certain we will ever know for sure."

As they walked back to the Green, she prayed, seeking God for wisdom, the right words to tell the children, and the courage to face the days ahead.

CHAPTER 29

Sunday morning a few weeks after the Duncans' visit, Heather steered the horse-drawn wagon down the drive toward the Green and wiped perspiration from her brow. It was warm for May. She removed her shawl and scanned the sky. It must be around noon. The children were as silent as she had been since they'd left the church service. She bit her lip, trying to hold back the tears. Friends at church had been kind, offering solicitous words, offering to help with whatever she might need. She had needed to get away from all their remarks, or she would have surely broken down again.

She knew her friends only wanted to help. She wished she could find a way to let them. But the truth was, even as those who loved her offered sympathy, Heather couldn't seem to convince herself Matthew was actually gone. There had been many times she'd sensed him as if he were calling to her, entreating her to believe in him, to believe he would return. She had not told anyone of her feelings, lest the entire town learn she was going daft.

Douglas looked at her from his seat beside her. "Mama, I wanted to stay for dinner after church." There was a furrow between his eyes.

"We needed to get home, laddie. I thought we could take a picnic down by the river today. Mark could even bring some fishing poles."

When the wagon stopped, Heather stepped off and helped Douglas down before reaching up for Mary to pass Sara to her. "Mark, please attend to the horse and wagon."

"Yes, Mama. Can we really take the fishing poles?"

"Aye. But 'twill be a few minutes while I take care of Sara and gather the meal. Go and change out of your Sunday clothes."

An hour later, they had spread the blanket and were all seated on the bank overlooking the Potomack River. Recent rains had increased the current, but the sound of the moving water and the warm sunlight helped settle her troubled spirit.

Mary passed around napkins. "Mama, you said you expected Mr. Macmillan to visit this month. Martha asked me at church if you had received word from him. She has not heard from James, and she hoped Mr. Macmillan would bring news of him." Mary leaned back against the oak tree and handed her little sister a cool damp cloth to chew on.

Heather rubbed the knot on the back of her neck. "Something must have interfered with Andrew's plans." She studied the food on her plate, barely touching it. "He may still come. There are a few days left in the month." Her hand went to her forehead to block the sun from her eyes. "Mark, do not let Douglas get too close to the water. 'Tis shallow there, but the current is strong, and I do not want him falling in."

Mark huffed. "How am I to bait his hooks, watch him, and fish at the same time?"

She looked at her two boys and shook her head. "Douglas, stand farther back from the pond or put your pole down and come over here and sit with us."

Mark yelled. "Do what Ma says, or you will ruin it for all of us."

Mark's sharp tone and scowl at his younger brother tore at her heart. They had all been short with each other. Had it only been a month since they had learned of Matthew's death? It seemed a lifetime had passed.

Their grief had gone from denial to anger, and now they all seemed to carry a general apathy toward life. She had been so preoccupied with her grief and set a poor example for the children. *This must change.*

"Mark, Douglas, please put your poles down for a couple of

minutes. I need to say something to all of you." The boys joined the girls and her on the bank. The children studied her with what she could only describe as dread. After learning of Matthew's death, it felt no good news could ever come again.

"I need to apologize for being so distracted and sad these past few weeks. The loss of your father is a tragedy, one we must learn to endure. He would not want us to go through life sad and hopeless and unloving toward each other. We must stop focusing on all we have lost and begin to count our blessings and be thankful for all we have. We have each other, our health, our friends, a home. More than all of that, we have faith that the Lord will see us through this."

Mark rubbed a rock back and forth in the dirt while Sara rested on her stomach, smiling, innocently unaware.

Mary shook her head. "We do not know about what happened to Papa. There are too many unanswered questions."

Heather put her arm around Douglas when he snuggled up next to her. "Adam said he would continue searching for answers, but he needs to work through certain channels. Your father worked in secret. Adam suggested one has to be careful in any investigation since further exposure might put critical plans or other people in danger."

Sara threw her ragdoll off the blanket, and Mary retrieved it. "But something else has troubled me. Remember when the Green was broken in to? Did that have something to do with Papa?"

Heather nodded. "I have wondered about that myself. Whoever ransacked our home must have been looking for something because other than a small amount of money, they took nothing of value."

Douglas looked up at her, a frown on his brow. "Are we safe?"

"I believe so, son." She ran her fingers through his hair. "We have new, strong locks on all the doors. The robbers must not have found anything, or if they did, we know nothing about it. Why would they come back?"

Mark took some bread and ham and began eating. "Besides,

we have two more rifles now, Douglas. I can protect us. Thomas showed me how to use them."

Heather shuddered and passed dried apple slices to Mark and Douglas. "I hope 'twill not come to that. I want you to continue helping Thomas and the boys finish the planting this week."

"Yes, ma'am."

A few minutes later, Mark tugged on Douglas' shirt. "Come on, there are fish to catch." The two boys picked up their poles and returned to the river.

Mary placed her shawl over her little sister. "She has fallen asleep. Lucky girl. She does not know how our world has turned upside down."

Mary's words broke Heather's heart. *How am I to guide this family through our grief?* "But Sara will never have known your papa, and that is a very great loss."

"Aye," Mary said. "A very great loss indeed."

After dinner the following day, a spring shower kept everyone indoors. Heather caught up on her mending, something she had been too restless to address the past few weeks. The sun came out mid-afternoon. Setting the mending on her lap and, resting her head on the back of the settee, she closed her eyes to enjoy the sun's warmth pouring through the window. *If only the rays of light streaming through the window would penetrate and heal my hurting heart.*

Douglas running into the room brought her back to the present. "Mama, may I go outside now? The boys are going to the front lawn with a ball."

"You may go out for a few minutes, dear, but if they do not want you to join in, you will need to watch."

Mary got up from the window where she was reading and sat on the settee next to Heather.

"You look as though you have something on your mind," Heather said.

"I wondered, how did you know when you loved Papa?"

Heather sighed. Was that a blush on Mary's face? "Why do you ask?"

"Is it too painful to speak about it, I mean with Papa being ... gone?"

"Nay." She glanced out the window again. Mary only wondered what every young woman wanted to know.

"How were you sure of your love for him?" Mary placed her hand on hers. "I want to understand how it happened with you."

"As you know, your father and I were not romantically attached when we married. We only met that very day."

"Aye. I thought Papa had lost his mind."

Heather chuckled. "Your father said his love developed for me not long after we married, but he always looked for the best in everyone. I was resistant. I did not trust others, nor did I trust even my own feelings, so it took me longer to realize that I loved him." The warmth she felt on her face penetrated to her soul. "Your father's character attracted me, the way he treated people with kindness and dignity. And how he loved the two of you touched my heart. I respected him, he made me laugh, and of course, being handsome and engaging did not hurt."

They both laughed.

"Is this about Donald?" Heather asked.

"I love Donald. But is the love of a friend the same kind of love one experiences with the one they should marry? I think about him often, I worry about his safety, and I miss him, but I also have enjoyed the company of others."

"Those are very honest and thoughtful admissions. When we are young and form friendships with young men, 'tis natural to wonder if we are suited to someone as a marriage partner. As we mature and know ourselves better, I think it becomes clearer. You do not need to make any decisions now."

"But 'tis hard not to think about," Mary said.

"Aye. When I was a young woman, a village chap and I cared for each other. Our families talked of us marrying someday, but the timing and circumstances never were right. After a few years, I realized two people could love each other but not be suited for marriage."

Mary sat back and shook her head. "There are different kinds of love. 'Tis confusing."

"You have time to search your mind and heart to know what you want. We can be praying God would provide the right husband for you when the time is right and to make it very clear to the two of you. I have no doubt you will know at the right time."

"Really?"

"Aye, and when it happens, 'tis amazing." She smiled and rested her head on the back of the chair. She closed her eyes again. The love she and Matthew had shared, all the special moments, could never be forgotten. After Mary wandered away, Heather glanced out the window. The sunshine made the raindrops on the leaves of the privet hedge glisten, a breathtaking sight.

Wait on Me. I am your help and your shield. I have never left you.

A jolt ran through her body, leaving the hair on her arms standing on end. A warm sensation of peace flowed through her. She looked around. No one was there and nothing had changed.

Is that You, Lord? I know you are with me, but what are You saying?

She scanned the room but saw no one. Had she dreamt or imagined the voice or the physical sensation?

Sara fussed upstairs. A glance at the clock on the hutch indicated it was six o'clock.

Mary came back into the room. "You stay there, Mama. I can see to Sara."

"Bring her downstairs. We will need to serve supper soon."

Mark came through the door. "There is a rider coming this way."

"'Tis late for a boarder," Heather said. "Mark, see to the horse, and I'll show him to his room."

She followed Mark to the porch and shaded her eyes as the rider approached.

"Mama, 'tis Mr. Macmillan." Mark ran toward him.

She walked down the steps as Andrew dismounted from his bay.

"I came as soon as possible. Your letter, Heather—" Andrew strode toward her and gathered her in his arms.

Tears ran down her cheeks as this old friend comforted her. "'Tis good to see you, Andrew."

"I'm so sorry." He held her until she stepped back.

She wiped her cheeks. "Forgive me. I weep too easily these days."

"I understand." The look in his eyes reminded her. *Aye, he too is well acquainted with grief.* "Your letter said you would fill me in on the rest."

"Aye, come inside. How is James? Mary will want to know also."

"I shall tell you both."

The sound of his voice gave her pause. *Please, no more bad news, Lord.*

CHAPTER 30

Heather ushered Andrew into the common room. The children followed. He reminded them of their father. He reminded her as well. She wiped fresh tears. "Join us for supper."

"I would like nothing better. I am famished."

"Please join me in the kitchen while I prepare supper." He followed her into the kitchen, and she poured him a cup of water. "You look well."

He drained the cup. "You are looking thin."

"Perhaps a little." They chatted about nothing while she ladled the cock-a-leekie soup into bowls.

After the blessing, Mark said, "Where is James?"

He set down his fork and took a deep breath. "James has joined the Continental Navy."

Silence followed, which Mark finally broke. "James is in the navy? That is fantastical."

Andrew nodded.

Mary's eyes were wide. "Continental Navy? Is that a Colonial Navy?"

"Aye," Andrew said.

"I read something in the *Gazette* a while ago about a navy being created," Heather said. "But I did not know the colonies had any ships."

Andrew shrugged. "'Tis still small. Some merchant ships have been refitted, and more are being built. The Continental Congress and General Washington want to rid the Chesapoyocke of Lord Dunmore."

Mary shook her head. "James never mentioned it. I feared he

might join the militia or the Continental Army, but I never knew he considered going to sea. Martha would have said something if she had known. 'Tis surprising James has not told or written her about this."

Mark grinned at the unexpected news. "He will have great tales to tell when he returns."

Heather passed a bowl of soup to Andrew. "We will keep James in our prayers."

"I appreciate that. James said very little about his decision to join, though I believe he gave it much consideration before telling me. He departed almost two months ago."

Andrew leaned forward and folded his hands on the table and looked at the children. "I'm so sorry about your pa. Your father was a good and courageous man who wanted to serve the cause of liberty in the best way he could. You can be proud of him. He was a well-respected member of this community and will be missed by many."

Mary sniffled. Andrew patted her hand.

Mark looked down at his lap, obviously fighting back tears. Douglas got up from his seat and climbed on Heather's lap.

Heather looked across the table to Andrew. It was hard to hear his heartfelt remarks. They were all still so tender. But his words would be remembered by each of them, and in time, they would be a balm for their hurting hearts.

Heather got up from her seat. "Mary, would you help me serve the pie?" What a relief to see smiles reappear on her children's faces. In the kitchen, she cut the apple pie.

Mary set plates on the work table. "How long will Mr. Macmillan be with us?"

"I'm not certain, but probably not long. He has a business in Fredericksburg to oversee."

After finishing their pie, Andrew approached the children. "Would you mind if your mother and I went for a walk? We will not be long."

Mary stood and gathered the plates onto a tray. "Of course."

Heather stood. "Put Sara to bed soon. I shall get a shawl."

It was dusk when they left the Green. The evening sounds of chirping crickets and croaking frogs filled the silence. She relayed what she had learned about Matthew's last days and his death and tried to answer his questions. When they reached the pond, they sat on the bench and gazed at the water in silence. Ducks huddled by a bush making soft sounds.

"Can you stay with us a few days, Andrew?"

"Aye. What can I do around here to be of assistance? Do you need any funds?" He reached into his coat and pulled out a folded parchment and handed it to her. "It is not much, but it may get you through any needs that come up."

She opened it slowly. There were several notes. "I cannot accept this, but I appreciate your generosity. We are not destitute."

"Please, keep it. You may need it in the future. Do it for me. I need to help in some way."

She smiled at his kindness. "'Tis challenging to learn how to receive graciously."

"Will the Gordon family stay and help you?"

"They have given me no reason to think otherwise. Polly, Thomas, and the boys have been a blessing and good company for all of us, now more than ever."

"I'm relieved."

She gently rubbed her fingers over the cross at the end of the blue ribbon hanging around her neck. "I have no reason to doubt what Adam told me about Matthew, and the limited evidence we have confirms Matthew is ... gone, but part of me still finds it difficult to accept." She turned and looked into Andrew's sympathetic eyes. "And there is still so much mystery. Why was he involved in some clandestine scheme, transporting intelligence packets? He shared none of this with me."

Andrew shook his head. "Matthew never told me of his involvement in the Patriot cause. He must have believed he could be useful." Andrew took her hand. "Heather, it takes a while to heal a grieving heart when you have lost someone to whom you have pledged your life."

The evening light almost gone now, she noted his eyes glistened. She fought back tears and looked down at her small hand almost lost in his large one. Sharing this intimacy with a man other than Matthew seemed confusing.

"With time, it does get easier." There was sincerity in his eyes as he searched her face. "In time, one remembers the good days shared and can again smile. You have friends who are praying for your family. If I can be of any help, in any way, get word to me, please."

"I will, Andrew, and many thanks, for everything."

"Let me pray for you."

She closed her eyes and listened to his strong and comforting voice.

"Father in heaven, You healeth the broken in heart and bindeth up their wounds. I pray You will heal Heather and the children's broken hearts and fill them with Your peace. Lord, help them to find the answers they seek, strengthen them each day, and meet all their needs. Lord, we trust in Your faithfulness."

Nothing had changed. Her circumstances were not altered, but her spirit was lighter, and for the first time in months, she felt encouraged.

A slight smile formed on her lips as she looked up at him. "That means a great deal to me. 'Tis dark, we'd best get back to the Green." They were both wounded people. She would need to be mindful to maintain her reserve and not compromise either of them.

CHAPTER 31

After the church service on Sunday a month later, Heather, Mary, and Amelia Turner walked toward the wagons to gather their food for the picnic.

Heather reached into their wagon for a basket and turned toward Amelia. "I'm eager to learn more about what this Declaration of Independence means."

Mary took it from her. "What does it mean that the colonies have declared their independence, other than it being the topic of conversation today while we eat?"

Amelia laughed. "True, little else will be discussed. 'Tis good to see you staying for dinner after services today."

Heather took another basket. "We would not have missed it."

Mark ran up to them, followed by Logan Turner and his sisters. "We are here to help carry food. I'm starving."

Amelia reached into her wagon and pulled baskets out. She handed them to Mark, Logan, and the girls.

Heather studied Amelia. She looked weary. "Have you any news from Cole?"

"Nothing lately. 'Tis difficult not to worry with all the things we hear. So many families have young men fighting, often away from home for the first time. We feel so helpless."

Heather placed her hand on Amelia's back. "I understand."

They made their way back to the group gathered outside the church and schoolhouse where some other ladies had already set out dishes of food.

Amelia wiped her brow and looked around at the group assembled. "What will happen now that we have formally separated from England?"

Heather glanced at Mark. Fortunately, he was too young to leave home to fight. "We wondered the same thing. Will the fighting increase, or will England give up and leave us alone?"

Aaron Turner joined his wife and family as they spread a quilt on the ground. "England, give up? We would be foolish to believe Britain will forfeit their investment in the colonies and sacrifice their pride as the world's most powerful nation and just walk away from her upstart colonies. No, their irritation with us has been piqued, and we will all experience their wrath soon."

Heather shuddered and placed a quilt beside the Turners'.

George and Hannah Whitcomb and their family spread a blanket and sat nearby.

Mama tapped Mark on the shoulder. "Please run back to the wagon and get the other quilt so the Gordons can join us."

When Mark returned with it, Thomas Gordon sat down beside his wife. "I understand Governor … well, former Governor Dunmore is encamped out at Gwynn's Island, and Maryland's former royal governor has joined him there in exile." He swallowed a bite of chicken before he continued. "My guess is they will use the island in the Chesapoyocke as a staging ground for attacks on Maryland and Virginia."

Polly elbowed her husband and nodded in the direction of Hannah Whitcomb.

Heather followed their gazes. Hannah seemed agitated. They had best keep the talk of war to a minimum or it would remind her of the danger facing Tobias.

Mark wasted no time jumping into the fray. "With our new navy, we can take on any old royal governors who want to hole up at Gwynne's Island."

Heather glanced at Martha. How did she feel now that James Macmillan had joined the navy? It was widely believed the navy's efforts were to be focused in the Bay.

Thomas Gordon's grin was jubilant. "No more king. We finally have a Patriot as governor, Patrick Henry."

Todd sat next to his father. "I suppose with Dunmore gone we would need a new governor."

Mark looked at Thomas. "If we have no king, who will rule the colonies?"

"No one will be in charge," Thomas said.

Mark looked confused.

Thomas put down his plate. "'Twill take time, but it means we will become free and independent and no longer a part of the British Empire. We are a new nation."

Heather looked around the group. Everyone seemed to silently process his words.

Mark got up and motioned to Logan to join him. "This would be an exciting time to be in Philadelphia. Come on, I think there is more chicken at the table."

She shuddered. This would be a frightening time to be in Philadelphia. "I'm grateful Mary and Mark are no longer there." She picked Sara up and made her way to the wagon.

When Heather was finished changing Sara, she heard Mary and Martha's voices. The Whitcombs' wagon was near enough to observe the girls.

Martha's voice cracked. "We are all living our lives as though nothing bad is happening. We go to church and picnic in safety, children play their games, yet we have fellow colonists, our young men, who are fighting and being injured and dying. Your mother understands because she has already lost someone, but so many others are caught up ... celebrating. Tobias and James and all the rest of our young men are in terrible peril."

Mary took Martha's hand. "People have not forgotten. They are glad we have officially separated from England. No one is making light of the danger."

Martha continued, "I do not know the ship James is on or where Tobias is. Your family has also suffered. My mother speaks of little else, and I am fearful."

Heather held Sara close and bit her lip. Hannah's depression was taking a toll on the Whitcomb family.

"Martha, whenever any of us are fearful, Mama reminds us to praise God for who He is and to thank Him for all He does for us. He is always faithful no matter the circumstances."

Heather's eyes prickled, hearing her own words offered as encouragement to someone else. She would need the reminder often in the coming months.

Over the next fortnight, numerous guests at the Green kept everyone busy. On a particularly warm Tuesday, Heather rolled the washtub outside and filled it with hot water. "'Tis too beautiful a day to stay in the wash house."

Mary reluctantly joined her with an armful of linens, which she dumped in the tub. "When the Walters stayed here, Mrs. Walters said many ordinaries have only a blanket on their mattresses, so there is far less wash to do."

"That may be why the Walters stay here when they travel. We Scots put great store in hygiene and cleanliness to maintain good health."

"Hmm." Mary picked up the paddle and stirred the soaking linens. "It takes more work."

Heather stretched. "Would you prefer working in the garden until Sara wakes up?"

"I would prefer reading or sewing."

"Good endeavors, but the chores need to be completed first." She glanced toward the lane. A rider approached. "'Tis Mr. Macmillan's bay, Stirling. Ask one of the boys to attend to his horse."

"Philip loves that horse," Mary said. "I will find him."

As Mary walked toward the barn, Heather took her apron off, set it on a basket, and approached the lane leading to the Green. "Andrew, how good of you to come visit."

Philip ran from the barn and took the reins as Andrew dismounted. Mary was right behind him.

"Good day, ladies." He nodded at Philip. "Stirling will want some water."

"Yes, sir. And I will give him some oats and rub him down, too."

They walked back toward the Green as Philip led the horse toward the barn.

"And how are the Stewarts?" He smiled, pointing to the laundry. "Again, I'm interfering."

"'Tis a welcome interruption," Mary responded.

Heather smirked. "Please take Mr. Macmillan inside and get him some cider. I will care for Sara and be down soon. There is a recent *Gazette* in there, Andrew."

<hr>

Heather spotted Andrew observing her more than once at dinner. Something was on his mind, perhaps news of James. *Dear God, please let him be well and safe.*

Thomas reached for more ham. "There is news a large English fleet arrived in New York. The fighting will increase now that we have declared our independence from England. Admiral Lord Howe and his brother General Lord Howe are our biggest threats."

Heather studied Thomas. He must have missed discussing current events with another man. With Andrew here, he finally had someone to debate war strategy.

Mary thumped her fingers on the table. "Have you received any posts from James?"

"No. No, but I expect no word from him when he is at sea."

"I pray he is well," Heather said. Was Andrew's modest smile forced optimism? "James is in our prayers, as are so many others."

Later, Heather and Mary went outside to pick up the dry linens from the hedges. She spotted Mary looking toward the field beyond the barn.

"Why did Mr. Macmillan go out with Thomas and the boys to harvest the wheat?"

"I think he wants to help."

"He does not need to do that."

"Nay, but he likes to help when he visits."

"His countenance at dinner ... he kept watching you like he wanted to say something."

Heather placed the folded laundry in a basket. Mary had also noticed Andrew's stares. "Perhaps he wanted a way to bring James into the conversation, and you did that."

"I never asked Papa or you before, and perhaps you will think me rude ... Do we charge Mr. Macmillan or the Duncan family when they stay here?"

"Nay, we never have. However, since ... last November, they always manage to pass a few notes to me. I initially resisted. But Maggie said they would not be comfortable visiting unless I accepted. She said I must learn to receive from friends just as I like to assist others."

"You know there is no use arguing with Mrs. Duncan."

They both laughed.

Around seven, the men returned, the Gordons to their cottage and Mark and Andrew to the Green.

Mark came through the door first. "We are here to get clean shirts. We plan to wash at the pond."

"Supper will be ready when you return."

After the meal, the family remained at the table, entertained by Andrew as he read a book of Aesop's Fables to Douglas. Heather reached for the few remaining dishes. "We appreciate your helping today. The harvesting would have taken so much longer if not for you. We are all grateful."

In the kitchen, Heather gazed out the window. She could focus beyond her hurting heart. The summer sounds and the rosy sky pleased her. "Red skies at night, sailors delight."

"Red skies in morning, sailors take warning." Andrew's deep voice was right behind her.

She flinched and pivoted. "I did not hear you come in the kitchen."

"I did not mean to startle you." His pensive look had returned. "Is there anything I can get you?"

"Nay. I, uh ... Do you think we might take a walk by the pond?"

As they walked along the gravel path, Andrew said very little. What troubled him? *Please ... nothing bad.* The breeze at the pond was refreshing. Why was he studying her so intently?

She gazed at the trees framing the far side of the pond. "What a lovely time of night."

Andrew led her to the bench. "Shall we sit?"

"Is something wrong?" She sat and turned her head to clearly observe his face.

Andrew laughed. "I do have something I want to speak about with you, and I guess I have not known the best way to approach the subject." He looked out toward the pond before turning back toward her. His right arm rested on the back of the bench. "Heather, you and your family mean a great deal to me. I know how painful it is to lose a beloved spouse. 'Tis devastating. When I am not at the Green, I find myself thinking about you and wondering how you are faring. I know it has been less than a year since Matthew left and only a few months since you learned of his death." He took a deep breath. "I think of you in other ways as well, and often." He reached over and took her hand in his. "I care deeply for you, Heather. Would you do me the honor of becoming my wife?"

CHAPTER 32

Heather caught her breath. Why had she not sensed Andrew's intentions? How was she to respond? He continued to speak, but the pounding in her chest and the thoughts racing through her head drowned out his words. She cared for Andrew, but she loved Matthew and still felt married. Perhaps she always would. "Andrew, I—"

"I will take care of you and the children." His blue eyes were filled with love. He drew closer.

She rose from the bench and stood in front of him. "I am deeply honored by your declaration, your generosity, and your affection. You are a dear friend. I apologize if I led you to believe I might enter into marriage again. I'm not ready to consider that now, and ... and I'm not sure I ever will be."

"'Tis too soon." The look of hurt as he stood and faced her tore at her heart. "I should have waited. Of course, I should have."

She stood as well. "You're so kind, truly. 'Tis just ... Matthew is ... Matthew was ..." How could she make him understand? How could anybody understand her feelings?

He tilted his head to the side. "What is it? Do you know something you have not shared with me?"

"Nay. Not really." She closed her mouth, opened it again. What could she say? Would he understand? "Think me foolish if you will, but when I pray, and at other times, I have sensed ... I cannot explain it. There is too much about Matthew's disappearance I do not understand."

He sat back on the bench, his gaze still on her. He patted the space beside him. "Sit down. I shan't press you." His charming smile returned.

She gazed at the pond. The dusky sky had lost its rosy hue. The evening sounds of owls and tree frogs had grown louder. "We were sitting here in April when Adam told me what he had learned about Matthew's passing. Someday, I may travel to Philadelphia to see his grave."

"That might bring some closure for you."

"I wonder." She turned to him. "I hope what we shared here will not alter our friendship. It would grieve me to lose it. But I do not want to be insensitive or selfish."

"We have been good friends for too long to let my ..." He paused, gathered himself. "Nothing will alter our friendship. We can let time take us where it will."

"I cannot make you any promises. Someday there may be another lady for you." She hated the thought of hurting him. Andrew was too good a friend.

His smile gave her hope that nothing would change. His hand came to rest on hers. "Please, if you reconsider, if you view things differently, do not be shy about telling me."

She chuckled, though it died quickly. "Have you ever known me to be shy about expressing myself? Nay, Andrew, I will not let pride keep me from being honest with you."

"Good. Now we best return to the Green, or your children may think I kidnapped you."

❧❀❧

The next morning, the family stood outside to see Andrew off as he mounted his bay and headed down the lane.

Heather felt Mary's eyes on her. "I'm sorry Mr. Macmillan left so soon. He is always so pleasant."

"Aye, he is a fine chap and good friend."

An hour later they had extracted all the honey they were going to get from the honeycomb. After storing it in jars and washing the honeycomb for later use, Heather fed Sara.

"May I go to Martha's after dinner?" Mary asked.

"Aye, and take one of the jars of honey to her mother. Sugar is in such short supply these days. Hannah loves our blackberries, so take some of those also. And watch the sky. 'Tis warm, and thunderstorms are always a possibility."

"Did Mr. Macmillan say when he might come back for a visit?"

"Nay. He keeps very busy in Fredericksburg. He may return before winter."

Mary left a few minutes later laden down with honey, berries, and her sewing project.

Heather and Polly walked outside to the kitchen garden to pick ripe vegetables.

They were in the midst of preserving when a bolt of lightning followed instantly by a thunderclap made them both jump.

Polly went to the window and looked out toward the lane. "That was close."

"I hope Mary is safe." Heather opened the door facing the barn. "I see Thomas and Mark penning animals, and Todd is securing things around the barn. Philip must be on the other side. I do not see him."

Rain that began gently picked up in intensity.

The door opened, and Thomas, Mark, and Todd entered, shaking the water off.

Polly looked up from the large kettle simmering over the hearth. "Where is Philip?"

Thomas shrugged. "I'm sure he will be here soon."

Heather brought towels for them to dry off. She used another cloth to wipe the water off the floor. "I hope Mary stayed at Martha's."

"I need to get to the cottage to close the windows," Polly said. She headed toward the center hall and the front door. Thomas followed.

A few minutes later, the pounding on the back door brought

Heather to her feet. She rushed to open the door, gasping when she saw Philip with Mary in his arms. "Quick, bring her in here. What happened?" She closed the door behind them, trying to keep the blowing rain from coming inside.

Breathing hard, Philip carried Mary inside. "Where do you want me to put her?"

Mary looked sheepish and in pain. "My ankle. I slipped and hurt my ankle."

"On the settee."

"You sure? She is all wet and muddy. I can take her to her bedroom."

"Upstairs?" He had to be exhausted from carrying Mary home from who knew how far.

Mark came alongside Philip. "I can help." They fashioned a chair with their arms and lifted her up the stairs.

Heather followed their slow climb. "Be careful not to slip, Philip. I am sure your shoes must be muddy."

The boys lowered Mary to her bed and helped her to recline. She groaned as they gently brought her legs up to rest on the bed.

Heather searched Mary's face. "What happened?"

"I was coming back from Martha's, and I slipped and twisted my ankle in the mud."

Philip panted. "I waited near the edge of the trees and saw her slip, so I got her home."

Heather wrapped her arms around him. "You are a treasure."

"Mrs. Stewart, I'm all wet."

Mary stared at Philip with a sheepish look. "I'm grateful you were there to help me."

Heather smoothed Mary's wet hair away from her brow. "I am going downstairs to get a basin of water. Do not move. I will be right back."

"Do not worry," Mary said. "I'm not going anywhere."

The boys followed her downstairs.

Worry etched Philip's face. "I will ride over and get Doc

Edwards."

"Nay, Philip, not now. The storm is so fierce. Go home so your mother knows you are safe and dry off. We can talk a bit later about getting the doctor."

"I will be back in half an hour to check on her, Mrs. Stewart."

"No need." She opened the door and gazed at the sky. "'Tis let up a bit."

"I will pray for Mary." Philip headed to the Gordon cottage.

Douglas stood in the doorway and sobbed.

"No fretting. Mary will be fine. Will you stay with Sara while I take care of Mary?"

"Yes, Mama."

Upstairs, Heather gently removed Mary's soiled, wet garments. "Where do you hurt?"

"My right elbow aches where I fell, but mostly it is my left ankle."

After Heather helped Mary into a clean shift, she checked the elbow and then ran her hand over Mary's leg. "The elbow will likely bruise, but it has not swelled. Can you move your foot?"

Mary winced as she moved her leg and foot around.

"Your leg and ankle do not look broken, but Doctor Edwards will know. Did you hurt your head?" She ran her fingers through Mary's wet, matted hair. "This could have been so much worse." Heather dampened the rag again and began cleaning the area at the back of Mary's head.

"The storm came up so fast. I came home as soon as the thunder began."

"Given the strength of the storm, you should have stayed at the Whitcombs' until it calmed. I am grateful your injuries are no worse. Thank heavens for Philip."

Mary wrapped a shawl around her shoulders, a chagrined expression on her face. She raised her shift and peered at her leg. "The ankle is swelling." She looked up. "I'm ashamed of how annoyed I have been by Philip's constant hovering. If he had not been there …"

Heather got up from the edge of Mary's bed. "Someone would have come looking for you. I hear someone at the door, probably Philip." She made her way downstairs and opened the door. "Oh, Thomas, 'tis you."

He took his hat off. "Philip wanted to get Doc Edwards, but I told him to dry off, and I would go if you needed me to. How is Mary?"

"She is sore. I would like the doctor to look at her leg and ankle so we know what to do for her."

"The storm has let up. I will go now. If he is home, we should be back soon."

"Please thank Philip again for being nearby and rescuing Mary. He is a fine young man."

Thomas smiled and nodded. "I should have figured he was waiting for her."

❦

Heather opened the door when Thomas and Doctor Edwards arrived a half hour later.

"'Twas good of you to come."

Doctor Edwards walked into the center hall. "Sorry to hear of Mary's fall."

Thomas turned toward the door. "I'm taking the doc's horse to the barn, then I'll let Philip know Mary is being tended to. Let me know when you are ready to leave, doc, and I will get your horse."

Heather ushered the doctor upstairs, then stood at Mary's side while the doctor examined her ankle. "It looks like a sprain. I am going to wrap it. You stay off of your feet as best you can for a few days. Let me see your head." He spent a couple of minutes looking at her eyes and then inspected the back of her head. "You are a fortunate young woman. I suspect you will have a goose egg and possibly a headache. 'Tis possible you may have some nausea." He turned. "Have you some ginger?"

"Aye."

"Make a tea and give her some of that if she gets sick to her stomach."

He looked over her elbow and rotated her arm. "This looks like 'twill be sore and bruised, but 'tis not broken."

Mary blushed. "I'm sorry I made you come out in this weather."

Two hours later, Mark came through the kitchen door, took his hat off, and wiped his feet on the rug. "I saw Doctor Edwards leave when I came from the barn. How is Mary? Can I go up and see her?"

Heather passed on what the doctor had told her. "I am sure she would appreciate that. Sara is sleeping so keep the noise down. I will fix supper."

Heather arranged a tray for Mary and took it to her room.

"I brought you some herb tea and a bowl of soup. Are you feeling any better?"

"I hurt," she said, "and I'm not very hungry."

Heather gently eased herself onto the bed. "Drink the ginger tea."

Tears filled Mary's eyes. "Mama, Mrs. Whitcomb is not well. When I arrived, she called me Elizabeth. At first, I thought it a simple mistake, but she did it again. Martha told me she sometimes calls out to Tobias and Timothy."

Heather handed Mary a handkerchief. "I suspect Hannah suffers from depression. Perhaps that is what has beset her."

"Martha said her mind wanders, and once she nearly set the kitchen on fire. I think they plan to keep her at home from now on. Martha fears if her mother does something bad, they might put her in an institution in Williamsburg."

Heather gazed out the window. "An institution? They must be devastated."

"Martha is very distressed. I feel sorry for her and her family. She thinks her mother might improve when Tobias comes home.

But who knows when that might happen."

Heather reached for Mary's hand and held it. "There must be something we can do to help." Almost dark now, the profile of the trees stood black against the indigo sky. "I hope Martha does not mind your sharing this sad news with me."

"I asked her if I could, and she said yes. She knows you will not tell everyone."

"We must keep their family in prayer. I will think about how I can help them."

"Yes, and I will thank Philip again. I have not been as kind as I should have been."

"It was a blessing he was there for you."

Mary smirked. "When Philip saw me headed towards Martha's, he asked when I would return. He would have carried my sewing basket all the way to Martha's if I had asked him."

"Poor Philip. It seems he is smitten with you."

"I told him not to wait for me and suggested he go fishing with Mark and Todd. My concern was he would be setting buckets of fish at my feet when I returned."

Heather laughed. "I fear someday, someone is going to take advantage of his kind heart. Now, drink your tea before it gets any cooler. 'Twill help you get a good night's rest. Call me if you need me."

CHAPTER 33

A fortnight later, Laura and Sara sat by the table playing while Heather, Polly, and Mary finished eating dinner. Thomas and the boys had taken the wheat to the mill to be ground into flour.

Polly set her fork down. "Did you hear something?"

Heather got up. "Sounds like a horse. It may be a guest."

Polly followed Heather to the front door. "'Tis just the post rider. We may still be able to do the preserving without interruption. I will get him a drink."

After the post rider left, they returned to the common room. Heather scanned the items he had left with her. "The *Gazette* and a letter from the Duncans with another one attached to it."

Mary hobbled toward her. "Perhaps they have word from Donald."

Polly stood. "I will take the girls to the cottage. You two rest and read."

Heather walked to the settee closest to the window. "Come over here, Mary, so you can rest your leg on the hassock." She opened the letter and began reading aloud.

"'Tis dated August twenty-fifth."

Dear Heather,

We hope this finds you and the family well. When I saw Andrew Macmillan ten days ago at Brady's, he mentioned that you had a good crop of wheat this year and seemed well. He was on his way to Philadelphia.

She looked up. "Andrew had not mentioned that he was going to Philadelphia."

Mary tapped the parchment. "Mama, read."

"Sorry."

"We were pleased when Donald came home. It was only for a day as he carried another packet to a location not far from here. He looked well, but thin. He asked us to extend his best wishes to your family when we next saw you.

Our main purpose in writing to you is to pass on the attached letter. 'Tis from an Oden and Anna Fleming, a couple in Swedesboro, New Jersey.

Patrick O'Brian brought it and told us of the providential encounter he had with the Flemings as well as the uncanny set of circumstances that led him to believe there was more about Matthew's disappearance than we had been told."

Heather stared at Mary a moment before continuing.

"Patrick said he had delivered some furniture to the Flemings. The previous fall, the Flemings had visited family in Philadelphia when they saw Patrick's work and commissioned him to build some cabinets. He told them he would deliver their order when completed and made that delivery about a fortnight ago. When his conversation with the Flemings turned to family, Patrick mentioned his brother in Alexandria.

Mr. and Mrs. Fleming told him about an injured Virginia man they found, sheltered, and cared for last winter. Apparently, the man had been shot not far from their village. The entire time they nursed him back to health the man would only tell them his name was Matthew. He would never give them his surname. One night, some British Regulars showed up at their home looking for him and identified him as Matthew Stewart. The soldiers took him. They told the Flemings he was a prisoner of the Crown, a Patriot courier, and would be imprisoned or executed."

Heather dropped the letter to her lap.

Mary muttered. "So, the soldiers took him back to Philadelphia."

Heather felt like she had been kicked in the belly. "Aye, that was where Matthew was passing the information he carried." The pain was as fresh as when they had first learned of his death. She began shaking and her voice cracked. "The brutes murdered him and left him on the ground to rot. 'Twas no different than the way they treated prisoners back home."

Mary placed an arm around her shoulder. "Is there more, Mama?"

Heather's tear-filled eyes traveled back to the letter on her lap. "Adam writes:

Tis believed that the soldiers took Matthew back to Philadelphia. This letter probably comes as a shock and opens up wounds, but we knew you would want to know.

We will make a visit before the month is out. Till then, take care and let us know if we can be of any assistance. Maggie sends her love.

Adam"

Heather opened the other note and held it so Mary could read over her shoulder.

Mrs. Stewart,

We just learned of your association with Patrick O'Brian. He writes this for us.

We are grateful to finally contact Matthew's family. We found him by Raccoon Creek. He had been shot and also suffered a head injury. We brought him home, and Anna cared for him. In time, he improved. Though we asked, Matthew never told us his full name or where we could find his family.

We thought he must be in some sort of trouble and hiding, but we were not afraid because we knew Matthew was a good man. When he was strong enough, he planned to go home, but then the soldiers came for him.

We send sympathy for your great loss.

Respectfully,
Oden and Anna Fleming

Heather put her arms around Mary as their tears flowed.

"Why would God let this happen, Mama? 'Tis so senseless, so evil."

"Some things we will never understand this side of heaven."

The two held each other and cried quietly. Heather sniffled. "God has not deserted us."

"It feels like He has to me."

Heather lifted Mary's chin. "Think about what we have just received. Through an amazing set of circumstances, we have learned what happened to your father, as unjust as it was. 'Tis powerful proof of God's faithfulness. The Lord did not prevent the evil perpetrated, but He revealed your father was rescued and cared for when he was injured. 'Tis some comfort."

Mary sighed. "We must share these letters with the others."

When Polly returned, Heather read the letters to her.

Polly wiped away her tears. "We can put off doing the preserves until tomorrow."

Heather tied on her apron. "Nay, work is a tonic, as my mother used to say."

Heather shared the letters with Thomas and Mark when they returned from Whitney's Mill. The grief came like waves that day.

Searching for things to be grateful for had been a struggle. Right before falling to sleep, thought of a blessing came. *I'm thankful we did not have any patrons today.*

Heather tossed in her sleep. She dreamed of a fire. She was running, trying to escape the heat and flames, holding on to Matthew's hand. Why was there no sound when she screamed? But the flames followed them, licked at their heels.

She threw the coverlet aside and bolted upright, out of breath, her skin drenched with perspiration. *No flames.* She smelled no smoke.

She glanced around, but no moonlight lit the pitch-black room. It was impossible to see. She made her way to Sara's bed in the corner. Sara slept peacefully, while Heather's heart beat rapidly in her chest. What would bring on such a nightmare?

She tried to brush off the images that had invaded her sleep and reminded herself that everyone was well. *Think on that, and not the terror that came this night.*

❦

Two weeks later after breakfast, Heather bounced Sara on her hip in the common room and looked at her son, who sat on a settee, engrossed in the newspaper.

"What are you reading so intently, Mark?"

"The *Gazette*."

"I see that. What has your interest? Is it a report of a missing servant or a farmer selling a prize mare?"

"We are to be called the United States of America." Mark held up the paper.

She looked over his shoulder. "Aye?"

"'Tis the name of our nation. The colonies … nay, the states together will be the United States of America."

"That sounds rather imperious."

"Sounds like our country has the authority to govern itself. I rather like it."

The United States of America. Is that what Matthew had died for?

Would his sacrifice amount to anything?

"I'm taking Sara up for a nap. Please keep care of Douglas while Mary and I pickle this afternoon."

Hours later, Heather wiped the perspiration from her brow and untied her apron. "Finally finished." Ten jars of pickled vegetables rested on the table at the far end of the kitchen to cool.

Mark put down the book he was reading. "I say we go fishing."

He addressed everyone but looked intently at Douglas.

Douglas ran over to her. "Yes, Mama, yes. May we go fishing?"

She shook her head at Mark. He had plied Douglas to do his bidding.

"Very well," she answered. "We can all take some baskets, and Mark, you carry a ladder. There are apples in the orchard we can stop and pick on the way home."

Two hours later as they returned to the Green, Philip and Todd relieved them of their baskets of apples.

Polly held Laura's hand as they approached. "Looks like you got some fish, Douglas."

Douglas grinned. "I did."

Heather reached where Polly and Laura stood. "If you have not already eaten, join us for supper. We can fry up these fish. Then I need to prepare for tomorrow's church picnic."

Polly nodded. "We would love to join you. I will come and help. I thought your gesture to go stay with Hannah tomorrow so her family could go to services was very generous."

She shifted Sara as the child waved at the boys. "I only regret I did not think of it sooner."

While the boys scaled and gutted the fish, Heather took Sara inside to the common room.

Mary stood by the window that looked out on the kitchen garden.

"Would you mind the girls while Polly and I get supper ready? 'Tis good to see you up and about and not in as much discomfort."

Mary turned and smiled. "Of course. I walked to the pond and back with little pain."

"No wonder you look so refreshed."

"It improved my attitude. I recalled happier times, times with Papa and visits from the Duncan family. Do you remember our game of Blind Man's Bluff when Donald tripped me?"

"Oh, yes, I remember that."

"Donald comes to mind more and more. I hope this war ends

soon. I hope all our friends come home without injuries."

Heather set Sara on the rug. "We all pray for that, dear, but 'tis not a realistic expectation with war. Some men may never return, and others may arrive home severely wounded. Our love for them should not depend on them returning home unscathed."

"I know. I just want everything to remain the same."

"Our world has altered drastically and will continue to change. We need to adjust to whatever comes, and we need to do it with a courageous and grateful heart."

CHAPTER 34

Heather patted her neighbor's hand. "Hannah, I know how you love sweets, so I brought you some apple fritters."

A subtle smile formed on Hannah's lips as she reached for the golden-brown pastry. "I love your baked goods, Elizabeth."

At least Hannah responded, even if she had confused her with Matthew's late wife. Heather spotted the clock on the mantel. She had been at the Whitcombs' for about a half hour.

Yesterday morning when she'd suggested to George that she would stay with Hannah so their family could attend Sunday services, he initially resisted. But a look at Martha and Teddy changed his mind.

"Are you certain, Heather? Hannah can get—"

"I am well acquainted with Hannah, and I will look after her. You and your children need to be around others, and attending church will do all of you good. Plan on staying for fellowship afterward. I will bring a basket of food you can take to share."

The sight of Martha's smile would be worth every minute she spent with Hannah, and giving this needy family some refreshment was a blessing to Heather.

When she told Polly and Mary of her plans, they said they would sit with the Whitcombs in church and at the fellowship.

It had been chilly when Heather arrived at the Whitcomb farmhouse. George, Martha, and Teddy were dressed in their Sunday clothes and ready to depart. Hannah initially looked confused but soon settled down.

While Hannah munched away at the sweet pastry, Heather opened her Bible. "While you eat, I will read from the fourteenth chapter of John. We can have our own service right here."

A gentle smile formed on Hannah's face.

"'Peace I leave with you, my peace I give unto you: not as the world giveth, give I unto you. Let not your heart be troubled, neither let it be afraid.'"

Later, the two women walked outside to a bench near the barn, where they sat. Heather asked Hannah questions about her childhood and youth, and Hannah smiled and laughed as she shared long-ago memories.

"Am I tiring you, Hannah?"

"No, 'tis been nice."

"If you are chilly, we can go inside and continue this while I heat up the beef stew."

Inside, Hannah sat at the table, and Heather served the stew. While they ate, Hannah's eyes darted from one thing to another around the large front room.

"Shall I read to you, or would you like to rest?"

"I need to clean. Look at the dust on the furniture." Hannah got up and grabbed a rag.

Heather joined her dusting the furniture. Hannah's demeanor improved when she focused on something outside of herself, even if it was only the dust. They spent the next hour cleaning each of the places Hannah selected.

Shortly after two o'clock, George and the children came through the door. Heather and Hannah had been laughing, and the surprised but joyful looks on the faces of Hannah's family members were ones Heather would long remember.

George walked outside with her when she readied to leave.

"I cannot believe the change in Hannah. What did you do?"

Heather told him what they had done. "When she was busy, she seemed more herself," Heather said. "I think changing her perspective helped. Be encouraged."

"Your being here today was a gift." George sounded and looked more at peace. "Attending Sunday services was what we needed."

"If you think it helps, I will come periodically. Let me know when you need someone to stay with her."

"I will."

Heather walked the well-worn path back to the Green. The change she had witnessed in Hannah's attitude and the joy she had seen in the Whitcomb family lifted her own spirits. The back of the Green came into view. Had the Gordons and the children returned yet from church and the social?

She had made her way to the side of the house to collect a bucket of water from the well when the sound of a neighing horse alerted her. They must have returned.

Carrying the full bucket, she walked to the front of the Green. Andrew's bay and another horse were tied to a fence rail, but when she looked around, her own wagon was nowhere in sight. Tucking some loose strands of hair into her cap, she headed inside to find Andrew in the common room.

"What a pleasant surprise. I assume the children told you I was with a neighbor."

Andrew's expression was odd. He smiled when he took the bucket from her.

"What is it?" She glanced around the kitchen. "Where are the children?"

"They are not here. We thought you were still at church."

She glanced around the kitchen. "We? How did you get in?" So much for her strong new locks.

"The hidden key, though it appears to be a different one." The raspy voice that came from the doorway leading to the common room took her breath away. She turned in the direction, certain her mind was playing tricks on her.

Her knees buckled at the sight of the tall, emaciated shape filling the doorway.

"Matthew!"

Heather reached for the side of the hutch as Andrew caught her and gently held her up. Her eyes never left the image before her.

She opened her mouth, but no words came out.

Matthew drew near. "I should have let Andrew prepare you, but I couldn't wait." He reached for her and took her in his arms.

"You are alive. I cannot believe ... How can it be?" She gazed into his tear-filled eyes, her shaking hands moving to rest on each side of his thin face. "You are real. I do not understand. We were told—"

"I know. Andrew explained it to me. I will tell you, but for now, just know I am home by the grace of God ... and with the help of some very good friends." Matthew tightened his hold on her and buried his face in her neck.

Her arms encircled his lean torso. She choked on the lump filling her throat. "Oh, Matthew, my heart. Thank God you are safe and home at last." Matthew's tears ran down her neck while her own fell on his chest.

When her eyes opened, she saw Andrew gazing out the window, his back to them.

"Andrew, Andrew, our eternal thanks."

He turned to face them, his eyes also tear-filled. "I'm going to the other room, or perhaps to take a walk." He looked happy but awkward sharing in their reunion.

"You shall do nothing of the sort, Andrew Macmillan," Heather said. "You have brought my Matthew home." She held Matthew's gaunt face in front of her. "Sit down and let me get you something to eat and drink."

Matthew sat. "I can wait for food. I'm more content than I can say just being home."

She caressed his face. "You look so tired and pale."

"I'm exhausted, but I will try to explain."

She jumped at the sound of a wagon approaching. "That will be the children. Let me go outside and prepare them."

Andrew turned back to the window. "They are coming up the lane."

Matthew stood beside her and gazed out the window.

She turned to Andrew. "Please take him into the parlor for a few minutes."

Andrew put an arm under Matthew's. "They will have recognized Stirling."

Thomas stepped down from the wagon first. He assisted Polly and Mary, who each carried the little girls. The boys stepped off the other side of the wagon.

Philip took the reins of the horse and unhitched it. "Mr. Macmillan must be here."

Heather turned toward him. "Aye."

Andrew came through the door.

Thomas smiled and shook Andrew's extended hand.

Polly came alongside Heather. "How was your time with Hannah? The Whitcombs looked very happy in church today."

"Aye, very well." Heather reached out for Polly's free arm. She pulled her aside and whispered. "Andrew has found Matthew and brought him home."

Polly gasped. "Alive?"

"Aye, Shh. Your family must come over later, but first we need some time with the children."

"Praise God! Of course," she whispered. "Tell us when you want us. May I tell Thomas?"

"Certainly."

Thomas and Polly walked to their cottage, little Laura between them. Polly looked back at her and grinned.

"What is it, Mama?" Mary held Sara on her hip and looked from her to Andrew. "Does this have anything to do with James?" Concern etched her face.

"Nay. 'Tis good news, the best news." She reached for Douglas and led him up the step.

"What is it, Ma?" Mark looked from her to Andrew.

"We have a wonderful surprise inside, though I know not yet how it came about." She winked at Andrew, took Sara, and led the way. "Come to the common room, children."

CHAPTER 35

Heather motioned for them all to sit. Broaching the news of their father's return needed to be done with care.

Worry filled Mary's face. "Is it Mrs. Whitcomb, Mama? Was she difficult today?"

"Nay, Mrs. Whitcomb is much improved." Still holding Sara, she looked into her children's faces. "This will come as quite a shock, but 'tis good."

Mark thumped his hand on the table. "Must we have all the mystery, Ma?"

"Mr. Macmillan has brought your father home."

A smile burst forth on Douglas as he jumped up from the bench. "Papa is home?"

Mary's blank stare met Mark's before turning back to her. "You said he was buried in Philadelphia."

"How can that be?" Mark's confusion matched his sister's.

A scuffling in the hallway had her turning toward the door. A moment later, Matthew stepped into the room.

"I'm very much alive." Matthew's pale face, full of joy, studied each of his children.

Douglas ran to his father's side and hugged his leg, nearly upsetting his balance.

Mary's mouth dropped open.

Mark's eyes grew wide. He stood, slowly approached his father. "I never believed it when they said you were dead."

Finally, Mary recovered from her shock. She pushed her chair back and ran to him. Tears ran down her cheeks.

With Douglas latched onto his waist, Matthew wrapped an

arm around Mark and his other around Mary.

Overcome by the sight, Heather could only watch and weep.

"Where have you been, Papa?" Douglas said.

"Are you ill?" Mark asked. "They said you were shot."

Mary stepped away to meet her father's eyes. "Who was the man with Mama's cross?"

"What happened to you, Pa? Where were you?" Mark's voice cracked. "Why did you not come home?"

"Children." Heather crossed the room and took Douglas, then focused on Mark and Mary. "Let your father sit down. I'm sure he'll tell us everything if we give him some time to speak."

Matthew made his way to a chair. He looked as if he would drop at any moment. When he reached for Sara, Heather placed the baby in his arms. He looked amazed at the sight of his youngest child. He kissed her forehead and her cheeks, which made her squirm in his arms. "My goodness, what a beautiful sight you are." He looked up at Heather, then at the other children. "All these months, I wished for this. Only this. To see you all again."

Mark said, "But Papa—"

"Children, your father is exhausted. We all have many questions, and he wants to answer them, but he is tired. Right now, let us thank God for his safe return and let him get some food and rest." She turned toward Andrew. "Oh, dear friend, we are indebted to you for finding him and bringing him home."

Heather put her hand on Mark's shoulder. "Please, go get some cider."

He headed toward the cellar, looking over his shoulder at his father, then to Andrew. "We are so thankful, Mr. Macmillan."

"Yes, we are so grateful." Tears ran down Mary's cheeks. "'Tis an answer to so many prayers." Still looking stunned, she looked back at her father. "Let me take Sara up and change her."

Heather addressed Andrew. "Sit with Matthew while I bring you both some food."

A few minutes later, she brought a tray with soup, bread,

applesauce, and cider to the table. After Andrew's brief prayer, she watched the men eat, her eyes still filled with tears.

Her heart full, her constant prayer answered. *You were faithful, Lord. You did the impossible.* The sight of Matthew, even ill and weary, was healing a broken heart. She was as impatient as the children. So many questions.

Mary returned with Sara and sat next to Douglas, who had not taken his eyes off his father. She'd never seen the boy so still and quiet, but they were all stunned. Mark brought the cider. They sat at the table, engrossed by their father's presence as he slowly ate.

Andrew sipped his soup. "This is much needed and appreciated. We stopped briefly in Alexandria on our way. The Duncans were overjoyed to see Matthew and said they would come soon."

Heather sat beside Matthew. "Wonderful."

Andrew's attention turned to Mark. "How has the fishing been?"

Mark looked dumbfounded by the question.

Heather nodded. "Tell him, Mark." Andrew was trying to lighten up the intense emotions around the table.

"'Tis been great. We caught some bass, walleye, even some trout." Mark's gaze traveled back to his father. "Perhaps ... we might go sometime, Pa, and fish ... when you feel better."

"I would like that. You have grown so tall, son."

He glanced to where Mary sat still looking stunned. "Mary, you have become such a lovely young woman. I look forward to hearing of your activities."

"You look so ill, Papa." Her face radiated worry.

"I will be fine." Matthew took a deep breath. "Once I get some rest and my strength back. Douglas, what a big boy you have become. And Sara—" Tears formed in his eyes.

When they finished their dinners, Andrew walked to Matthew's side. "Let me help you up the stairs."

Matthew tried to wave him off.

"Not the time for pride, my friend." Andrew placed an arm

under Matthew's.

"I can help also." Heather went to her husband's other side.

Once the three of them reached the stairs, she stood back and allowed the men to maneuver the climb together.

Matthew's breathing was labored as they took each riser.

Her eyes followed them. *Praise You, Lord … so much. My heart overflows with joy.*

Heather entered the room after them and closed the curtain while Andrew led Matthew to the bed. She removed his shoes and draped a quilt over him. "Get some rest now. We will hear more when you wake."

Andrew followed her back downstairs. At the foot of the staircase, she turned toward him. "Come and share what you know."

"Of course."

When they reached the common room, all eyes were riveted on Andrew.

Mary stood. "Please tell us how you found Papa."

Andrew glanced around at each of them. "Not long after my last visit here, I went to Philadelphia to learn more about Matthew's time there and his disappearance. I wanted to find out who killed him and why."

Andrew sipped his cider. "Adam had already been to Philadelphia in pursuit of answers, so I stopped on my way there to seek his advice, which was most helpful. He gave me details about his encounter with Jones and Stephens and let me know how to contact Patrick O'Brian. When I arrived in Philadelphia, Patrick told me of an encounter he had that added more clarity."

Mary leaned forward. "What did he say?"

Andrew proceeded to share much of the information about Matthew's time at the Flemings that Adam had already shared in his letter.

Heather glanced at Mark and Mary, who were as absorbed as she was in Andrew's story. Douglas had a troubled look on his face. "Laddie," Heather said, "please take the bucket to the garden and pick the ripe beans for me." The child looked relieved to leave the table. When the door had closed behind him, she said, "Please continue, Andrew."

"Patrick already knew from his and Adam's meeting with Stephens that Matthew had been passing information. So, when the Flemings told Patrick about the sequence of events, it raised some questions in his mind."

"What kinds of questions?" Mary's brow furrowed as she sat back in her chair.

Andrew poured himself more cider and took a drink. "If the British suspected Matthew Stewart of passing information and took him prisoner in New Jersey, how had he been found murdered in Philadelphia? The body, believed to be Matthew's, was found before Matthew was taken prisoner in Swedesboro." Andrew set the tankard down. "Which meant that the injured man the Flemings had cared for could not possibly have been the murdered man found in Philadelphia."

"Oh, my." Heather's hand went to her chest.

"Patrick and I returned to Swedesboro to get more of our questions answered. Oden and Anna Fleming told us they were very troubled when Matthew was taken prisoner. They wondered how the British soldiers learned of his location at their home, so they began asking questions of their neighbors. Apparently, Oden had been overheard speaking with a friend at a local tavern about taking care of a Virginia man named Matthew who had been shot. A man in the tavern overheard the conversation and informed the British encamped nearby."

Mark stood up. "Who was the informer?"

"Some of the townsfolk recognized him as a man named Cranford," Andrew said.

The man who had aided her at the schoolhouse.

"Cranford." Mark turned to her. "Do you know him?"

"Only slightly. Sit and let Andrew continue."

"After Oden Fleming left the tavern," Andrew said, "Cranford asked the tavern keeper where Oden lived. Since Cranford was from Virginia, they assumed he had an acquaintance with the wounded man, so they told him. The Flemings figured Cranford told the Regulars."

Heather got up and paced. "That does not explain how you found Matthew. You said he was taken prisoner. So Cranford had Matthew arrested. Then what happened?"

"From what Matthew told me, the Regulars took him from the Flemings and imprisoned him on New York Island. He said he was there nearly six months."

Mary leaned on the table. "Did the British let him go?"

"I bet he escaped." Mark's expression displayed a mixture of wonder and pride.

"In a manner of speaking, yes, he did escape." Andrew took another swallow of the cider. "Apparently, on September twenty-first, a horrible fire broke out on the southern end of New York Island. Strong winds and dry weather spread it to the north and west. A large part of the city was destroyed. The building Matthew and others were held in was in the middle of it. He said someone unlocked the bolts and the prisoners, as well as everyone else in the building, ran to escape the flames."

Heather stared at Andrew. A chill traveled up her spine. "A fire, in late September?"

"What is it, Mama?" Mary tilted her head to the side.

"I'm not sure." She remembered the nightmare, the fire, and fleeing with Matthew. It had been near that time.

Unaware of her thoughts, Andrew continued. "Matthew said he believed a miracle took place amid that disaster. He likened it to St. Paul's escaping his guards after the earthquake. There was a lot of confusion, but Matthew and many others escaped. They managed to find boats and cross the Hudson River to Jersey City."

Heather sat at the table, shaken. "Then what happened?"

"Matthew walked until he could go no farther. A farmer

spotted him on the side of a road and asked him where he was bound. Matthew told him Philadelphia. The farmer took him part way to where he lived near Princeton. He and his wife fed and sheltered him two nights. Matthew walked and caught transport the remainder of the way to Philadelphia."

The sound of Sara crying interrupted Andrew's story.

Heather stood. "Not another word until I return."

Everyone erupted in laughter.

Mary shook her head "It has been too long since we laughed. Hurry back, Mama."

"I needed to catch a breath, anyway." Andrew stood and went to the window overlooking the garden where Douglas was still picking beans.

Heather ran up the stairs and crept into her bedroom. She stopped inside and gazed at Matthew sleeping soundly on their bed.

'Twas true. He was really there.

Fresh tears filled her eyes at the wonder of it. She looked up, mouthed *thank you*, and allowed the tears of gratitude to come.

Sara smiled when Heather walked into the room, so she lifted Sara from her cradle and returned down the stairs.

"He is still sleeping. So, tell us, Matthew arrived in Philadelphia—"

"Yes. I was sharing a meal with Patrick O'Brian at the City Tavern when a shopkeeper, a neighbor of the cabinetmaking establishment where Patrick worked, came by looking for him. He said a rather sorry-looking fellow had come by the shop asking for him. The neighbor wanted to know when he might return.

"When Patrick and I arrived back at the shop, his neighbor pointed to a tall, thin ragamuffin in the alleyway. The man faced us. It was Matthew. We were shocked."

Mary stood. "But Mr. Macmillan, how did Papa end up at Patrick's shop? Philadelphia is a large city."

"Your father remembered Patrick O'Brian from your visit to Philadelphia. He recalled Patrick was a cabinetmaker who worked for Thomas Affleck. Matthew sought out that shop because he believed Patrick would help him get back to his family. Matthew said he no longer had any other contacts in Philadelphia, and he did not want his whereabouts known by those aligned with the Loyalist cause."

They all digested Matthew's odyssey in silence.

Douglas came inside with a bucket of beans, which Heather traded for a basket of toys. "'Tis nothing short of a miracle."

Andrew glanced at the children and back to her. "Once Matthew was rested, he told us about when he was attacked. He had gone to a location near Swedesboro where he was to meet his contact. When he was on foot near a creek, someone approached him from the rear. The attacker shot and robbed him and left him for dead. We believe it was the man who robbed him who was found dead near Philadelphia with your cross, the sealed packet, and a document with Matthew's name on it. The body found had det ... well, he must have been of similar appearance, hence was identified as Matthew."

Heather sat back in her chair, gazing around the table at her children and Andrew. "God has been so good to us. And you, Patrick O'Brian, the Flemings, and the others who helped him have been the Lord's agents. No words can express our gratitude."

Concern etched Mary's face. "Papa was shot? No wonder he looks so thin and ill. Will he recover?"

How could she reassure the children when she had her own worries? "We will do everything we can, and with God's help, your father's health will improve. But we need to be patient and not press him for details."

Mark got up. "Mr. Macmillan, do you think Pa will be safe here? I mean, will the soldiers come looking for him?" The boy's comment drew everyone's attention. "Do you suppose that Cranford man knows where he lives?"

Heather took a deep breath. "Mr. Cranford knows where your father lives. Many months ago, he came here looking for him."

CHAPTER 36

Matthew opened his eyes and stirred when he heard Sara's babbling coming from her cradle. Her sweet sound choked him up. A month ago, he could never have imagined being here. The bedroom door opened. Heather stood in the doorway, her trim figure defined by the candlelight from the lit sconce in the hallway.

"I'm awake. Come in."

"Did I disturb you?" Her voice, such a welcome sound. She approached the bed.

"Not at all." He turned on his side and pushed himself to a sitting position.

"Do you want to come downstairs for supper or shall I bring it up for you?" Heather picked Sara up and bounced the tot on her hip.

"I will come down. I'm eager to be with all of you."

She set Sara beside him and bent down to help him with his shoes.

"I can do that." He took her hands in his.

Their eyes met. His hands caressed her face. He leaned in and kissed her. His guarded emotions, long held at bay, burst forth. Their kisses flooded with tears. Her fingers ran through his hair, a longed-for sensation finally realized. His breathing grew rapid.

She pulled away. "Do not tire yourself." In the dim light, he studied her face, her eyes, remembering every feature and expression he loved and had missed so much.

"Where were you shot? Let me see it."

He pulled up his shirt, exposing a large scar on his left side. "It has healed very well thanks to the ministrations of Anna Fleming."

She ran her fingers over the ropey wound. "I hope to thank that blessed couple someday. Does it hurt?"

"Not so much. I am not at my best right now, but I will gain strength." He stroked her face and kissed her lips again. Sara crawled onto his lap.

Heather laughed. "Someone has come between us." He joined in the mirth as he scooped Sara into his arms.

Heather reached for her. "Let me get her into dry clothes."

He had missed most of Sara's life. Getting to know this precious child would be a priority. That and becoming reacquainted with the rest of the family.

"I'm going to get Andrew to help you down the stairs. We will not risk you taking a fall and further injuring yourself."

"Fair enough."

She picked up Sara and walked to the doorway, turned back to him, and smiled. "Andrew has been telling us about how he discovered you and some of what you have been through. I must warn you to expect questions."

"Understood." He rose. "Did you find my Bible with the notes?"

"Aye, 'twas what alerted me that your trip was more than you had originally told me."

"I could not tell you, but I also did not want to leave without letting you know how much you mean to me." He leaned against the chest-on-chest.

"'Tis behind us now. I will send Andrew for you and ask the Gordons to join us for supper."

Later, as they all gathered around the large table, Matthew offered a prayer before they began passing the food around.

Mary smiled. "While you were upstairs, Mr. Macmillan told us he received word from James."

"Oh, that is wonderful. How is he?" Heather asked.

"He is now a lieutenant and serving on the *Alfred*, a thirty-gun converted merchant ship. James joined the ship before they headed to Nassau in the West Indies. They took Fort Montague and recovered some of the powder and armaments they believe Dunmore stole from the Williamsburg magazine. They also took two British ships before they took a serious hit from the *HMS Glasgow*. It forced them to New London, Connecticut, in April for repairs, additional crew, and a new captain."

Mary looked relieved at Andrew's news. "May I tell Martha Whitcomb? She has been so concerned for him."

Matthew studied Mary. She had grown quite comely, and there was a new softness about her. Evidently, her wounded relationship with Martha had healed.

Andrew pulled a small sealed parchment from his waistcoat. "You can do more than that. You can give Martha this note James included in my letter." He handed it to her.

"I will."

Heather smiled at Mary and Andrew. "'Tis relief to know he is well. When you write to James, do give him all our best."

Thomas reached for the bread. "How is he finding life at sea?

"Other than being at war, he said it has been an education, meeting and working with all kinds of people he had no exposure to in the past."

The men and boys continued their conversation while Mary took Sara upstairs to put her to bed. Later, after the younger children fell asleep, the others gathered around the large fire in the common room, catching up on the events of the past eleven months.

Andrew stood and squared his shoulders. "I believe you are gaining strength, Matthew. You hardly needed me to get downstairs. 'Tis my intention to travel back to Fredericksburg tomorrow. I have been absent a long time."

Matthew stood in front of their friend, extending his arm. "There are no words to express my deepest gratitude to you, Andrew, for all you have done to aid and encourage my family these past months, as well as your valiant efforts to find and assist me in returning home." The two men embraced.

Polly picked up Laura and motioned to Todd and Philip. "I think we will head back to the cottage and let the Stewarts get the rest they need after this incredible day."

Matthew turned to the group. "I'm indebted to all of you for everything you have done for my family in my absence. I will be indebted to you for the remainder of my life."

CHAPTER 37

The next morning, while the boys and Matthew still slept, Heather carried Sara downstairs. Voices came from the kitchen.

Heather entered. "'Tis a crisp October morn, Mary ... Andrew." She put Sara on the floor near the toy crate.

Mary was slicing bread. "'Tis. I was just about to gather the eggs."

Andrew sat at the kitchen table, drinking coffee and reading the *Gazette*.

When Mary opened the kitchen door, Philip was on the stoop with a basket of eggs. He handed Mary the basket. "I gathered the eggs for you so you could be with your pa."

"That was thoughtful. Here, you take some for your family." She reached up for another basket and placed some of the eggs in it.

"You are nice."

Her shoulders sagged for a moment. "'Tis the least I can do since you collected them." Mary watched as he turned and made his way around the side of the Green. She set the basket on the counter.

Heather pointed to a pot. "Please feed Sara. There is some porridge over there."

Andrew looked up from reading the paper. "The *Gazette* is full of meetings between General Washington, members of the Congress, and General Howe. It sounds like Britain has not yet accepted the fact we are a free nation and no longer under their control. They continue to hope we will recognize the error of our ways and return to the fold."

Mary struggled getting the porridge into Sara's mouth. The tot only wanted to play and maneuver the spoon herself. "Perhaps they want to end the war with us, so they will take their troops and return to England."

Andrew's laugh sounded sarcastic. "Wishful thinking, Mary. No, they will not give up all their holdings here without a serious fight."

Matthew opened his eyes and looked around. Alive, sleeping in his own bed, living with his family. Could life be any better? He washed and dressed and headed toward the stairs. He reached for the banister and stepped slowly down each tread, then crossed the common room to the kitchen.

He entered to see Heather working by the window and Andrew seated at the table. Mary was slicing fresh apples, while Sara played on the floor. "'Twas so good to be home, I obviously slept later than all of you."

Mary looked up and smiled. "Papa!"

Sara echoed her sister's enthusiasm. "Papapapapa!"

Heather rushed to his side. "You came downstairs by yourself? You look better than you did yesterday."

"'Tis what rest and decent food will do for a body." After receiving a kiss from his eldest daughter and ruffling Sara's curls, he sat across from Andrew. "Good day, everyone."

Heather brought fried ham and eggs.

Andrew set the paper down. "This is it, news of the fire in New York. But 'tis hardly covered at all. More space is given to stray mares and cows."

Heather poured coffee. "Perhaps it bodes well if there is no mention of escaped prisoners as a result of the fire."

Matthew shook his head. "There was so much confusion that night, people everywhere. It would be easy to believe the prisoners perished in the fire."

Heather sat beside him. "Do you think someone may come looking for you?"

Mary's eyes grew wide.

He took Heather's hand. "No. I think not."

Andrew stood. "I agree. The British in New York have more to worry about than one escaped prisoner. 'Tis time for me to leave. Philip is outside, so I will have him saddle Stirling."

Mark and Douglas came into the kitchen.

Douglas climbed onto Matthew's lap. "I missed you, Papa."

He ruffled his son's hair. "I missed you too."

The whole family accompanied Andrew outside.

Matthew hugged him. "Good-bye, my friend. I will be forever thankful for all you have done for me and my family."

"I'm grateful to have played a small part in your happy ending."

Matthew stood next to Heather, placing his arm around her. She leaned in, a sensation he had dreamed about for months. They watched as Andrew rode away from the Green. When he disappeared around a bend, they returned to the kitchen.

Mary handed Sara the spoon and the bowl, and the room filled with her thumping music and splashed porridge. "Papa, was the man who exposed you to the British soldiers the same Mr. Cranford who came here looking for you in June of last year?"

He turned to Heather and listened as Heather reminded him of her encounter with Mr. Cranford.

Mary sat at his side. "After you disappeared, I visited the Duncans. Jean and I were in town and ran into Mr. Whitney and Mr. Cranford. During our conversation, Mr. Cranford stared at me the whole time. He and Mr. Whitney are both Loyalists."

He looked out the window. He wanted to be honest, yet he still needed to be cautious about what he shared. "He came to the Green and spoke to me once."

Heather cocked her head. "What about?"

He shook his head. "Cranford wanted to enlist my services in support of the Loyalists. I believe Cranford later suspected my mission."

Mark gasped. "Perhaps it was Cranford who broke into the Green."

"What?" Matthew's gaze snapped to Heather. "A break-in? When did that happen? Were you home?"

Heather placed her hand on his and told him all the details of the ransacking of their property.

"The whole place was a mess," Douglas added.

Matthew shook his head. "If the culprit was Cranford, he no doubt was searching for one of the packets, evidence to use against me. Thank God you were absent at the time." There was so much he had missed.

Mark grabbed a biscuit. "Mr. Duncan put new locks on, Papa. No one was hurt."

Mary passed the plate of biscuits to him. "Mr. Duncan and Mr. Macmillan went so many places looking for you, Pa."

"I'm grateful to our many friends who assisted you and tried to locate me."

"Here, Mark." Heather came around the table with more eggs. "I think we need to let your father eat his breakfast. We do not need to review the past eleven months today."

Mary continued to stare at him. "Mama said you believed you needed to help the Patriot cause. That was why you left, but you might have died. You will not do that again, will you?"

He looked around the table. All eyes were on him. They deserved an answer. "I was approached for a specific mission because I had some helpful connections, and I was the best person to carry it out without raising suspicion or being identified. I never sought to get involved with this fight. But many others have put their lives in peril to win our independence. Should I stand by and let others sacrifice and take all the risks if I'm not willing to help?" He studied each of them. "I do not foresee a situation like this coming again, but I cannot promise what the future will demand of me or any of us. No one knows how long this war will last. Young men like Donald Duncan, James Macmillan, Tobias Whitcomb, and many others throughout the colonies are fighting to protect our freedoms. We have an obligation to support them, pray for them … possibly take up arms with them."

Heather gazed at him, her eyes brimming with admiration and love. None of them wanted this war, but liberty would not come without a cost. Strange. Instead of feeling weary, he was energized.

"Pa, what was it like in prison?" Mark asked. "Did they torture you?" The expression on his son's face suggested he longed to know but dreaded the answer.

There were elements of his imprisonment he might never share. "They did not torture me, but I also could not anticipate from one day to the next if it might begin. They were brutal with some prisoners." He sat back in the chair and glanced to where Douglas and Sara sat at the far end of the room. "I suspect those of us jailed in that building were treated better than some prisoners. From what I understand, they did not have much in the way of evidence against us but were holding us until they would determine how, or if, we were involved with subversive activities."

Heather stood. "Mary, Mark, please watch Douglas and Sara while your father and I take a walk around the farm."

"Yes, Mama," Mary said.

Heather flushed. "Do you feel like taking a walk, dear? I should not have presumed—"

"I would like nothing more." He stood, and his eyes met hers as a slow smile formed. In truth, he longed for time alone with her.

Heather reached for her shawl and wrapped it about her shoulders.

At the door, he said, "Which way?"

She nodded to the right, the path leading to the pond.

He breathed in the fresh fall air. "I suspect I will need to harvest the corn."

Heather pointed to the left. "You will be relieved to know most of the harvesting has been completed. Thomas, his boys, and Mark have been busy."

He followed her gaze and stopped at the split rail fencing and looked about. "I see." He turned and faced her. "I cannot tell you how often over these last months I have longed to be back in these beautiful rolling green hills."

"I will never be able to tell you how much you were missed."

He took her hand, slipping his fingers between hers, and pulled her close. "The children, how often I prayed for them and for you, to keep you safe and at peace."

For minutes they just held each other. Having her in his arms brought a lump to his throat. He could have lost all of this.

He glanced again toward the path leading left. "How are the Whitcombs?"

She informed him of the changes at their neighbor's home.

They passed by the open barn door. Sunlight filtered through the cracks in the walls as well as the open top of the Dutch door opposite them.

"Everything looks the same, as if I had never left."

"I think not. I would have been lost without Thomas and the boys' help and without Polly's constant friendship and assistance." She looked up at him with those blue eyes he could drown in. "Shall we keep walking, dear, or do you want to rest?"

"Keep going … to the bench at the pond." He took her hand as they made their way down the path. She was really there beside him, walking with him, something he had longed for and feared would never happen again. *I will never stop thanking You, Lord, for all you have restored to me.*

Heather answered all his questions about neighbors. When they reached the far end of the wheat field yet to be harvested, he placed one foot on the bottom rail of the fence and leaned on the top. "Was there a good crop?"

"Aye, very good. Again, we were fortunate. All pitched in to help. Even Andrew assisted when he was here."

Matthew sighed. "I am indebted to so many." He faced her. "It appears you all did quite well without me."

"Nay, Matthew. We never do well without you. We suffered and felt your absence every day. But God was good. He has been faithful and provided what we needed when we needed it. He gave us good weather, a healthy crop, and most of all, good friends who prayed for us and offered encouragement and assistance. I will never forget that."

He slipped his arms around her, holding her close. It thrilled him to hear the beating of her heart. Lifting her chin, he leaned down and kissed her, and kissed her again. He cared not whether the family, the Gordons, or anyone else saw them in such an intimate embrace.

⚜

Heather looked up at him. 'Twas not a dream, he was really home. "Are you tired?"

"A little, but not enough to go back." He smiled at her.

They walked to the pond and sat on the bench, still holding hands. Geese at the far end splashed in the water and fluffed their feathers, while others sat on the bank preening. Many of the trees had rained golden and amber leaves. This was where she came to think, to pray. This was the place they came to talk.

Matthew rubbed her cheek with his hand. "And what has you so deep in thought?"

"How much this spot means to me. Think of all the times we shared here."

He laughed. "I remember ... it must be about six years ago now, also in the fall, when I returned from selling the Philadelphia property to help you get established on your own. We took a walk around the farm. I was so proud of the way you had maintained it. We ended up here. I was desperately in love with you and hated the possibility of losing you, but I needed to set you free to find out if you wanted to stay."

"Oh, Matthew, that was so long ago, and our problems were nowhere near as serious as the world we face today. Tell me, was what you told the children about your captivity true? I sensed there was more you were not sharing with us."

He rubbed his chin.

She bit her lip. She should not have brought up the prison again so soon.

"I have said all I care to about that time. I want to forget those months." The furrow on his brow overshadowed his tentative smile.

It must have been terrible. She reached for his hand, holding it in both of hers. Honoring his request might prove challenging.

"I did not mean to be gruff." He took her in his arms again, kissing her gently on her forehead. "I clung to Scripture, and it strengthened me. 'It is of the Lord's mercies that we are not consumed, because His compassions fail not. They are new every morning: great is Thy faithfulness.'"

"I depended on His Word also. And I was thankful for your letters." She brought his hand to her lips and kissed it. "Do you think we have a chance against England?"

"'Twill not be easy, and the cost may be great, but I believe and support the principles set forth in the Declaration of Independence. Our cause is just, and I believe we all must be willing to support those who are fighting to secure our freedoms."

"I am proud to be your wife, Matthew Stewart. I am so grateful for the life and family we have here. Whatever the future holds, with God's help, we will face it together."

The Revolutionary War will rage on for another seven years as a new nation is birthed. Lives will be changed, and the war will exact its toll. Battles sometimes extend beyond the end of a war. The story continues in the final book in the trilogy.

Made in the USA
Middletown, DE
29 September 2018